Matthew Waterhouse has worked extensively as an actor in theatre and for the BBC. He lives in New Haven, CT, visiting Europe frequently. This is his first novel, and a second – Vanitas – is due for release in November 2010.

FATES, FLOWERS

A COMEDY OF
NEW YORK

MATTHEW
WATERHOUSE

Fates, Flowers
Matthew Waterhouse

First Published in the UK in May 2010 by Hirst Publishing

Originally published in the USA in 2006 by ThisPress

Hirst Publishing, Suite 285 Andover House, George Yard, Andover, Hants, SP10 1PB

ISBN 978-0-9557149-5-5

A CIP catalogue record for this book is available from the British Library.

Cover by Tara O'Shea
Printed and bound by Good News Digital Books

Paper stock used is natural, recyclable and made from wood grown in sustainable forests. The manufacturing processes conform to environmental regulations.

www.hirstbooks.com

The roads from the West were dotted with bones
with plants sprouting fates and flowers

- APOLLINAIRE,
Trans. Anne Hyde Greet

Take me to the river, wash me down

- AL GREEN

O now, my minor moon, dead as meat

- GEORGE BARKER

SARA

Here in New York City on the island of Manhattan, on a lane called Minetta in the heart of the West Village, there was an old Town House. Number 33. It was divided up into three apartments, with an empty store in the basement. In the second floor apartment lived Sara Smith. She'd bought her cosy little residence in 1986, so she'd been here sixteen years.

Three years ago in a fit of reckless expenditure she had treated herself to a lovely new blue leather sofa and thrown her old one out. Her old one had been lumpy and uncomfortable. She much preferred the new one. It was her favourite piece of furniture.

She was sitting on it now.

She wasn't happy. The sofa cannot be blamed for this.

She sat looking towards the windows and the fire escape stairs. The light was beginning to soften.

Steve, her beautiful sweet 'Huck' as she had sometimes called him, was gone. She could scarcely believe she'd seen him for the last time only yesterday. So long ago. He would never return, never return. She said this aloud, very slowly into the silence of her lonely room:

7

"Never... ever...to... return." She let out a sad little sigh. She let out a sad little laugh. She felt a terrible hollow, a literal physical hollow somewhere in her body, as a sympathetic response to the emotional hollowness in her heart.

How long had she sat there? All she knew was, a long time.

What was she to do?

Her plan (she decided) was to get back into the cycle of her old life, the life before Steve. She would go back to her old drinking haunt, *Mulligan's,* see her old friends again and pretend the whole thing with Steve had never happened. This was surely the wisest thing to do, the best way to wash away the last few days. That old life, after all, was only a week in the past. How long ago it seemed.

But she wasn't in the mood for loud laughs and Guinnesses and slaps on the back, not yet. What she really wanted was silence, silence like the stars above. No – she shook her head to chase away whatever particular train of thought her dwelling on the stars was leading her towards. Anyway, the stars were not yet out, even as far as the stars could ever be said to be out in New York City, whose man-made lights would always dim them.

Mulligan's? Hmmm. Maybe not. Maybe it would be wiser to take more drastic action.

She placed a hand unthinkingly on her sofa and felt the leather soft on her palm's skin. She did not like having to leave her sofa behind, but maybe she should. Because what she really wanted was to get far away from the Village, far away from New York. Oh, if she could get on a plane and fly back to London! London again after all these years! She reflected fondly on all the London tourist traps, realizing as they flashed through her head like a flicked deck of cards that she was thinking not like a British native but like the sort of tourist she'd hated there as she hated here.

8

Just goes to show how long it's been!

The Changing of the Guard came into her mind, Tower Bridge, the ducks in St James's Park, big red buses and Trafalgar Square, the National Gallery into which she had never been but past which she had walked many hundreds of times. Black cabs and more big red buses. The number three bus to Brixton! The National Theatre on the South Bank disturbed by the rattle of trains into Charing Cross. She thought also, with relief – the native reasserting herself - of Berwick Street market and Boots the Chemist. The number Sixty-one to Putney.

In the midst of these reminiscences she dwelt for an instant on whether when she thought about England did she think in English spelling - programme - or did she think in American? Program? But this sort of reflection is too abstract for Sara, immediately she switched back to matters of substance. BBC voices, the Northern Line, (Mind the gap!), *Coronation Street*. Rain. Things you could see, things you could hear, things you could touch.

Then she pushed these thoughts from her mind in a sort of muscular mental thrust. It irritated her that she'd allowed herself to become dreamy and nostalgic like this, it reeked of weakness to her. I'm a practical woman, she reminded herself, and I must deal with the situation I find myself in, in a practical way. I'm not in London, I'm in New York, and for now I have to get on with things. Even as she pulled herself together a little indulgent tear lit her eyelash. It may have been a tear for London or it may have been a tear for poor Steve who she'd lost.

I must get back into the cycle of my old life fast as possible, it's the only way. I must go to *Mulligan*'s and start all over again whether I bloody want to or not.

This was unusually far-sighted of her: she was not a woman who foresaw consequences and outcomes as a matter of course. As she herself said, a phrase that came to her lips

9

on the slightest pretext, "I live for the moment, ducks! I live for the moment!" Sitting there on her sofa, she found herself smiling over that word, "ducks." So English, so solid working class. It'd been old-fashioned even when she'd lived in London, an older person's word, not hers, a word she'd never used until she'd come out here. She had in truth held it in that easy mild contempt children hold for their parents as somehow signifying simplicity, lack of ambition, acceptance of a lowly status. It had crept into her speech as a wry tribute to "my old mother" whose term it had been, affectionate and ironic all at once, and somehow it had stuck to the tip of her tongue. Now, it cropped up of its own will in her speech. But she thought of it at this moment because an adjustment had taken place in her life and in the aftermath she was thinking about all sorts of things. She was herself aware of this new working of her mind, of this mulling over matters, and she was shrewd enough to appreciate the cause. After a crisis you find yourself reviewing everything, even the trivia. That morning, for instance, she had bought six rolls of pink toilet paper. She had always before bought blue, without making a deliberate choice that it was her preference. Blue had become her habit. Now, things would be different and she might as well mark that difference in the small ways as well as the big. Moreover, enough small differences added up to a big difference. But not all things would change. The word 'ducks' was stuck to her tongue and would not unpeel just because she was freshly aware of its presence. Anyway, they loved it at *Mulligan's*. Some ex-pats blur into their country of residence, the imprint of their place of origin fades away, but Sara: I've become more English than ever! And I know I bloody well play up to it - Sara, the salt of the earth! - But why bloody not?

Yet Sara had been away from London for so many years that unknown to her, her Englishness had become diluted with New York's idioms. In London they would have thought her transatlantic, foreign even. This would have horrified her, for if she was not rooted in New York and could no longer pass as London-born-and-bred, was she not a nomad, a placeless person? But unquestionably an English listener would have noticed that for every time she said "ducks" there was a time she said "kiddo," for every time she said "bloke" there was a time she said "guy", for every "quarter to twelve" there was a "quarter of one."

A sudden urge to *see* herself came upon her, to remind herself that she still existed, still had a body, was still of the earth, was not merely a cloud of melancholy reflections floating in a greyish light.

She stood up and looked in the good-sized mirror which hung over the sofa. The street lamp beyond the three windows overlooking her balcony glinted in the upper right of the glass. The fire escape stairs slashed across at an angle.

Evening after evening after evening she had looked in this mirror before going out to *Mulligan's*. She'd always checked her thick sun-blond hair, the roots. She pretended she was looking at herself now for exactly the same reason. The roots? Yes, they were blond too, she nodded in plump satisfaction. You're still a looker, you are Sara, you still look pretty damn terrific. Any man would be bloody lucky to have you for his lady!

She pursed her red, red lips, red like a London bus. She tapped a puff caked in powder onto first one cheek then the other.

She went into her compact windowless bathroom and splashed on some perfume, which made her smell like factory-made roses. It was only after she was perfumed that she realized she was re-enacting her regular ritual. Her body, her actions, in making preparations, had chosen for her:

Mulligan's.

She breathed in deeply and could almost make herself feel everything was all right.

"Here we go then."

Her voice cracked, not because she was emotionally moved but because after long silence her vocal machinery needed warming up.

She smoothed her skirt and picked up her handbag and put on her nice shoes with the fairly high heels. She didn't think she'd need her coat, it wasn't yet October. She closed the door to her apartment and went down the wooden stairs, past Tony and Pete's door.

But arriving outside at the top of the stone steps the cool breeze of late September brought Steve to her mind again. A shiver ran through her. A flash of worry.

The balcony windows - did I lock them? She chastised herself: You know, Sara, you silly cow, did you ever check the balcony for marks? No! Cow! Who knows what clues you could have left for some nosy busybody to find? You silly old fool! She said it aloud this time:

"Bloody silly cow, you are!"

She went back up. Tap tap tap tap went her heels on the stairs.

The windows onto the balcony were unlocked. She climbed through the left one, looked at the wrought-iron strips under her feet, the black-painted balcony railings with little twists of rust. On the right was the fire escape ladder. She scanned the balcony for traces, for anything that might catch a searching eye. There had been no blood, there had been no violence, yet she wouldn't feel comfortable until she could say to herself, I looked, I'm safe as houses. She glanced up to the slats of the balcony above, and down to Tony and Pete's balcony. Just as she looked, a light was switched on in Tony and Pete's apartment. It flooded their balcony for a moment, catching the black paintwork, until the glare was filtered and reduced by the closing of white curtains. At dusk, they always drew their curtains. Good old Tony, good old Pete. The boys, she called them, to herself

12

and to their faces, as though they were the only gay couple in the Village.

Standing in the fresh breeze, she thought it a good idea to put on her brown coat after all, her coat with its one missing button. She must remember to sew that button back on! She went into her apartment, put on her coat, felt it comfortable and enclosing her.

Now, *Mulligan's*.

"Suddenly I'm really in the mood for that Guinness. What a changeable one you are, Sara."

Tap tap tap tap went her heels.

She came into Bleecker Street and joined the dusk crowd going about its businesses. People carrying bags of groceries, people carrying briefcases, people in jeans carrying nothing at all. A man asked her for change, but she didn't catch his eye. Another man stood hopelessly, blearily, pressed against a wall, hand held out, saying nothing and receiving nothing in return. In the streets of New York people didn't often catch a person's eye. Occasionally someone would look over to Sara and she would look back to them. She had always been the kind who pulled gazes to her. Twenty years ago she'd been a real looker, a girl who took wolf whistles as her due, and still she got her share of attention. She no longer looked young and she was certainly full-bodied, but her apparent age could alter with a change in the light so that sometimes she looked older than her forty-five years but in the right atmosphere she could knock ten years off. As long as she didn't smile too broadly and allow the crow's feet to bunch up.

She had deluded herself only a few days before that *Mulligan's* was in her past, she would never have to go back there, yet here she was, walkwalkwalking to it just as if everything were as it always had been. Before Steve.

Before Steve.

13

Oh, silly romantic Sara! All this is what comes of living for the moment, see.

All of a sudden, she was standing on *Mulligan's* stairs looking down into the cellar bar. The burr of familiar voices. She knew already what they would say when she got to the foot of the stairs, when she, as she thought of it, made her entrance. This was the most important event of her life perhaps, this easing herself back into the drone of this familiar monotony, but they must not know it. To them, Sara must be the same old girl, the same old hilarious girl she always was.

When you've spent six out of every seven evenings for God knows how many years sitting in the same old bar, at the same old table, four days away can seem like forever, if not to you then to your friends who rely on your sour humour to spin the evening through.

She could tell by the noise that it was packed, but then it was always packed on a Saturday evening.

From a river of indistinguishable voices, a laugh she knew came to her, like a log floating upon the Mississippi. She wanted to weep. She wanted to scream.

Oh I don't want to see these people; I don't want to be all merry and laughy for them, not tonight. She felt a tingle of self-pity. Not tonight! An Enya song came up to her suffocatingly. She might have turned back and left but two things happened to arrest her. First, she caught a whiff of hot food and remembered that this was Saturday night and during Happy Hour *Mulligan's* gave away spare ribs and chicken legs and buffalo wings, and the smell and the thought of them combined to make her hungry. You need to get some food in your stomach, girl. Second, after she had gone a couple of steps down, she clapped her eyes on Eddie McGovern. A big heavy guy with a little moustache and thinning hair. An easy laugh. It was his laugh she'd heard. She knew his laugh! He was at the bar waiting for the barman to get to him. He looked around and met her eyes. She saw him hesitate a second in something like disbelief, then run his eyes over her face and her body. She knew what he was thinking: Those familiar feet in their familiar shoes, those familiar legs slim at the ankles and ample at the knees.

"Oh my God!" he said to some people she could not see from the staircase. "Sara!" A new tune began to play, a limp m.o.r version of 'Danny Boy.'

"Hello, Eddie!" she said as brightly as she could, and she went down to the foot of the stairs and Eddie caught the barman's eye. He ordered an ale for him and a Guinness for her, and standing behind him were Ernie and Jackie Sleet and Eddie's girl Bea King, and Leanne and Lawrence Fortune. Sara felt a mild boredom at the notion of passing an evening with these people, the same old people she'd passed hundreds of evenings with before Steve. She could not bring herself even to pretend to like them any more. But she had to, she had to. For her sanity. For her future.

"Where've you been?" Eddie McGovern asked, as if he hadn't seen her for years.

She shrugged.

"Life happens," she said. "Thanks."

Eddie handed her her Guinness and sipped his ale. The others had half-full glasses.

Mulligan's was an astonishingly ordinary Irish cellar bar, with exposed brick walls and large colour photographs of Dublin all over the place. It was ill-lit, the air was smoky and the atmosphere muddy. There were a number of high round tables with three or four stools around them. There were stools along the bar. Most people were standing in huddles.

Beyond the circle she knew, a mash of suited men and neatly dressed women made a general, indecipherable noise. At the back of the cellar near the men's room were three trays of food, already half-empty. A man plucked out a buffalo wing and sauce slid from it onto the floor. Then

15

sauce dribbled down his chin. He picked up a napkin and wiped it away.

A group of strangers left a table which was a couple of feet from the bar, and Eddie sort of leapt towards it, making a claim before anyone else could get their hands on it. There were four stools around it, so all the ladies sat and Lawrence sat. Eddie McGovern and Ernie Sleet remained standing.

'Danny Boy' finished and then 'Raglan Road' finished and then an Irish fiddle tune circulated inoffensively, but Sara wasn't in the mood for it. As a long-time regular, she was perfectly entitled to ask the barman to change the disc. She called loudly so that the boy behind the bar heard her over the babble,

"Why do you have to play all this emerald isle crap? Why can't you play something good?" A rim of foam from the Guinness lay on her top lip. Her tongue lapped over it.

Eddie McGovern laughed. "It is an Irish bar, Sara!"

She was sick to death of Irishness. Sick to death of it! When she had first begun to frequent *Mulligan's* there'd been a guy, what was his name? Never been to Ireland and so held strong views on it, was always rude to her as though she were a representative of the British Government. (It'd be a bloody better world if I was!) So she'd invented an Irish mother from Wicklow, a fiction which would have infuriated her real mother who had thought all Irish people a lot of grubby layabouts. Sometimes Sara agreed with her. At one time or another Sara agreed with nearly anyone about nearly anything, though not for long and not very deeply. Right now, she wanted to disown her Wicklow mother and praise her London mother. She was sick to death of Irishness.

"Go on, put on something good, Seamus!" She craned her neck toward the barman. She had to shout. "Don't you have something seventies?"

The barman was very young and tall and lanky with a long thin face and a dark complexion. He had a little tuft of hair

16

between his eyebrows. He had long, thin fingers. His darkness made her think of Steve. This lad could probably use a lesson or two in love from me, Sara said to herself. He probably looks quite good naked. A bit thin. I like thin. Perhaps one day we'll get together if he's lucky. But not tonight. It would be a betrayal of Steve tonight.

"We've got a Barry Manilow CD."

"Gawd no, something good, I was a wild girl in the seventies, got happy memories, play something good. Al Green. Got any Al Green?"

Seamus looked blank.

"Al Green? Who's he?"

"Oh my God! Kids today are such philistines. Al Green! Only the best pop singer since Elvis!" Ironically, Sara had never much liked Elvis, she was a little too young to have heard the good stuff when it was all the rage, to her he was a bit soupy and thick- voiced. But she knew that this philistine barman would at least have heard of him.

He shrugged. She pursed her red, red lips together. "'Let's Stay Together'! 'Take Me To The River'! 'Love and Happiness'!"

"Oh sure," he said, "'Take me to the river'. That's Talking Heads, isn't it?"

"Well," she said, eyelids drooping critically, "They did a version of it, yes. Not a very good one. But Al Green did it first." She began to sing the melody softly but coarsely, missing notes. "'Take me to the river, wash me down, cleanse my soul, put my feet on the ground...'" She fell silent and looked for a moment very sad.

"Gets to you, that song, does it?" said Eddie, smiling. His neat moustache, raised by his lips, looked like an insect climbing into his nostrils. He'd already reached that pitch of sentimentality that often came on him halfway through his second pint. She glanced up at him as though he'd interrupted some other train of thought and there was something accusatory in her eyes.

"You what?"

"That song. It moves you."

"Oh. Yeh. Yeh, it does." She was in her head a long way from the bar. Dark inky water. Piers. Wooden pillars rising out of the river. A compacted smell of salt. A hugging couple a few hundred feet from her on a bench arm in arm looking across to the Jersey shore. She'd hated them with their romantic embrace and their cosiness and their foreverandevers, which - she'd wanted to go up and tell them - which will not last forever and ever, I assure you, never let a man tell you otherwise. One thirty in the morning, and in New bloody York there were still bloody people about. The City that never sleeps! But don't these kissing wretches have work to go to?

She was unmooring, losing her sense of real place, real time. She pinched herself to bring *Mulligan's* back to her. She pulled her compact mirror from her handbag and flipped it open to remind herself that she was still alive, still corporeal. She looked old and tired even in the muddiness of the bar. But she was still here. She dropped the mirror back into the bag. It seemed to her the bar was getting noisier. Oh, how she yearned for silence!

The barman was sorting through the short pile of CDs behind the bar.

Leanne said, "Do you know what song always makes me tear up?" Leanne was pretty in a vacant way, but her neck was a bit wide. She was a nurse and could colour the simplest remark with generalized compassion. Her husband, Lawrence, sold railroad tickets at Pennsylvania station and could colour the simplest remark with curtness.

"Hummmph," he said, sceptically, before she'd had a chance to answer her own question.

"What?" said Eddie, interested.

18

"You'll laugh."

"No I won't."

"It's my age, you see. 'Puppy Love.' The Donny Osmond version." Eddie did indeed laugh. So did Ernest and Jackie and Bea, even Leanne's husband Lawrence. "Because it was the first single I ever bought. I knew you'd laugh." She was a little hurt. Lawrence patted her on the back. The conversation had turned formally to pop music, as it often does in bars. It was revealed that Lawrence had briefly been a punk rocker, which not even his wife knew. "You sure keep secrets, honey," she said, not altogether fondly.

"That from a girl who never told me about her crush on Donny Osmond!"

"Would you have dropped me if you'd known?" They'd married at nineteen, only shortly after his punk phase.

"Of course I would!" he said dismissively. "I couldn't have lived down Donny Osmond."

"We've got this," called Seamus the barman, waving a double CD towards Sara called 'Soul explosion – 40 classic R&B Hits'.

"Oh, well it's better than a lot of fiddling leprechauns!"

Otis Redding sat plaintively on 'The Dock of the Bay'.

"Give us a fag, Eddie."

Eddie passed his half-empty package to her, saying in mock criticism, "Not fallen off the wagon, have you, Sara? Not after five years?"

"Six." She unfolded the Guinness match book sitting in the unused ashtray. "Nearly seven, actually. But I want a fag right now and so a bloody fag I'll have." She puffed on it just as familiarly as if she were still a twenty-a-day girl. "That feels bloody good."

"Apparently that slimeball of a mayor wants to stop smoking in bars," said Jackie. Jackie had flame red hair and a flame-red temperament which was suppressed in her secretarial job but sometimes came out with her pals.

19

"Well that bloody mayor can stick his ban right up his arse and smoke it, can't he?" Sara inhaled a huge gasp as if in protest, and expelled it full and fat into the space over their heads.

Otis Redding faded away and 'The Midnight Hour' punched through the speakers, promising raunch after dark.

"For me, John Lennon's the man. I really like Lennon," said Eddie McGovern. Sara sighed, over something not to do with Lennon, and brushed hair from her forehead. The smoke curled around her ear. "'Imagine all the People', 'Jealous Guy.' Lennon was a genius. It was awful when that Chapman creep shot him." Eddie exterminated cockroaches by day and talked about The Beatles at night.

"Genius? He was a meshuganer, that one," said Ernest Sleet, who wasn't Jewish but liked Yiddish expressions.

"But he was," said Jackie. "Though he was better with the Beatles than after." She touched Ernest's hand. They worked different shifts in different departments in *Macy's* and were always glad to see each other.

"Well, The Beatles were all geniuses," said Leanne kindly.

"No way!" said Eddie." Lennon was God. McCartney was sort of okay. The other two were useless. It was Lennon who made them."

"Have you ever been up to Strawberry Fields?"

"Every year we go up on the anniversary of his assassination. Sort of a tribute. Look at the Dakota building and light a candle in the park. Don't we, honey?"

The Dakota Building. Sara blinked. Her lost Steve had never heard of the Dakota Building. How could anyone be so young and unsullied they'd never heard of the Dakota building?

"Yeah," said Bea. "One time we saw Yoko. I'm sure we did."

"We saw a shadow moving in the apartment. It might have been Yoko."

"It looked kind of thin and Japanese."

"You know what I thought? I thought maybe it was John's ghost. Maybe around the anniversary of his death he comes back. Makes a visit to the earthly plane. Because the shadow looked tall and had, well it looked like little round glasses."

"You said that at the time, but I don't think it was. It was Yoko."

"Yoko's crap," said Ernest.

No-one felt like debating this, Sara least of all. Unconsciously, she sniffed her palm. Her rose scent was a powerful one, but it could not withstand the stronger wafts of beer and smoke and fried chicken. She looked over to where the free food was arrayed.

Three big mass-catering pans, one with buffalo wings sinking into a glutinous sauce, another with very deeply fried chicken legs, the third with dark delicious ribs.

"God, I'm hungry!" But before she could move, Eddie McGovern said with clumsy kindness,

"Let me! What do you want?"

"All of it! I'm bloody hungry!"

"Don't wanna get fat," he said with humour. She wasn't amused.

"Edward, I'll get as fat as I bloody well like, actually!"

"Yes, ma'am!" he raised his hands in defence. But it was the way he said 'ma'am' that made her really angry. Wounds were too fresh for even unintended mockery. For a paranoid second she wondered if Eddie knew something, was mocking her in full knowledge? At this moment she felt her re-entry into the old dull life was beginning to fail. She flashed eyes at him.

"Look, I'll get my own fucking food!" And she stalked through the crowd. She pushed a man's elbow and a splash of wine dampened his shoe.

"Watch it, lady!"

21

"Don't you 'lady' me!"

She piled her plate with seven legs and seven wings and three ribs. It was a very full plate. She didn't care if she looked greedy. She'd be as greedy as she bloody well liked.

She wolfed down alternately a leg and a wing and a leg and a wing, then a rib, then a leg and a wing and a leg and a wing, then a rib, then a leg and a wing and a leg and a wing, then a rib, and lastly a leg and a wing, until all that remained was a smear of sauce and some meatless bones. In her head she was a long way from *Mulligan's* again. She was thinking of Steve. She was always thinking of Steve. What a beautiful body he'd had. Even at the end, there had been an odd beauty in his stillness.

She pictured him in embrace, but it was not an embrace with her. She could not see the face of the lucky woman, knew it was not her only because she was, as in a dream, looking at them; though of course in a dream you could look on at your own embrace. So perhaps it was her after all. She hoped it was.

The vision popped into nothingness and she was back in the banality of the bar and the talk had turned to the price of gas and how awful Arabs were.

I cannot stand it, she said to herself, but the thought was so near the front of her mind that her lips shaped it, although no sound emerged. I cannot stand this, I don't belong here. I would rather die. I do not belong here.

Suddenly she said,

"I've had enough of this prattle. I'm getting out of here. Goodbye, all." And she downed the dregs of her stout in one gulp and pushed her stool away from the table with her bottom.

"But you've only just got here!" said Eddie, in sentimental offense. Oh Eddie, she wanted to say, you big dopey fool with your kindness and your lumpy body, oh Eddie, what can you possibly know?

22

"Goodbye, all," she said. She did not look back. She wanted her goodbye to have the ring of finality to it, because she really did not want ever to return to this place and these people, but the cautious part of her nature did not allow her to slam the metaphorical door too firmly. Just in case. She clomped to the staircase. She heard Bea say in what that silly woman supposed was a whisper,

"She's in an odd mood." She heard Eddie quietly agree.

"Yeah…"

She climbed to the exit.

Well, they were right, her mood was odd. Whose wouldn't be under the circumstances? After what she had lived through, the trivia of *Mulligan's*, the chat and noise and booze and food, was contemptible. The last few days had changed her. She would never be able to go to *Mulligan's* again. *Mulligan's* was a part of an old life. She could not pass another evening listening to those people talking rubbish. They were more distant to her even than the boy whom she would never see again.

She walked north, shoes tap-tapping, her left leg moving forward, her right, her left again. Sara's mind blanked, so that it was not she herself in control, but her body, her limbs, her limbs were deciding for her where she would go. Her feet in their elegant heels. Walk, walk. Tap, tap. Walk, walk. Tap, tap.

To Washington Square.

The square was quite busy. A man sat on the edge of the fountain smoking a roll- up. He looked unwell. A young black kid, all alone and in his own world, kicked his skate board into the air and leapt up to it, his feet making contact, soles flat to the wood, and they hit the ground as a single being. It was a beautiful action, like dance. He must have practiced for hours, days, weeks, to get so good. He had a nice body, she saw, wiry and fit. He looked ecstatic.

He and his skateboard for that wonderful moment were to him, Sara saw, the whole world, like the universe before the Big Bang, all packed into that little space of joy. If only he could keep that sensation forever. That sensation, eternally sustained. If there was a heaven, that would be it. If there could be a heaven on earth that must be it.

Was it the gift of youth that even as they looked out into the world, looked for romance or just for warm easy fucks, even as they began to engage other people in a grown-up way, at the same time they were happy in their own sealed world into which they could at any time retreat? Their bodies could become the whole world. This could not happen when you were older and you had been soiled by experience, by contact with too many other people, by knowledge of your dependence. Sara pursed her red red lips. Steve, like this boy with the skateboard, had been able to live entirely within his body. His fleshly, sinewy universe. How Sara envied that easy, uncorrupted narcissism.

Couples kissed. A flouncy woman walked her poodle. Sara passed so close to the bench on which she'd once from a distance seen Steve that if he'd been there now her coat would have brushed his knee. Coming towards this specific bench was a deliberate action. She thought as the hem of her coat blew in the light breeze against the bench's outer slat, that's it, that's the one. She fancied that the tug of the breeze was in fact Steve himself, invisible but present, pulling fondly at her coat as if to say everything was all right.

She crossed the street and came to the foot of Fifth Avenue. Fifth Avenue, like Elvis, was something she'd never warmed to, partly because she lived like a person who didn't have very much money and partly because she wasn't much interested in material things. She was interested in people. I like people, she thought, and because there were none near her to spoil the illusion she felt this was true. I'm a kind of psychiatrist really, she decided, I see people more clearly than

24

most. I've an eye for the tell-tale clue, the mannerism or the statement that gives a person away. She was willing, looking at the lights running all the way up to Central Park, to buy into her own flattery absolutely. But the lights of Fifth Avenue made her think of the lights of Broadway which made her think of sweet 'Huck', sweet Steve, who was gone for good. But sweet Steve had never actually been anywhere near Broadway except as a paying customer, and then not often because he couldn't afford it. He'd had no money, Steve. What actor starting out ever does? Steve's dream had been Broadway, but it was never going to come to anything now.

Will I ever be able even to walk in the vicinity of Broadway without thinking of that bloody boy? Oh, maybe I should just get out of New York, go back to London.

She gazed out at the lights of the city, the great big city, the wonderful city. She felt only an ill-focused hatred for it until the Guinness came sour into her mouth and her self-pity rose again and she felt tears in her eyes and the round red lights of cars became many-pointed stars which dazzled her.

Perhaps she had been too greedy after all, had eaten too many ribs and legs and wings, because she began to feel slightly unwell...

ALICE

Sara's world before Steve had been a different world, she knew that now. How could it feel so different, the same places, the same people? It was as if she had moved from Iceland to Samarkand, that's how different it felt. Yet she hadn't moved anywhere.

That day she had met him, it had been an ordinary day, as boring and repetitive as any other. It had started out promising nothing. Indeed, the morning of that day had been if anything less wonderful even than usual.

Sara knew that Dave and Ruth wished she wouldn't be so snappy with patrons she took a dislike to, usually on a whim, but as she often said over one or another matter to them, to Dave Mann and Ruth Fowkes-Mann, the co-owners with her of *Make Someone's Day Cards and Gifts* on Seventh and Fifteenth, "look, ducks, I am what I am and I don't tolerate fools gladly, that's how I am," and just as a nice smile from a charming man could make her day so a difficult customer could ruin it.

The mother came in with her cute little girl and her baby in its stroller. Before the poor woman had so much as opened her mouth Sara felt her, Sara's, day collapse into ruins. Dave and Ruth were out to lunch.

"Hi," said the woman.

"Hello," said Sara unwelcomingly.

"I'm looking for a birthday card for a six-year-old child."

"We've got plenty of them." The cute girl beamed up to Sara like a very, very good little madam.

"It's for my fwend Jonathan," said the girl in a very high voice. "He's having a party and I've been invited."

"Have you, dear, how nice." Sara avoided her eye. She looked instead at the child's golden curls.

"Yeah, it's gonna be cool. His daddy is real rich."

"How nice for his daddy. Kids' cards over there."

She pointed to a section against the left wall of the store. The kid ran to it. The mother struggled with the stroller. The baby awoke and yawned and closed his eyes again. Sara took it he was a he because his stroller was blue and so was his coat.

The mother riffled a few cards that said "6 today," or "Happy Sixth Birthday" in gold or silver or a dusting of red sprinkles. One had a removable pin which said "I'm six." Sara couldn't envision a child bedecked in such a pin without feeling dizzy, but *Make Someone's Day* sold quite a few of them.

There were Carlton Cards, Clinton's cards, Marion Heath and Caspari and American Greetings. There were Snoopy cards and Batman cards and Thomas the Tank Engine cards and an old and curling My Little Pony card.

"Which do you like, honey?"

"I wanna Disney card," said the child in her delightfully chiming voice. "'Finding Nemo' or Mickey Mouse."

The child could not know that mentioning Disney within Sara's hearing was a big mistake.

"Sure," said the mother, riffling some more. The child pulled out a card, not a Disney one. An arrow in the corner pointed to a plastic button. 'Press me,' it said, like the bottle in 'Alice in Wonderland.' This was appropriate because the child shared the name of that figure of literature. The mother said, "Don't touch things, Alice." But of course the

27

little minx couldn't resist. A thin, mean rendition of the melody of Happy Birthday grated the ear of Sara at her counter. The mother snatched the card away.

"I said, don't touch things!" She shoved the card back into the rack with such force that the top left corner creased downward, making the card unsaleable. "There don't seem to be any Disney cards. This one's nice." Snoopy the dog and that strange yellow bird whose name Sara couldn't remember held between them a sign saying 'SIX!'

"Nah, I want Disney."

The mother turned to Sara.

"Please, where are your Disney cards?"

Sara said with deliciously excruciating politeness,

"We don't stock Disney. We've lots of great cards, but no Disney."

"Snoopy's a bit out of date."

"I don't want Snoopy, I want Mickey Mouse! Donald!"

"Look," said Sara, "there's Batman. All boys like Batman. I take it this Jonathan is a boy?"

"Mom. Can we go to the Disney store?"

"No, Alice, we're going to pick out a card right here! There's a big choice."

"Mom, I wanna go to the Disney store."

"Alice, if you don't shut up we'll go home without a card and you won't go to Jonathan's party."

As often in the negotiations between an adult and a child, the child's complete lack of reason resulted in the opposite effect to the one the parent plotted. Any adult can tell you that if it's a choice between on the one hand a Snoopy card and a party or on the other hand no Mickey Mouse card and no party either; you swallow your reservations and buy the Snoopy card. Children's minds are alien. Alice wanted both the Mickey card and the party and could not see that she was endangering both.

"I wanna Disney card, Momma."

28

"Alice, choose a card, please," said mother with quiet, stern finality. She aged seven years.

"I wanna Disney card! Jonathan hates Snoopy." It is probable that Jonathan held no strong views on Snoopy, but Alice certainly did at that moment. Just as Sara held strong views on Alice.

"Well then, like the lady said, Batman." There was desperate appeal in the mother's voice.

Alice's face fell. She said, so quietly it could not be heard but for its intense emotional force, "Disney."

"Choose, Alice!"

"I wanna go to the Disney store."

"Choose! We can't take all day. We've got to go and visit Grandma in the hospital. Now choose!"

"I wanna go to the Disney Store! Please, momma! Pllleeeaaazzz!" The 'please' did not come out as a courtesy but as a demand.

Sara's patience had run out. She said, in a tone of utmost pleasantness, of flattery even, just as if she were saying, *my what a lovely little girl you are, look at your big smile*, only the words coming out wrong:

"Look, little Alice, why don't you sod off and get a Disney card then, eh?" The mother gaped at her. "Because frankly I hate bloody Disney cards, I'd like to cut Mickey's nose off if I had a pair of scissors to hand, which in fact I do in this drawer here, and if he's not anywhere nearby," she made a move of the head to indicate she was looking out for him, "I may have to cut your nose off instead. So if I were you I would piss off out of my store and get you card somewhere else."

The girl's face screwed up in a terrible look of horror. The mother had recovered enough to say,

"Don't you talk to my child like that!"

Sara said, level, reasonable, "Kindly get out of my shop."

"This is a disgrace! I'm going to lodge a formal complaint. Where's the manager? I want the manager now!"

"Dear, I *am* the bloody manager. Complaint noted. Now piss off." Sara held the door open. The mother rather meekly swung the stroller around and pushed it through the door. But Alice did not move, so her mother had to look back for her.

"Come along, Alice!"

The girl ran to her, and as she crossed the threshold she burst into sobs of lovely tears. Sara let the door swing shut, but just before it closed, she said on her breath so that only the girl could hear,

"snip, snip."

The door touched the back of Alice's little pink shoes. She ran off.

Sara went back behind the counter, feeling a little better for the confrontation.

"I expect the last bloody thing I'll see on my deathbed is that fucking mouse!"

She flipped open the 'New York Post.' Dave and Ruth came back arm in arm from lunch.

"Your turn," said Dave as he always did, meaning she could go to lunch. "How's it been?"

"Quiet." She didn't look up from the paper, turned a page.

"Be back ASAP," said Dave, tapping his watch. He grinned, because the term 'ASAP' enraged Sara. That's why he used it so often. Sara's temper wasn't ideal for the management of a card store, but it was fun to annoy her.

"Oh Dave!" said Ruth. "Don't make her mad! He doesn't mean it, Sara."

Sara didn't take offense today, because after all she'd driven a potential customer away, and Ruth and Dave needed the money more than she did. So she laughed and only pretended to be annoyed.

"I will kick your ass ASAP if you don't watch it, young man."

Ruth and Dave went into the office.

Make Someone's Day Cards and Gifts was a genuine if modest success story, though Sara herself was marginal to its success. She'd put money into it when David and Ruth were looking for what they'd called an 'investor'. They had not expected their 'investor' to become the ongoing presence that Sara was, but merely to receive a percentage of the profits. Dave and Ruth did all the real work, such as it was: ordering, accounting, organizing, arranging the shelves. They had to keep it dusted, too. It was one of those stores that gave the impression of never being entirely free of dust, despite Ruth's daily round of flapping a cloth over the stock. Sara simply turned up for approximately eight hours a day on approximately five days out of seven, with varying degrees of sweetness and sourness, in the expectation that Ruth and Dave would be suitably grateful.

Dave had walked past the sad, empty building and had looked about him and had said first to himself and a few minutes later in a phone booth had said to Ruth, "This is the perfect place for a card store!" The reason for this inspiration was the presence round the corner of St. Vincent's Hospital. "We'll make a million bucks in 'Get Well Soon' cards!" And they had made, if not a million bucks, at least enough to keep the store chugging along while others around them folded and changed hands. They did sell a large quantity of 'Get Well Soon' cards, and nearby apartments purchased Birthday cards and Christmas cards and Valentine's Day cards. Office buildings in the vicinity snapped up 'Good Luck in Your New Job' cards.

One of the keys to business success is using your space to its utmost capacity. Occasionally adventurous tourists might throw their guide books away and wander out of the sight-seeing districts, heads up, in the hope of spotting some life as it is actually lived in this unsleeping city. They were drawn into *Make Someone's Day* to acquire trashy gifts for the folks back home. If they wanted a plaster model of the Statue of Liberty or the Empire State Building *Make Someone's Day* was the place for them. (Dave and Ruth had tearfully thrown away their stock of the World Trade Centre after that black day over a year gone. Less ethical businesses had put the prices up, but Dave and Ruth couldn't bring themselves to profiteer in so unconscionable a way.) If they wanted a mug which said 'To my special Grandmother' or 'Hug a policeman - it's the law!' *Make Someone's Day* could supply them. If they had a disagreeable child, their very own Alice, they could placate her with a Ty Beanie animal or a stuffed Bugs Bunny or a talking bear. If their little monster was an Alan, could he be satisfied for a few minutes with a 'Star Wars' ceramic mug or a 'Lord of the Rings' action figure? If the pangs of hunger arose there were Oreos and Ritz Sandwiches, if of thirst there were bottles of Snapple and cans of Diet Coke. If they wanted to get rich they could buy their Lotto tickets. If they needed cash, there was an ATM in a corner.

Of course even Dave could every so often make a misjudgement. He had ordered fifteen three-dimensional NYPD plates, made and hand-painted in China, and at $28.00 they had not sold a single one. Reduced to $19.99, they still sat there, unwanted. Ruth had said he should get rid of them, but he'd said they could stay there forever as a reminder that even he was not perfect. Then he'd pecked her on the cheek.

Sara picked up her handbag and swung it, perhaps not accidentally, dangerously near the upright NYPD plate on its plastic stand, atop its box. She went to find lunch. She felt rather lively as she always did after inspiring the spilling of a few tears.

32

Lunch for her was usually from the *Blimpie* sandwich shop two doors down or from the *McDonald's Express*, or one of the countless Pizza places within a minute's walk - *Pedro's Pizza*, *The Crispy Pizza Café* - but today she decided she'd forgo her usual quick snack and treat herself to something more exotic: Chinese. So she went down to the *Empire Szechuan Village* at 12th, opposite the *Village Vanguard* jazz club. The *Empire* was novel in that it had both a Japanese and a Chinese menu, but she didn't like seafood so it was always Chinese for her. She settled at her table on one of the upright chairs with bright pink cushions. She could see the *Vanguard* across from her and the nail salon above it. An attractive black man in early middle age wearing a baseball cap went through the jazz venue's bright red door, red like her lips, red like a London bus, and disappeared into the basement.

(Sara didn't know much about jazz. If she'd known more, she might've been excited to witness the great Sphere Masters on his way to rehearse in the dark of the club, playing his tenor saxophone all alone because he loved it, his music swirling in the stillness, licking up the stairs to the door. Sphere was a genius.)

The special of the day was sliced duck sautéed with basil leaves for only $12.00, and very good it was too, served with countless little cups of tea. She crumbled her fortune cookie.

'Just as you feel old, youth will revive you.'

Now what on earth could that mean? Sara mulled it over. She repeated it three times in her head. Just as you feel old, youth will revive you. Just as you feel old, youth will revive you. Just as you feel old, youth will revive you. Hmm. It didn't make much sense, but it sounded like good news so she permitted it to warm her. Sara did not precisely believe the prophecies of fortune cookies, just as she did not precisely believe the horoscopes she turned to in magazines; but she did not quite disbelieve them either. If

33

her friends at *Mulligan's* said to her, "Sara, you don't actually buy that shit, do you?" she'd say of course she bloody didn't, it's just a bit of fun. Yet a particularly memorable prognostication, one that promised something unusually good or unusually bad or something rather mysterious as this one did would linger in her mind, and she would for several days watch for evidences of its coming to pass in one way or another.

In the afternoon she manned the counter again. She couldn't actually see the parts of St Vincent's that mattered to *Make Someone's Day* from the store. The main hospital, including the Emergency Room, was round the corner out of sight. If she were to put her nose to the glass she could just see the sign, *Emergency*, and an arrow pointing left. All she could easily see from her counter was the Medical Training Centre directly across from her. It proudly displayed the St. Vincent's insignia: an orange V on an ochre blue cross. As the hospital was a Catholic institution, Sara supposed that the 'V' was intended to be an abstract representation of Christ.

Dave fingered catalogues selecting new stock. Ruth pretended to do some accounting but spent most of the time sitting next to Dave, rubbing his hand now and then fondly. Customers wandered in and out. A few birthday cards were sold and the first Halloween cards of the year. A youngish couple came in and the man selected a dreadful plaster model of the Empire State Building. He handed over a ten dollar bill and when she gave him three back he said,

"Cheers!" and turned to leave.

"You English?" asked Sara.

"Yes."

"Same here," said Sara.

"Oh."

"Same here," said the woman.

34

Not knowing what more to say, the couple tried to pretend to be impressed that here in NY was a fellow import from Blighty.

"Been here the best part of twenty years," said Sara.

"Oh." He crumpled the brown bag containing the Empire State Building.

"You? Just visiting?"

"Yes, just a tourist I'm afraid." He shook the bag as if to say, who on earth would buy this horrible little thing if he wasn't a tourist?

"Do you get back often?" asked the woman.

"Not since my old mum died. I'm settled here now."

"Like it?"

"Love it. The City That Never Sleeps! Who wouldn't? Your first visit?"

"To New York, yeh. We've done Florida. Disneyworld." She put an arm around her husband's waist, perhaps in a sharing of happy memories.

Disney! Disney! Sara gritted her teeth. Why did half the world have an obsession with Disney? If only they knew... if only they knew.

"How nice. Still, it's better to visit a real place, isn't it, where real people live? A glimpse of real life's always a good thing, eh?"

"Oh of course." It was not clear the woman believed this, though she nodded vigorously.

The couple left. Ruth wandered out from the office, indifferently clutching a glossy catalogue which she hadn't opened and never would.

"English?"

Sara was sharp.

"They've been corrupted. No English person thirty years ago would have gone to Disneyworld. They'd've thought it was plasticky rubbish. What a bunch of philistines this younger generation is! At least in France they still have a

35

sense of their own culture." In France they hated Euro Disney. Or Disney Europe, or whatever it was called now. (The corporation had renamed it in a desperate attempt to salvage it.) The French hated *McDonald's* too, and farmers drove their tractors through the plate-glass windows of that estimable chain in protest. Sara liked the French.

The afternoon unwound without any enlivening interest, so shortly after four Sara decided she would go crazy if she stayed another minute. She went into the back room.

"It's nearly five," she said, "so I think I'll be heading out." The clock very blatantly said four oh seven but Dave didn't put up a fight. He never put up a fight.

"Sure. See you tomorrow."

So she left the store in the capable hands of Ruth and Dave and headed off to her Village apartment which a claim on life insurance had purchased. It hadn't cost much at the time, but inflation and overcrowding had made it a valuable piece of real estate these days, so valuable that letters from realtors begging her to let them sell it for her at a soaringly high price turned up frequently in her mail box. But she wasn't going to sell it, because where would she go? She remembered the English couple, and thought: I love it here! I love NY! I heart NY! Who'd want dark, dank old England after this? New York, New York, it's a wonderful town! The park is up and the Battery's down!

When she got to her apartment she'd do what she always did   because, just as she had nowhere else to live so she had nothing else to do.   She was – she thought - not an imaginative woman and had never quite worked out how to use the City, how to 'make it work for her' as that loathsome financial advisor had once said to her of her modest but not unenviable nest-egg, this too the result of life insurance. She was the kind who fell too easily into routines, which through sheer repetition became fixed.   So tonight as on other nights she'd open a can or a box of something flavourless but

36

quickly prepared, and she'd flop onto her lovely leather couch and make an effort at watching the news, then she'd head out to *Mulligan's* for the boring and unchanging company there. She had long before given up any pretence of enjoyment of these evenings. The novelty of new friends sixteen years ago had soon after turned into the mildly dull but comforting buzz of familiar faces, familiar conversations. But that too had fallen away, the dullness no longer intimate, only leaden.

Her own sense that she'd done nothing for a decade except sit in *Make Someone's Day* and drink in *Mulligan's* was an edited version of the facts. There had in reality been adventures, a vacation every now and then, the odd fling with a man. She'd even screwed Eddie McGovern from *Mulligan's* a few times before he'd met Bea, and even after, which she was sure Bea had no inkling of. But their encounters had brought no pleasure on her part except the satisfaction that comes with doing one's duty: She had felt when he had put his hand nervously to her breast that to let him make love to her was indeed a duty, an act of generosity. She remembered his heavy body pressed on her, her head uncomfortably bent against the arm of the couch so she'd feared her neck would break, (her old couch this was, not the nice comfy leather one she had now), the suffocating pressure which she recalled so clearly she could feel the weight from memory, her knickers round her ankles, his quick sharp penetration, his rolling off her which relief was the nearest to enjoyment she got from the act, a drowning woman breaking back into air. Then, his well-meant whispers afterwards in his thick Brooklyn accent,

"That was great, you're a great gal, Sara."

"It was nice," she'd said kindly. "You know me, Eddie, I live for the moment."

He'd gazed at her with his wide sentimental eyes. He'd looked like he wanted to cry.

37

But it was the starker version of her life, the one without love or sex, which she liked to dwell on. Its austerity allowed her to indulge her well-developed martyr complex. Anyway, her impression was that this cycle remained unbroken for month after month and year into year.

Until, that evening, it broke. The boy broke it. He shattered it.

STEVE

It's not often a boy falls over outside your apartment building, especially one who is notably attractive, speaks with a shimmery Southern lilt and is apparently not drunk or drug-crazed or simple-minded.

He fell a split second before Sara rounded the corner, so when she first sighted him he was sprawled flat on the sidewalk at the foot of her steps at 33 Minetta Lane. She saw his top half lift a little as he folded to his knees and his arms dropped back to the pavement, palms splayed, in the shape of a slim graceful four-legged animal, a well-kept cat perhaps. She saw his bottom, the blue jeans tightening around it in his movement, the legs bent into right angles, two sides of a perfect square. White sports shoes were on his feet, the right with laces untied. Then she saw his back, the leather jacket catching a pool of gentle light shaped like a match head's flame between his shoulder blades and down to the hem. Above the jacket the thin line of pink flesh at the collar, the brown-black hair above. Two small pink ears.

But it wasn't his body that made the first important impression.

No, it wasn't his body, slim and neat and well-shaped as it was in his blue jeans and black leather jacket over - she saw as he looked up to her - a burgundy red shirt which looked quite expensive.

Nor was it his face, the right cheek of which was grazed from the fall, a streak of broken skin under the cheekbone like a swordsman's scar. She could not see the streak at her angle.

It was, first, his eyes.

It wasn't because his eyes were necessarily deep or beautiful. Perhaps they were; she couldn't at that moment tell. As he looked up to her the fuzzy Autumn evening sun touched his face and perhaps a cloud broke apart because the light hardened for a second, he squinted, the lids half closed, the yellow sun washing the eyes and reflecting back to her. All she saw was sun-yellow light, and was there - she couldn't be sure - some water in them as if he had been crying or was about to cry? Or was that an effect of the sun too? His hand shot up to his right cheek, his fingers touched it, and only then did she see the thin red strip, red like her lips, red like a London Bus.

That must hurt quite a bit, she thought. Poor hurt boy. When he took his fingers away from the flesh, the tips were dotted with little pricks of blood.

Sara's mothering instinct came out. She was proud of this instinct, discerned occasionally by her like the spirit of an unborn child but never gleaned by anyone else. Sara was certain she would have made a superb mother. The girl with little pink shoes was long forgotten. Anyway, if she'd had a child it would have been a boy. She didn't like girls.

He looked down to the pavement and reached for his sun glasses and said, not to her particularly,

"Shit, I sure hope these didn't break." Shee-it, ah sho' hope theise didn' brake.

Sara did not object to this coarseness, she'd been known to use a few 'direct' words in her time, it's only natural, the salt of the earth, only prissy people look askance when someone uses a word which, after all, best expresses the mood. The voice was so liltingly Southern and so sun-

40

warmed he might have been quoting romantic poetry to her. As he put the sun glasses on his nose she saw that a little blurry fingerprint of his blood coloured the thick portion of the left arm near the lens.

"Careful, ducks, you don't want to get blood in your hair."

The boy hesitated again, a glimmer of confusion. This might have been because he'd forgotten his bloodied fingers, or it may have been that he'd never heard the word 'ducks' as a term of address and had to digest it for a beat. Perhaps at first he took it to be an insult. But the beaming face of the plump blond woman could not have been friendlier.

"Oh. Yeah."

"Your glasses."

He took them off, saw the fingerprint.

"Shit."

"You'd better wash them off."

"I will, ma'am."

She reached out her hand to pull him to his feet. He looked at the hand in another moment of puzzlement. He was very boyish when puzzled, strangely uncorrupted. He was perfectly able to get to his feet without help. When he accepted her offer, wrapped his bloodied fingers round the full pillow of her hand, it must have been purely out of courtesy, out of a wish not to spurn a Samaritan. She scarcely felt the pull of his body as he rose up; he was not using her strength but his own, holding her hand limply, his own legs and thighs the leverage.

On his feet, she saw that he was under-sized, her own height in fact, five foot six.

"This is my building you're outside," she said. He looked up to it: a narrow old brick townhouse nestling between taller buildings. Brown steps leading to a porch, a wrought-iron black rail running up either side, three floors above. An apartment on each floor. The fire escape stairs and balconies

41

which had been added when the house had been broken up into apartments were so much a part of the tone of the Village that they were rather attractive, rather "authentically New York." There was a basement room at street level beside the run of steps. In the basement window a sign said *Boyle's Travel,* the most recent of a number of businesses to hire the space. *Boyle's* had withered like the others before it. Now the basement was empty, the window opaque with dirt. No doubt some sucker would be found to take it on for a while. There were plenty of suckers to be had. But anyone who thought they'd find customers here was a fool: People did not shop in Minetta Lane. Sara, a successful business woman, had nothing but contempt for suckers. The sole success on her street was a Mexican restaurant, its wall painted bright red like her lips, with crude illustrations of cactuses breaking up the redness. In front of *Boyle's* was a small square yard with a single unhappy tree in it, struggling to survive but somehow hanging on, its branches leaning against the steps as if exhausted. Behind it, pressed to the wall made by the rise of the steps, were three trash cans, one for each apartment.

"You'd best come up, you need a dab of cotton wool and some ointment."

"Oh, ma'am, I wouldn't want to bother you."

"No bother. Come on, lad."

He looked at her building, up to her window. He was nervous.

"I'm not going to eat you, kiddo! Come on!" She was on the first step up to the porch. He followed, she thought not because he wanted to but again because he did not wish to offend.

"Well, if you don't mind…"

He did not seem comfortable following her. He seemed on edge. Why should he be afraid?

42

They went up the steps. A mildly metallic smell, the distinctive odour of City waste, rose from the three trash cans standing neatly in a row to the side of the flight like three wise monkeys. Just before Sara reached the door she glanced down into their cold dark mouths. They'd been emptied that morning. Their lids rested against their sides.

A bronze plaque was attached to the wall beside the porch: 1836.

She pushed her key into the lock. She walked right past the mailbox which could wait. She rarely got any mail worth opening anyway, bills, circulars, begging letters from charities and realtors.

The door on the first floor was Peter and Tony's, she was on the floor above. A little bald man she hardly knew lived over her.

One day, thought Sara, I won't be able to climb these stairs, then the realtors can have the bloody place all they want.

She switched on the light and she saw with a touch of shame how cramped her apartment was, how mean and bare. She wished she vacuumed more often.

The boy passed her at the open door and when he turned around to face her she saw his eyes without the sun in them for the first time. For a moment she did not take in their richness. Her first sensation was one of relief, for there was no criticism in them as he looked around. He was finding no fault in her threadbare surroundings. His room in a shared apartment, she supposed, wherever it may be, was no doubt smaller yet, but he was young and, she speculated, venturing out into the City for the first time. The world and all its fortunes lay before him. What was he, a student, a waiter somewhere? The eyes did not say. They spoke of nothing except their own richness. They were a deep brown, nearly black. But there was something else to them, which at first appeared a trick of the light like the sunlit flood, but when he

43

stood back a little to give her a direct path to her bathroom the strangeness did not fade. Laid into the blackness were tiny little golden drops. She had never seen eyes like them before. She had looked with concentration into hundreds of eyes, not only those of the men she had loved (if love was the right word,) but into unknown faces which drew her attention, in the street, in the store. She had always liked nice eyes. The eyes were the window of the soul it was said and she thought you could read character through them. She'd seen pairs of eyes where each eye was a different colour, the one brown, the one blue. The one blue, the one yellow. She had once seen into pink blind eyes. She had seen the unnatural paleness of the eyes of an albino. She had seen the red eyes of alcoholism. Once on a TV documentary she had seen the eyes of the novelist Graham Greene, cool and observant. She had thought them striking. She had vowed to read one of his books, but her interest had foundered before the bookstores had opened the next morning. She had seen the dark eyes of hatred. She had seen in her dreams many times the eyes of her unloved husband full of terror as the water rushed over him. But she had never seen eyes like these. It was like looking through a window not into a soul but out into the night sky, a black night sky with very few stars but how bright they were.

She wanted to ask him about them. Were they the result of some accident in childhood perhaps, were they a rare medical condition, were they trendy contact lenses, concealing perfectly ordinary eyes? They looked strong. They looked weak. Did they mean he was doomed to die young? Did they signify potential wisdom? He was too young yet for actual wisdom, but who knew what the future might reveal? But wisdom was a very human trait, one which Sara prided herself in having a share of, and these eyes were not wise with knowledge but silent and indifferent like space itself. And whereas they had seemed kind and mysterious

44

just a moment before, now were they hard and unloving? Yet they had not changed, they had not blinked. They had not moved away. Sara held them a little longer than was polite, but they held hers with equal rigor. They did not slide away, they just looked at her. They looked now, though without any change, soft and unhappy and she was drawn back to the boy with his grazed cheek and his loose-hanging shoelace.

"That's a bad habit, that," she said pointing to the shoe.

"You're right, ma'am." He was shyly apologetic. "I do it all the time. Tie them all I might they don't stay tied."

"Well one day you'll do yourself an injury, my lad. Worse than this one." She tugged on his upper arm, pulling him towards the bathroom. He came without a fight, though there was the slightest resistance, a stiffening of his bicep under the jacket.

"Just a moment," he said. She let him go and he took off the jacket, threw it on the sofa, black leather over blue. "I wouldn't want anything to spill on it." It lay, pockets and three buttons, over the middle cushion, and the top half bent upward against the back. The black on the blue looked like a design, for a catalogue cover perhaps. They belonged together. Sara remembered an old song: Wherever I lay my hat, that's my home.

The bathroom was a windowless square. When she flicked on the light a loud and inefficient air purifying system growled into operation. There was a shower cubicle, a W.C. and a small sink with a mirrored cabinet above it, these items fitting compactly into the small area leaving hardly standing room for two.

She glanced into the mirror at herself, (looking good,) and at him behind her. Strange eyes, strange eyes. Gorgeous face. Then she opened the cabinet and took out some ointment and a ball of cotton wool.

45

She splashed the lotion liberally onto the wad and lifted it to the poor boy's cracked skin. She had been possibly overly generous with the fluid. The bathroom smelt like a compressed hospital. The boy flinched a little as the wad passed near his nose.

"Hold still, dear, it's for your own good."

She pressed the cotton wool to the cut with three flat fingers, more firmly than Leanne the nurse at *Mulligan's* would have considered necessary.

"Ow," he said. "It stings."

She felt as she applied pressure the firmness of her palm against his face, the meeting of skin with skin, curving her wrist so that the fleshy part of her palm near the thumb lightly cupped his jaw. The small bathroom brought out the scent of her perfume heavily, mixing it with the medicinal ointment into a uniquely sweet, unnatural aroma. It may have been the force of her arm or it may have been the sticky smell which made the boy move back a couple of steps.

"It stings," he repeated with a charming little whine.

"That's as it should be. Be brave, dear."

Sara had a superstition that any cure should hurt a little, that if you really felt the sting it meant the chemicals were getting under the skin and melting the cuts one into the other. This was how she pictured the healing process. "There, all done." The boy lifted his finger to touch the cut. He looked unhappy. She slapped his hand away. "Don't touch, dear! You haven't washed that hand. Don't want to soil the wound!" He looked at his fingertips with the speckles of blood, a little shamefaced. She turned on the tap, ran the water until it warmed a little, guided his open hand towards it. "Wash yourself, down, dear," she knelt to the cupboard under the basin while speaking, "and I'll get out the Elastoplast."

He washed, she took the lid off the cookie tin where she kept her first aid supplies. There was a box of Band-Aid.

46

She tore the paper away from one. His hands were still wet when she got to her feet leaving the tin on the floor, and applied the Band-Aid.

"Towel," she said. The nails holding her towel rail to the wall had been pulled loose over the years, after all those wet towels had weighed down on it, then been flipped away from it. So when she drew her towel of the moment to her, with its red and blue and yellow waves, the rail made a rattling noise, surprisingly jarring in this closed space. The towel was damp from her morning shower and smelt of powder. The boy wiped his hands and for no practical purpose he ran the towel over his face too. This licked his hair up at the fringe and she patted it down again.

"There. Better?"

He nodded, seemingly grateful. She looked into his eyes. For the second time she really looked into them. It was not to be the last time, though there was to be a last time not too far ahead. They were lovely, they were deep brown, like rich black coffee, like Al Green's skin. For the first moment, the lighting in the bathroom not being terribly strong, she could not see any of those little flecks of yellow, but then she could, they were still there, like little crystals splashed from a liquid sun. Sara said to herself again, I've never seen eyes like them. He held her gaze as he had held it earlier. Strong-willed, she thought, a good sign in a man. They held for a second, then she stood back as he had stood back: the sheer force of those eyes pushed her away from him. Their intensity. It was in that stepping back that she first saw him as physically beautiful. Not ethereal at all as the eyes suggested, but flesh and blood and bone, well-shaped and of the Earth. My God, she thought, your girlfriend's a bloody lucky woman. Or your boyfriend's a lucky man. Whichever it is.

47

She hoped he was straight. There were already plenty of gays in New York City. What a novelty it would be to find a good-looking straight boy in this city!

He said, simply,

"Thank you." His voice cracked, apparently with feeling but perhaps because the full medicinal smell had dried his throat. He went back into the sitting room and she followed.

"Well," he said, standing at her front door which he had opened, much to her annoyance, "thank you very much again, I appreciate it." He put his fingers to the Band- Aid.

She knew then that she did not want him to go. She wanted him to stay and chat with her. She wanted to know about him. She didn't make new friends in the City often and she did not want this encounter to pass so quickly and shallowly. She wanted him to sit on her nice leather sofa and tell her about himself.

"In a hurry?" she said, she hoped not rudely. "Got an appointment? Seeing your girl or something?" She threw him her best have-a-nice-day card store smile.

"Oh, not really," he said, but he turned to go.

She looked at her watch.

"It's a quarter past six," she said. She was going to say, supper time, do you want to stay for a bite? But that was too forward, and anyway she had nothing in her cupboards she could conjure into even a barely adequate meal she could call to a stranger's face 'supper'. 'Dinner' to her, in the English way, meant lunch. She wondered if under his burgundy shirt he was not, as many young men who are not already obese tend to be, a bit thinner than was healthy. Lads new to the City as she was sure he must be, if they're intelligent enough not to stuff their faces with *KFCs* and *Popeyes* until they exploded, but too young and cool and modern to try serious cooking, too impecunious to try serious restaurants, overcompensated by eating only salads. Yet in fact she preferred a certain under-nourished quality in males. She

48

thought of Eddie from *Mulligan's* weighing down on her, she thought of her husband with his unsightly paunch. Thin was good. But were those strange eyes a result of meals inadequately planned and balanced, were they a manifestation of unhealthy habits? There had once many years before been a mild scandal over an anti-drugs campaign because the boy in the posters, designed to appall with his waif-like misty-eyed sadness, had in fact driven teenage girls into a frenzy of desire so beautifully lit was he, so vulnerable and erotic his downcast features, so cute his suffering. Perhaps these eyes looking back to Sara were the lustrous outcome of debauch with certain early death to come. Or - regretting the comparatively unglamorous spin of her thinking - simply too many vegetables, not enough meat. Plenty of lettuce leaves but not enough bread? You need fattening up, young man, she felt inclined to say.

All this pondering brought only one clear conclusion: Tuna Helper was fine for her, but it wasn't the sort of thing you offered if you wanted to charm. She was not sure that she did want to charm exactly. She wasn't sure what she wanted except that she did not want him to close her door and go down her stairs and disappear forever into the crowds of New York. It would be pleasant to chat to a nice-looking young man, that was the extent of it. Tuna Helper would not suffice, so she said,

"Want to go for a bite to eat?"

She feared that this was too casual, and though she did not want to be pushy, she wanted at least to make it a little embarrassing for him to refuse, so before he had a chance to say thanks but no, she added, "on me." Her nature was parsimonious and she felt an enjoyable flutter of irresponsibility in this offer.

"Oh, ma'am, that's very nice, but no. I've gotta be somewhere."

49

"Oh," she said, more lightly than she felt, "I thought you were free. I'm sorry."

But impecunious boys who do not eat enough think twice before turning down a free meal. So he said,

"It's not that, I've a bit of time, but I wouldn't want to impose."

"I offered, dear, if it was an imposition I wouldn't have offered."

"I know but..." he shrugged.

She adored his Southern politeness, yet also felt he was overdoing it.

"Yes or no, dear?" She meant this to sound final, but of course her training in card selling had taught her to make (sometimes) even the most barbed of remarks nicely, so it came out quite friendly.

"Well," he spread his hands and laughed, a small nasal laugh she noticed, "I guess." Wale, ah gaiss.

"Is that a yes?"

"I guess."

"Good! What's your fancy?"

"I beg your pardon?"

"What food do you like?"

"All sorts." He shrugged again. Yes, his shoulders were a little thin. She ran her eyes down to his pants. Were the legs a bit too thin as well?

"Choose."

"I don't know. It's up to you."

"Well, how about Indian?" Indian restaurants made her think of London. "There's a terrific Indian on Bleecker Street."

"Great."

So they went to the splendid *Indian Taj*.

But things did not start well. There was an air of unease, as much on Sara's part as on the boy's, as they sipped on their waters and pored over their menus. He frowned deeply, his eyes running down the list of selections with, as became increasingly apparent, bafflement.

"Ever had an Indian meal before, dear?"

"Oh yeah," he said. Then, apologetically, "well no, not exactly." Which she knew meant 'no, never,' but she did not challenge him on it. She leant into his menu and recommended a couple of dishes.

"The Bhuna is very nice. You can have chicken Bhuna or lamb or if you're really brave you can have goat."

"Yuk."

"Chicken or lamb then. It's quite light, too. Tomatoes. Onions. And the Chicken Tikka Masala is great too. It's cooked in a Tandoori oven. Has a wonderful orange glow. Do you like yoghurt?"

"Yeah."

"Then you'll love Chicken Tikka Masala."

"Okay."

"So I'll have the Lamb Bhuna, my friend the Chicken Tikka Masala," she said to the waiter. "No, make mine the goat." She wanted to encourage him to experiment. "And your special Nan bread stuffed with Almonds. And a bottle of the house Chardonnay." The waiter went off and came back with the wine. "Cheap and cheerful," she winked at the boy opposite her. "Well," she raised her glass, "cheers."

He raised his, they clashed.

"Cheers," he said, without celebration. Once he'd downed his first glass - quite quickly, she noticed with pleasure - he relaxed, but when she asked him what had brought him to New York he looked away and shrugged and said,

"Nothing much. It's a place. You've got to be somewhere, don't you, why not here?"

She laughed at his blatant evasion and said,

"Kiddo, it's none of my business," and she began to talk about herself. This was a clever move. He seemed happy

51

enough to listen to her going on about *Make Someone's Day* and her old life in London. When she tried to turn the conversation over to him, he became hesitant and said very little, mumbled politenesses which contained no hard information. She learnt to ask about him without pushing for an answer so that when he shrugged and said next to nothing and she turned the talk to her own life it was comfortable for both of them. Thus the one-sided conversation felt deceptively like a genuine exchange. But she hoped that by applying this very mild pressure she would get something out of him before the meal was through. She called over the waiter and asked for another bottle, the first having only a drop left.

The boy was relaxing but he gave nothing away. It crossed her mind that though they had now been acquainted for ninety minutes or more she didn't yet even know his name.

"I feel very silly but I forgot to ask your name!" She laughed, loudly but soberly. His laugh in return was no louder than it had been but it was pitched a tone higher. He was no longer completely sober, though no-one would have called him drunk. He sipped his wine with pleasure, she observed. No, pleasure was too sophisticated a word. He sipped his wine with happiness.

"And I don't know yours, ma'am! And you saved me from a visit to hospital! I should at least know the name of the person I have to thank! "

"I'm Sara," she said, "without an aitch."

"And I'm Steven with a V. But normally people call me Steve, without an N." He fingered the Band-Aid on his cheek.

"Okay, I'll call you Steve. With a V, without an N."

"And I'll call you Sara without an aitch, ma'am."

They ordered Gulab Jamon for dessert.

"I warn you it's sweet," she said. "And another bottle of the wine, please."

"Oh ma'am, I can't go on drinking this stuff like it's water!" Lahk it's woatuh.

"You're young, Steve with a V. You should learn to enjoy yourself."

Did he look somewhat guilty at this finding of a fault? Was he a boy who had not yet learned that enjoyment was the only point to life? Southerners were notoriously earnest and right-wing and self-important, not to say pompously religious. My God, she thought, I hope he's not some wretched virgin full of ideas of "saving myself until I find true love." But no-one came to New York to "save themselves", in either meaning of the phrase, did they? Sara would almost prefer that he was gay than that he was "saving himself for the right woman." Mind you, being Southern, claiming to be saving yourself for the right woman might itself be cover for homosexuality. Southern fathers were liable to beat up their gay children, it was a well-known fact. Poor boy! Poor hurt boy! She wanted to hug him close. She wanted him to feel her warmth. She would be his friend, he could always trust her. It's all right if you're gay. This is New York, not Memphis, Tennessee. We embrace gay people here. In fact, we like them more than straight people. Except in our beds, then we like straight people more, if they're men of course. Even this was doubtful. Would the ideal lover not be a man with a gay sensibility and a discretely gay manner, with gay friends and gay humour, who nevertheless through some weird alchemy was actually heterosexual: would he not be every woman's dream come true? Like Bryan Ferry from Roxy Music? Bryan Ferry, after all, was very nearly perfect. Al Green himself had an attractively gay manner too, without ever even going to art school! She found herself praying that Bryan Ferry would not find God like Al Green. But people who collected art by

53

the Bloomsbury school were not the God-finding sort. Phew.

He spooned into the dessert. "Wow, it is sweet," he said.

She leaned towards him. "Like you, dear." She was confident that she was still sober, yet her mother from London, perhaps also the one from Wicklow, would have recognized the broadening of her accent into a definite cockney, with a little music hall self-pity in her inflection. Her London mother, were she still in the land of the living to have an opinion of any kind, would have said to her as she had done when as a wild teenager Sara had sometimes rolled up at home at two in the morning drunk and loud, "You may think it's clever, but you're only making a fool of yourself, Sara." The Wicklow mother was more relaxed about it. "It's good for a girl to be a little wild, it's an introduction to life. So you enjoy yourself, girl, you enjoy yourself. Just be careful."

"Huh?" Steve blinked.

"You're a very sweet boy. It's been a fun evening."

She reached out her hand to his, which was resting on the table cloth, and she tapped his fingers. It was a motherly rather than an erotic gesture.

She had been thinking it for a while, but only when the dessert plates were empty and she had ordered coffee and brandy for herself, leaving Steve to the remains of the wine, did she actually say it directly:

"You're a very good-looking young man."

"Thanks." He didn't know where to look except not at her. With the little strip of bandage on his cheek he looked easily hurt, not only physically. The light caught the yellow spots in his eyes and they shone like liquid gold.

"No, I mean it, you are." She leant across the table and said in a conspiratorial whisper, "I bet I know what you're doing in New York."

"Yeah?" He looked disconcerted.

54

"Yes, you're an actor, aren't you?" She smiled triumphantly. He smiled shyly. Did his head drop in just the smallest of nods, or was it an illusion of the light and the brandy? "I'm right, aren't I? You're an actor. I'm often right about these things. My old mother from Wicklow once said to me, 'Sara, you can tell a person a mile off. A priest, a farmer, a barman, a lord, a labourer. You'd know instantly even if they all swapped clothes.' And she was right."

He expelled a rush of air as if with relief at not having to keep his secret any more.

"Ma'am, you amaze me. That's what I am. An actor. And," he raised an eyebrow as if this were a new discovery, "a dancer." A daincuh, which seemed more beautiful than a mere dancer, more rarefied, more otherworldly. Did the golden flecks in his eyes catch the light and themselves dance, in reflection of his own dancing body which moved gracefully over the boards of stages?

She reached across to his hand around the water glass and tapped his fingernail.

"You stand a real chance, you do. You'd be great in a soap opera."

"That would be really cool. But I like doing plays too."

"What's your real first love? Musicals? Do you sing?"

He was silent for a beat.

"Yeah, I sing, too. Sing, act and dance. I like dancing best. I've always danced. It's like a release to me." He flicked his wrist as if this were a gesture he'd learned in dance class. It was a lovely gesture too, this batting rather tenderly of the air.

If he was a dancer, what chance was there he was not gay? One in a million, reflected Sara ruefully. She wanted to bring up the issue immediately.

"I hope I'm not being forward, but you're not gay, are you? You don't seem to be." In fact, as she had already

55

deduced, in the lightness of his voice and the airy quality of his movement there was a homosexual tinge, but then nearly every male in New York these days gave a homosexual impression to Sara if they were any more sophisticated than the regulars at *Mulligan's*.

"Oh, ma'am." He blinked like a little lost bird.

"I don't mind, I'm not prejudiced. There's a gay couple lives under me and we get on like a house on fire." She felt a sinking disappointment however.

"No, ma'am. I like ladies." What an old-fashioned way of saying it! Sara mused.

Not I like girls, I like ladies. Is that how it was down South, all old world charm?

"Sorry if I offended. It's just, Broadway and that, I always think it's only gays. Chorus boys and so on."

"Well, not all."

Sara was disciplined enough not to talk further of sex or sexuality. She neatly switched the subject.

"Resting at the moment, are you?"

"I'm what?"

"Resting? Unemployed?"

"Oh. Yeah. Right now. I'm auditioning a lot. I've got a call back on Thursday."

"Good! Good! That's exciting. It must be hard starting out. It's a tough world isn't it, theatre? Well, good luck to you ducks. You stand a real chance, you do."

"Thanks."

"And when your name's up in lights I'll be able to say 'I knew him when! I bandaged his wound!' I hope you won't be like some stars get, all full of themselves. If I come round to your dressing room will you speak to me?"

"Ma'am, if I get my name up in lights you will have a free ticket to all my first nights!"

"But not if it's 'The Lion King'. I don't like Disney. I like Andrew Lloyd Webber. I like 'Cats'."

56

"Yeah, I like 'Cats' too."

"You'd be great in that. You have to have a good body for that."

She paid the check in silence. He pulled out his wallet, but before he had to pretend to be willing to pay his share she'd slapped her card into the plastic folder.

"On me," she said, as if this had not already been agreed.

Outside, the first thing he did was dance on the spot for a few moments, clicking a few beats on his tongue for rhythmic guidance. Sara was no judge of a dancer's skills but he certainly moved well, he moved in a flow like water. He was physically very relaxed. Sara looked back through the restaurant window and the waiter was looking out at Steve. There was proof. He drew eyes, he had what it took to entrance an audience. He was like her in that he naturally drew people to him. As a woman who saw herself as charismatic she felt a bond with other people of charisma.

"Want to come back to my apartment for a coffee?" she asked.

The boy did not hear her, or pretended not to hear her. At least he didn't run away! He was preoccupied with the rhythm on his tongue and the ripples through his body. He was delighted by his own movements, taking a huge pleasure in what his body could do as if he were only discovering it now. Oh, the joyful discoveries of youth! Sara felt envious. She felt stale, she felt past all possibility of joy.

"Want to come back for coffee?"

The boy heard this time. He did not stop dancing, but said, with a small embarrassed grin and exquisite Southern courtesy, looking down at his tapping-tapping shoes,

"Oh, I don't know that I should."

"Don't be a spoilsport."

He stopped, stood quite still.

"Ma'am, I'd love to as long as... as long as you don't think..."

57

She exploded forth a sound designed to illustrate amusement.

"I'm not that sort of girl!" She patted his bottom, a gesture that was supposed in its forwardness to subtly suggest chasteness.

"Well, I didn't mean to... you know... but I wanted to be clear."

"That's fine. You're right to be clear. So you're coming back?"

"Sure. I mean, I guess so..."

"Then I guess so too."

He blinked at her. He was certainly no longer able to pass for sober. But he wasn't drunk either, not so he was loud and obnoxious. Perhaps he was a rare person who was never loud or obnoxious. He was sweet when sober and when he'd had a bit to drink he became even sweeter. Sara remembered her husband. He'd drunk beer by the gallon. He'd not been nice when he was drunk. He wasn't violent, but he was objectionable, he was a complainer. He was very boring when he was drunk. He was fairly boring when he was sober as a matter of fact. He turned the TV up loud. He sat there bathed in its flickering retarding glow. He said next to nothing except to be rude or to moan. Mostly he stared into the screen. His mouth would fall open. He looked stupid. He looked like a person in a sci-fi movie whose frontal lobes had been removed by some horrible scientist. He dribbled a bit sometimes. *How on earth did I end up with him?* she wondered again, as she'd wondered so many times. It wasn't that he'd been much good in bed, even at the beginning when he'd been quite horny. He stuck his prick in her and came and then he snored.

But Steve with a V was not boring, he was lovely. He was happy. He was relaxed. He took such pleasure in his talent for movement that he kept breaking into little dancing steps

58

on the short walk to Minetta Lane. Sara felt very young. His moving shadow brushed her softly.

Bringing him into her apartment for the second time she felt more conscious of its shortcomings, because she supposed they reflected her own shortcomings. Now she knew about him, how interesting he was and how ambitious, she felt ordinary and unsuccessful. Now that his dancing shadow was not on her she felt old again. When you were forty-five and lonely and you lived in a little cramped space like this people could rightly suppose that this was it, your lot for life, loneliness in a box. Behind a store counter by day. Guinness at night with the same old crowd. She wished her lounge - she insisted on the English word - gave if not more space at least a more intellectual impression, a set of Shakespeare, a collection of poetry, some classical CDs, instead of these stark white walls, a grubby folded out-of-date 'New York Post', two framed flower prints from K-Mart on the wall, (albeit they were pretty enough,) a bookcase with a plastic plant on top and some photographs of relatives she never saw and a couple of Jackie Collins novels and some pop CDs of what would no doubt be called 'her era.' There were also some curling vinyl album sleeves leaning against a wall. The CD player was portable and the turntable was second-hand when she'd bought it twelve years ago. The TV was small, the video player dusty. She bet his room had copies of well-thumbed plays all over the floor, show music and an Opera or two, actors' trade newspapers. The chaos of a clever ambitious boy with a talent for the arts. There were two things in her apartment, however, that she loved. Her glorious blue leather sofa pushed against the wall to the right of the door, and the large rather flattering rectangular mirror above it. She'd bought the couch on an impulse because she deserved a little luxury, and all this time later, three years or more, she still loved it, the way she sank into it, the way it

59

received her and all the troubles of the day melted away in its folds as if it were a lover.

But, imagining his room full of intelligence and artiness, she corrected herself: I don't know he's actually clever. He must be a college dropout because he's too young to have graduated. He didn't say anything clever at the *Taj*. Actors don't have great minds, do they? He may be good-looking yet empty-headed. (Like me.) But oh he's sweet and handsome and charming. (But then so was I once. So am I still in my way. I'm still a charismatic woman. She looked in the mirror. Men still look at me. They want me.)

It was a matter of moments to get the cafetiere bubbling. Steve was in the middle of the floor, breaking into little dancing movements every few seconds.

"My, you love it, don't you? You love to dance?"

"Oh, yeah. Sorry!" He stopped still. "You see, I have to keep practicing. It's my art."

"Well don't you stop! I wasn't finding fault, I was complimenting you. And I hope I'm not being a nag but you really must stop   apologizing all the time!"

"Sorry."

"Like that."

"Sorry!" He frowned in secret puzzlement, and then said beguilingly, "I think I may be a bit drunk."

How Southern he was, how delightfully courteous and humble.

"Lord, you're not drunk! You're merry! So am I! This coffee'll pull you round anyhow. I made it extra strong."

"That's how I like it." If she'd said she'd made it extra weak, he'd have said he liked it best extra weak. He'd say anything to please.

She indicated the sofa and he fell into it. It made a whispering noise as it took his body. She sat opposite in a chair near the windows. The light from the street lamp made a pool on the floor. It lapped at his shoes. Backlit, her face

60

was in darkness: she saw this in the mirror. He sat there and drank his coffee in complete silence. She watched his left hand, wrapped around the cup. The fingers of his right were stretched flat to make a surface for the saucer to sit on. The thumb over the saucer's edge kept it secure. He sipped. She sipped. She looked into his eyes, his strange eyes. He must have known how very strange they were? Perhaps he'd got used to people's amazement just as someone with a purple birthmark running down his face gets used to the moment when his birthmark is noticed, the moment when another's eyes flick to it and flick away, pretending that no disfigurement had been seen. Sara supposed that those golden drops were themselves a sort of disfigurement, if any unusual facial feature could be termed such. But they were not the sort of mark that would make a person harder to love. Yet that may not have been true when he'd been a schoolboy. Perhaps then he'd been mocked as a weirdo. Kids will pick on anything unusual to make another kid suffer, because pointing out someone else's oddity takes attention away from their own. The Indian restaurant's brandy, still to be tasted on her lips, blending with the bitterness of coffee brought to Sara an onrush of affection, even of love. You are not a freak to me, she wanted to say. You are beautiful and mysterious. She finished her cup and put it on the table. Without any calculation she moved over to the sofa and dropped into it right next to the boy, so near to him his body rocked sideways and an overspill of coffee wetted his saucer.

In the boldness of both alcohol and her age it seemed okay to put her hand right on his knee and pat it affectionately.

"It's been such a lovely evening, ducks. It's been great." She felt the shape of his knee against the denim. He flinched, which was disappointing, but he did not move away, which was reassuring.

61

"Oh, no ma'am, I don't... I did say..."

"I know. I didn't mean anything by it. You're a very nice guy, that's all. I didn't mean to get too close." She shifted an inch away from him, towards the sofa's arm.

"You're a very nice lady."

"Thanks. It's good, that *Indian Taj*, isn't it?"

"It's great."

"I expect you don't get to eat in restaurants often, do you?"

"Not really."

"Being an artist and all, in New York City. You've made a tough life choice, you have. I admire it." She moved back towards him. "You're great. I bet you've got a great body. I like a beautiful body. You may not think I'm an arty type but I like beauty. I always have."

"Oh, I'm not beautiful."

"Now that's just false modesty. You know you are. You wouldn't be a dancer otherwise."

She did not know she was going to say it even once it was halfway out of her mouth:

"I'd love to see you naked. I really would."

He let out his shy nasal laugh. Perhaps it was the only reaction he could come up with which would not have seemed rude to the woman who had, after all, bought him a great dinner. And to release the tension between them she laughed too.

"I'm not making a pass, kiddo! I'm just saying. My old mum from Wicklow always said, 'you speak your mind, you do, Sara, and that's a good thing. It gets things out in the open.' So when I say I'd like to see you naked it's only the truth. But I'm not seducing you! I'm just saying." She patted his leg a few inches above the knee. Her voice was modulated so that she sounded more romantic than her words. There is a way of saying I am not seducing you as a prologue to seduction and it may be that Sara had this skill.

62

She would have denied it. Anyway, she'd have said, it was wine and brandy talking, not her at all.

"Sure. I understand."

"I expect you've had a lot of girlfriends in your time."

"I'm only twenty, ma'am. I haven't had too much time to have lots. Not lots." He smiled with delightful cheeky self-knowledge, to confirm that, indeed, women loved him and he could hardly help it.

"Well, some." She knew it was lots by most people's standards. She pressed her hand against his leg, palm flat. This time it stayed there. He looked down at it. He did not move it away as he could have done. He sipped his coffee. He did not stand up and say, I think I'd better leave. He looked at it, plump and warm against him.

"See, it's just that I'm not into, like, older women…"

She said straight out as if she had not already asked it:

"You're not gay, are you?"

Even in the dim light she saw that his cheeks pinked a little.

"Oh no, ma'am. I… I'm not into older ladies I mean."

"Like me? I'm an older lady, am I? How old do you think?"

"Oh, shucks, I don't… like, thirty-five?"

She laughed.

"I wish! So. Like them young?"

"Not young, but… My age, you know?"

"And what's your age, dear?" She wanted to hear him say it again.

"Twenty."

"Think a twenty-year old girl knows all about how to please, do you?" Just in case she seemed to be pushing too far she let out another sound which was supposed to symbolize mirth. "Drink your coffee, dear, it'll get cold. Then you'd best be on your way."

63

"Sure." He slurped it. He was for the first time obviously uncomfortable. How strange that when she released the pressure, when he could have left without too much difficulty, it was then that he seemed most put out.

"Then you'd best be going," she said again. She thought: I don't think this boy is going anywhere.

"Yeah."

"Would you like another cup? I can put on a fresh brew."

"Oh no, ma'am, I wouldn't want to bother you." How lovely that Memphis speech was. It sung. It made her think of deep muddy water, of the Mississippi as it just kept rolling along. It made her think of the dark masculine America, violent and sexy and absent of effeteness. She touched his arm. She narrowed her eyes. Of course, he was a would-be actor and he loved dance which was undeniably a bit effete, but still.

You little bastard! If you get the chance you're going to screw me, aren't you? Just to see what it would be like. You're dying to know, aren't you?

He put the empty cup on the floor next to his feet.

"Sure?"

"Well, if you're having another cup yourself." He checked his watch. It had a luminous dial, and when he pressed it a touch of green stroked the Band-Aid on his cheek.

"But then I must be going. I have to get uptown. My room's on Hundred and Eighth. I have to be up early tomorrow."

"You would be a very good Puck, you know."

"I'm sorry?" He laughed a little, but he wasn't so embarrassed now, they were playing a game (she was fairly sure of this) and he knew his part in it and wasn't pretending any more, or rather he was pretending on the understanding that she could read between the lines and the silences. But he did not catch her eye. He pressed his hands together

64

between his legs, squeezed his knees into them. There was something cat-like in this movement.

"Puck. Shakespeare." The fact was that Puck and Hamlet and Romeo and Juliet and King Lear were the only Shakespeare characters Sara knew and she was sure he wasn't cut out for Hamlet and of course he was far too young for Lear. She had been forced to read King Lear at school. How boring it had been! Yet she had never forgotten the gouging of the eyes in it, the bickering daughters, her own image of Lear as a long- bearded white-haired rheumy-eyed old man, a cross between a fly-weight Santa and an alcoholic tramp. Also, Steve was perhaps too slight, too slim, to be any but an unlikely Romeo. (But I've known a few unlikely Romeos in my time, and not on any stage either!) So Puck it was.

She thought fondly of the London Underground, which closed at one a.m., and had provided the opportunity to her in her younger days and to millions of others for plenty of adventurous sexual encounters on the grounds that it was too late to get home, I'd better stay here, I'll use your settee if I can, oh of course let me find you a blanket. How many love makings that would otherwise have been evaded to the regret of both parties had occurred because of it, not to be spoken of ever again but to be remembered in secret, in private moments, in masturbation perhaps. Bugger the New bloody York twenty-four hour Subway! No wonder New Yorkers were all so stressed out. They didn't get laid enough. They didn't have an excuse to stay.

She and Steve had to play a different kind of game.

She was prepared to no longer believe a word he said and she was certain that he was not expecting that she should. In the dim romantic lighting with the sounds of the City and the cool breeze from the balcony and the room now not so much overly compact as inviting and intimate, she thought,

65

you little bugger! You little angel! You're randy as hell you are. You want me, I know you do.

"When I said Puck you thought I said something else?" She squinted knowingly.

"Yeah. No. I mean, yeah, I get what the joke is but that's not it. You see, Puck is very near to my nickname. So I thought, how does she know people call me Huck?"

"Huck?"

"As in Mark Twain. 'Huckleberry Finn'."

"Why?"

"Well, I come from Tennessee." He said this as if it were too obvious to need explanation.

"I know, but so does everybody else in Tennessee! They can't all be nick-named Huck!"

"No, I mean here in New York. My friends call me Huck."

"Oh. I didn't know Mark Twain was Tennessee."

"Well, he wasn't, but to Northerners the South's all one place."

She felt this to be true. She had lived in Florida for many years and yet she did not think it authentically a part of the South because it did not have steamboats and old jazz. All it had was theme parks and fruit and drug dealers. Florida was hell. She hated it. But Memphis Tennessee she was willing to believe she would like. Al Green made his records in Memphis. She heard his song in her head. 'Take me to the river, wash me down. Cleanse my soul, put my feet on the ground.' Bryan Ferry had done that song too, quite well. Talking Heads had messed it up. They'd tried to be clever. Bryan wasn't even American and he'd done it better!

She was still thinking of 'Take Me to the River' when she put her hand back on Steve's leg. This time it was further up his thigh. She might not have been fully aware of this contact; she certainly might have given the impression of thinking of something not in the room, something other than

66

his body. It was only that her hand had to go somewhere. It is possible that even when she moved her face towards his and put her lips momentarily on his cheek she was being very friendly rather than suggestive. When she pulled it away again like a curious hen she looked into his eyes. He had four of them, because she was too near him for her vision to focus. They were looking at her. They were not lit with romance, there was no love in them as she would have liked, but nor were they appalled and they were not frightened. They were cool and they implied a distant half-concentration as if he'd seen something mildly interesting which caught his attention for a moment. Close up the golden spots looked larger; they flowed into the brown like expanding puddles. They seemed indeed to float, but Sara thought this was a deception of her own crossed eyes. Her hand swam up to his fly and her thumb and first finger pulled the zip down, all this in one smooth motion, a floating motion like his golden splashes. She felt a tiny jolt run through his body but he did not move away. She felt his breathing near her ear. She pulled out his penis. It was half erect when the tip of her first finger touched it and fully erect before she pulled the head out over the blue of his denims. She remembered her own first experiences with boys and young men, how easily they became erect. They were usually hopeless at the actual intercourse, clumsy and rhythmically graceless, but the arousal sprang up with the lightest of touches, even at the anticipation of the lightest of touches.

They were still serving nature's whim, not mankind's, and arousal was the first biological requirement, the point of nature's urgency. The pleasure of sex was irrelevant to nature herself. What mattered to her was the erection, the penetration, the orgasm. The subtler pleasures, which you discovered as you got better at it, were beside the point for nature's purpose. Those glorious pleasures, thought Sara, were developments of mankind for him- and herself, as

67

cordon bleu cooking was a human development on top of nature's necessity for food. People often said sex was 'a natural urge.' Well, the urge was natural, yes, but really terrific love was artificial.

This was the great revelation, the magical discovery, of gay sex. Sara's views on homosexuality were variable but at this moment she thought of Tony and Peter downstairs who were probably fucking each other. Queer love, she reflected, was a creation of the human creature as astonishing and brilliant as Grand Central Station or rockets to the moon. Truly human in the grandest sense of that word, an imaginative achievement like the invention of God. A transcendence of nature.

As you got older you wanted your lover to be skilled and wonderful and dazzling as a magician, and after nature's demand for reproduction had been fulfilled, or not fulfilled as the case may be, the human dimension of sex had only just begun.

And now it could go on until you dropped! Nature had been conquered yet again! Viagra meant a guy could have fabulous orgasms when he was ninety-five! For no earthly reason except the wonder of it!

There was more wish than reality in these ideas, Sara knew it, but now with this wonderful beautiful male on her leather sofa, aroused for her, for her! Now she could - she was sure - experience something approaching perfection. He was still urgent, still under nature's instructions, but she was beyond that, she had moved into artifice.

"Oh sweetheart," she said, very quietly. She pressed her ear to his chest and she could hear his heartbeat. "Oh sweetheart." She felt like weeping. She looked up to him and he was smiling, delightedly. She undid the button at the top of his jeans and folded back the opening at both sides, like the masts for a paper boat. The curls of his pubes ran over his shorts in a thin line, up to his tummy button. "Oh

68

sweetheart," she said again. She kissed the head of his penis, while tugging at his jeans.

"Let me," he whispered, and he stood and he pulled his denims off. His shorts came with them. He bent to drag them over first one foot and then the other. They caught on his left foot and he let them drop, his foot wrapped up. His bottom was perfectly shaped. The mellow lighting marked the roundness of the cheeks in light and shadow.

Then he took his shirt off. It was her turn to feel a sizzle. He was in her apartment. He was nearly naked, he was horny, he was happy, he liked her and he liked the adventure of it. He could have any girl, any boy, and yet he was happy to be with her instead of any of the others, at least for now he was. She felt her eyes water. She had not felt such intense erotic joy in years. Perhaps not ever. He had a body and she had a body and they would use them for each other's gratification and her head spun at the thought.

He turned to her.

The light from the table lamp cast a soft triangle over his torso, his genitals. His face was slightly shadowed, but she could see his sweet boyish smile. My God, he's beautiful, she thought. Then, aloud:

"My God, you're beautiful!"

He grinned. He was pleased with the compliment.

He wasn't actually beautiful, her critical radar told her. Sara's critical radar was never inoperative. She could reduce its intensity but she could not switch it off. He was fit, certainly, and lithe, as a dancer must be, but perhaps a little too thin, the nipples a little too small. The flesh a little pale. His penis curved upward, not big. (She didn't care for big, Steve One had been too big really.) He was very hard indeed. Though he was short his legs were proportionately long, a touch bony, the knees protruded sufficiently to be called knobbly. He stood there with that silly sweet grin as seconds

69

went by without either of them speaking or moving, his pants and shorts around his ankle.

"One thing about my naked men, I like them properly naked!" She hoped he caught her humour.

He looked at the heap of clothing at his feet and said, "Sorry!" kicking the pants away, and the shorts.

"And your socks, kiddo!"

He removed first one, in a stylized stripper's motion as though it were a sheer stocking, threw it all the way across the room. Then the other, threw it. It landed on top of the standard lamp near the balcony and hung there from the shade.

"Now you come here to me, kiddo!" And shyly but excitedly he came forward three paces, his penis level with her mouth. She put her lips on the tip and gazed up at him. He looked like a dumb, stunned animal, wide-eyed. "I can do this better than any of your girls," she said, "because some things you get better at with experience, see." And she slid her head forward, the whole of his penis was in her mouth. He moaned boyishly. "But we don't want to blow a gasket just yet, do we?" She pulled away. He looked disappointed. She knew he would, she knew men. They're all stupid. I can give him an hour of pleasure, and all he wants is to get his rocks off as quickly as possible. Why is it that all men are so awful in bed? Yet they all think they're so bloody great. Especially the young. But this time he's going to learn that patience is a virtue for the un-virtuous.

And in time when she was lying on her leather sofa completely naked, her ample breasts and the curves at her belly proof of her earthiness, her substance, he approached her. She saw in his eyes as he climbed on her that though his maleness told her he was aroused, it was not she who aroused him but he himself. He was probably no more narcissistic than any other young man of his age, no more narcissistic than she herself had been. She recalled herself at

70

eighteen with Ted, her first. She hadn't much fancied Ted. He worked in a fish and chip shop on the Brompton Road and he smelt a little of vinegar. But he was her age and they'd lost their virginity together, and it had been wonderful. Ted himself had not been wonderful. He had been frightened and inexpert. Who could expect otherwise? The wonder for her had been in the discovery of the possibilities in her body, the hint of the layers of pleasures it would find, which that first go had only begun to unveil. So it was with Steve, she perceived. He was still young enough to be awed by what he could do, what he could feel and what he could make another feel, awed that someone else, it hardly mattered who, might shiver at the sight of him. His was a contradiction, a generous self-centeredness, the pleasure he knew he could give the raison d'etre for the only pleasure he wanted, which was his own. So in his weird eyes she saw not so much lust as fascination, because he had never seen a body like hers. He put his hand on her breast as if it were a strange smooth new object which he wanted very much to touch, but at the same time feared might give him an electric shock. His mouth was open slightly. He was scared and awed and excited. He was an explorer, he was an adventurer, and she was the strange new land. She put her hand over his where it lay on her breast and touched it ever so gently.

He said in a whisper,

"I've got a rubber in my jacket." But she said,

"Dear, I'm past all that." And they were together. It was beautiful. Very sweet, very tender, very intense. It was sublime.

MARTIN AND ERICA

She woke to sounds from what she liked to call her kitchen, which was a stove and a refrigerator in the corner near the front door. She remembered with complete clarity all of last night's lovemaking, and put a hand onto the empty space where the boy had slept. His place was warm. I hope he's still here, she said to herself, comfortable in the clatter which told her he was.

She got out of bed feeling only dully awake and yet 'ready for anything' as she would sometimes put it, and pulled her dressing gown around her, over her big breasts, as if to be modest.

She lent on the doorframe and watched him. She loved the ease of his nakedness. He was happy to fry bacon without a stitch on, very different from the shy boy of the last evening, the boy with the untied shoelaces.

"You should put on at least a shirt, kiddo," she said, "don't want hot oil scarring that pristine chest of yours." Actually, she thought, a little scar on the chest like the scar on his cheek, a little bit of damage, might add a new dimension to him. It's a pity the graze isn't going to leave its mark. He turned around and pirouetted gracefully, grinned, bowed for applause which was not forthcoming. But still he grinned, turning back to the bacon. Belatedly, she did applaud.

"Bravo," she said. Then, "Do you not have work to go to?"

In the ordinary light of day Sara had the habit of becoming efficient. It turned men off. Eddie McGovern hadn't liked it, her way of acting as if nothing had happened the night before. Yet this time Sara's practicality had nothing to do with wanting to be rid of a man, but rather a disbelief that this boy could have found her attractive. Her sudden efficiency was a defence mechanism, though she did succeed in reminding herself that she had been really good in bed with him. Really good! He'd been really good too.

He didn't reply so she asked again.

"No work?"

He didn't turn away from the stove.

"Well, I'm a motorcycle messenger, if I don't turn up I don't turn up. What they gonna do, sack me? There are a thousand jobs like that to be had."

"I thought you were an actor."

"I am but... it's hard, you know. I've got rent."

"Which you're not going to pay by cooking me breakfast."

"What about you?"

"Late shift. Twelve to Eight. If I decide to go at all. See, I'm a business woman, I own the store."

"A store? You said last night. What kind?" Had he been so drunk he couldn't remember their conversation? She was sure she'd told him all about it. He didn't seem to have a hangover at all. He was bright and sparkly.

"We sell mainly cards. Birthday cards, Christmas. Hanukah. All that."

"O yeah, I remember. Mother's day, father's day, bar mitzvahs, births, christenings!" He broke an egg into the pan and it sizzled. "Martin Luther King day! Congratulations on your new baby. Congratulations on you new car. Your new

73

house.   Your new porch!   Happy graduation, happy dropping-out-of-college. Get well soon. Sorry you died!"

The way he said Martin Luther King, the airiness, like music. Mart'n Luth'r Kaiyng.

"Okay, don't take the piss, kiddo, it's a living. Yeh, they're always trying to invent new reasons to sell cards."

"I like the way you say 'don't take the piss.'"

"I like the way you say Martin Luther King."

"Martin Luther King, Martin Luther King. Martin Luther King."

"Piss piss piss piss piss!"

"Does well? The store? " Duz wale? thu' stower?

"Does okay. There's a big margin on cards."

"Good." He flipped three rashers onto a plate, two eggs sunny side up. He handed it to her. When his torso swung around to her he saw that his penis was half erect.

"My, you're a one! Horny as hell."

He looked down and that tinge of pink returned again to his face.

"Aw, shucks. Sorry ma'am."

"Don't apologize, I'm not complaining."

"I brewed some coffee too."

She poured for herself. He finished making his own breakfast. She watched him, the way the cheeks of his buttocks moved and their shape changed as the pressure of his weight switched from one leg to the other, the cheek taking the weight compressed slightly, the other rounder, fuller; the curve of the back to the narrow shoulders and the arms which were very thin. She ran her eyes back down him. The legs in this light were very thin too, but the calves were quite fleshy and strong.

"I thought actors and dancers and those types ate nothing but fruit for breakfast."

"This is all you had in," he said, as if that explained everything, which she accepted it did.

74

She sat at her tiny table, pulling her dressing gown more tightly around her. He took his plate to the sofa and almost collapsed onto the leather. His neat tummy button winked at her as he folded himself down. "Wow," he said, "this is cold on my butt!"

"It warms up."

His pubes were very dark, she saw, darker than his head hair, and the balls, visible below the penis which was lifted slightly outward, hung fairly low.

It's nice to see in the cold light of day the body of a person you've made love to and not be disappointed. She felt sure her nakedness would be a disappointment to him and bunched her dressing gown tighter. He ate his bacon by hand, folding a complete rasher into his mouth. Is that the Southern way, she wondered, having no idea. She sliced hers up. His left knee, she saw, was freshly scarred. That must be from yesterday's fall, she mused. Poor thing! I didn't notice that yesterday. Well, I was thinking a little damage might improve him and that's a start.

"By the way, I've been in America for nearly nineteen years, almost your whole life, and I've never actually heard a single human being say 'aw shucks'. Are you ..." - she was aware of her own use of an Americanism - "... for real?"

He felt his pulse in a spirit of research.

"I guess."

He cleared his plate very fast, as though he were starving.

"You eat fast," she said.

He smiled, an apologetic lift of the eyebrows. He's so polite, she thought, how few polite men there are nowadays, of any age. He put the plate on the leather cushion next to him, picked up his coffee from the floor. One hand was lightly touching his penis, quite unconsciously she was sure.

"I guess I do. Everyone says that. My mom hates it that I do." He slurped coffee, a loud impolite slurp of which he was oblivious. Sara felt very sentimental.

75

"You're such an angel," she said, with syrupy affection. "Such a sweetheart."

"Oh, ma'am, I'm not an angel." He looked down at the evidence of his humanity. "Anyway, I thought angels were blond."

"Perhaps you're a fallen one."

He looked a little disturbed by this.

"I was brought up in the South, ma'am, where they have strong opinions on biblical things, and I hope a very lot I'm not a fallen angel."

"By the way, you're allowed to call me by my name. Sara."

"Sorry, ma'am. Sara."

She still had a full rasher to go and an egg. She knifed into the yolk with the tip of the knife as though she were stabbing an eye, the blade as it broke through hitting the porcelain below hard enough for it to make a dry scraping noise like chalk on a blackboard, but only momentarily. The yolk bled yellow over the plate, damping the crisp bacon.

"Come on, Kiddo, you'd best think of getting away."

He was looking over to the photographs in the bookcase. A portrait shot of a man with a beard, full faced, wispy hair already beginning to thin though he could only have been thirty.

"Steve," she said.

"Huh?"

"He's Steve too. My Steve. Was."

"Left you?"

"You bugger! No, he didn't bloody leave me. As it happens, he died. An accident at work." She felt the lower rims of her eyes begin to water, experiencing an obscure relief that she could, Oprah-like, summon some feelings to impress the boy. "He was a great guy, my Steve. A great guy." Her voice fell away.

"What sort of accident?"

76

She wanted to sniff loudly, an in-drawing of breath to stem flowing tears, but she decided this might be a little overdoing it, so she let her lips curl slightly downward instead, a study of feminine stoicism.

"We were in Florida then. He worked for Disney World, you know. Maintaining the rides. He was working on the rail of one of the roller coasters, some fool who didn't know he was up there gave it the test run they do before opening, to see if it was working right. It was." She put her hand to her eyes. "That was the end of my Steve. Squashed, he was. Drowned, too, it was a water ride."

"I'm really sorry, ma'am."

"Sara. Well, it's fate isn't it, ducks? I wouldn't have a stake in my card shop, I wouldn't have this apartment, if it wasn't for the life insurance. Poor old Steve. Dear old Steve. I miss him still, every day. And the worse thing of it is, that... " a word she rarely used and did not approve of, came out, "that fucking mouse is all over the place and every time I see him I want to blow everything to do with Walt fucking Disney sky high."

"I bet."

"None of this sniffling. Come on, get your pants on, get out of here."

She hadn't meant to sound bossy. Steve reached for his clothes which were still bunched on the floor from last night and he pulled his shorts on. Then his denims. The first sock. She wished he would not hurry. She wanted him to dress slowly. She wanted to see each movement of his limbs, the folding of his tummy as he bent, the swaying of his cock. It was her own fault. She'd frightened him. He looked about.

"Uh... I've lost my other sock."

"Calm down, Steve from Memphis, I didn't mean to snap. I was thinking of my Steve, see, gets me worked up."

She stretched behind her chair to the lampshade from which the sock hung like an ear muffler. She threw it to him. He put it on, then his shoes.

"You look very sexy undressed, just as sexy dressed," she said, mainly as an apology for her churlishness though she felt it was true. He couldn't have looked more pleased if she'd written him a check for a million dollars. "When you find the right girl she's going to be very lucky. I wish I were nineteen, kiddo, so I could be the one."

"Well," he bowed from the waist, "thanks for everything, Sara."

"Thanks, dear. Now, you best be off." She flapped her cushiony hand towards the door, but she cocked her head and smiled so that he would not think she was trying to get rid of him.

"Well, thanks again." He hesitated a second.

"Thank you."

At the door he put his hand on the knob but did not turn it.

"Ma'am."

"Yes?"

"It was really great."

Of course it was, you little idiot! Sex hasn't anything to do with a slim waist and a short skirt, you little fool, it's experience. It's knowing about when to apply pressure and when not, what to touch and when. When to kiss and when to slap just a little, just enough to sting. When to hold back in exquisite torture. Only women know this. Men know nothing except that they want to feel the flood as soon as they can; but the flood's more intense when it's delayed. That's why they're all rubbish in bed, men. That's why women have the power.

"It was great for me too."

78

"Sara, would you...?" He looked at her, the pink on his cheeks deeper than she'd seen it before. "Like last night... it was really great..."

"Kind of like for old times' sake?"

His laugh backfired and came out through his nostrils. She could see through the jeans the outline of his penis.

"Yeah."

"Better then any little twenty-year old girl can do, eh?"

"Yeah."

Last night she'd said she liked her men naked, but now, as he unzipped and pulled out his penis, she decided she liked them clothed. She put her hand on his bottom, the feel of the denim on the ball of her thumb, rough and soft all at once.

When he went through the door afterwards he was bouncy as a boy who got the best gifts at Christmas. That's what I am, Sara analyzed herself. I give gifts I do. I'm a giver. I make the lives around me just a little bit better.

Should I have given him my number? Should I have taken his? Well, if he wants to see me again, he knows where I am. I'm certainly not going to pursue the little whippersnapper. If he wants me he must come to me. If!

Well, of course he'll come to me! If I know men he'll be back! Because he didn't know you could get such a great feeling as I gave him. Twice. Those girls of his, they're like water to him now. Me, I'm a bracing shot of whiskey. He'll be back.

She took the plates to the sink and ran water over them, let them sit and drip.

It was only after she'd showered and dressed for work that she looked at the photograph of Steve again, her Steve. Oh Steven you bastard, what do you think of that then, eh? You were always a jealous little bastard, you always thought you owned me, didn't you, even when you were full of beer and couldn't get it up you still owned me and I had to be the good little wife who didn't mind that hubby couldn't get a hard-on twice a year, and now all you can do is stare out of that frame and I can screw anyone I like right in front of your eyes and you can't stop me, you can't get at me any more. She reached out a hand sharply, making a slapping motion, and the tips of her nails scratched the clear plastic.

She was happy for the next half hour. She hummed a tune. It happened to be 'Eleanor Rigby'. She was scarcely aware of this. It was a tune she'd plucked out of the air. She was wholly detached from the lyrics which had originally accompanied it. So she hummed the melody which supported the line "all the lonely people, where do they all come from?" with an upbeat, almost a gospel spirit.

Yet it did not take long for the emptiness of her apartment to encroach on her, for the sparseness of the furnishings and the layer of dust on everything, for the flat whiteness marked here and there with streaks of brown or black where a splash of coffee sprawled like a discoloured snowflake, where a heel had brushed the skirting board, where the back of the sofa had etched a grey strip like a tidemark, it didn't take long for all these things to touch her with their faint unhappiness, the distant clue of depression to make itself known to her. Such grubbiness may have suggested to a neutral eye an indifference to neatness on the owner's part, a resigned shrug of the shoulders when dampening a cloth had seemed too much like hard work. To Sara herself they yelled out her loneliness, neglect not of a boxy living space but of the woman herself. All those years past in her childhood her mother - not the one from Wicklow - had often chastised her for her self-indulgence, for the pout which came so easily, the crossed arms and the frown and the refusal to move. The stamp of the foot. Sara, everything's such a drama with you, her mother said how many times, you think you're the centre of the world and everyone should just drop everything and make things right

80

for spoilt little Sara. You mark my words, girl, people aren't like that and when you purse your lips and frown you make yourself ugly and unattractive so no-one likes you.

Her mother had not understood her, just as Steve One had not understood her. She was more sensitive than most people, that was all, she felt more deeply. And of course people did like her. They liked her in *Mulligan's* even if she did not much like them, quite a few men had liked her body. Steve, the new young Steve, he liked her. His penis told her he liked her, his tiny little grunt as he came.

Most women of my age couldn't charm a boy into her bed and give him such a good time he'd want to come back. She felt bright again at the thought and began to whistle as she undressed. She whistled the chorus to 'Hot Legs,' a dreadful record - even she had thought so - which had been a big hit single for that hopeless Rod Stewart in the seventies. Halfway through the first line the words clicked into place and she looked down to her own legs and rubbed their flesh. They were very nice, her legs. Very hot. Sexy. She liked them. She was proud of them. Hot legs. You've worn bloody well, you have, girl.

The day sped by in anticipation of her new young lover's return. She was polite to all her customers, even to a group of Brownies who came in shortly after lunch. Their teacher - what was the proper title? Squirrel Brownie or something? Brown Owl? - anyway, she said they were making a day trip to the Empire State Building. Nineteen smiley girls lined up to buy tubes of candy, wanting to be liked by the lady with the funny accent behind the counter. How lovely they are, thought Sara, convinced that she believed it. She made a special effort to beam at each individual child as she took her coins. She wanted to make each one feel adored, just as Bill Clinton, that superbly empathetic man, could make anyone feel they were of outstanding, even unique, interest to him with just a hug and a twinkle in the eye. Sara wanted to go

81

round the counter and hug each happy child in her sweet brown uniform. Her eyes were nearly watering so fond of them she felt, and so were theirs. Life is so hard, she thought, the thought itself (she did not doubt) received and understood by each nearly weeping Brownie through some telepathic transference, that every one of us must offer a little bit of love to each person we encounter, the unspoken bond, yes, I'm human too, I know what it is to suffer, oh my dear we will make it to the end with positivity and love and optimism and hope.

"And what's your name?" she asked each child.

"Erica."

"Nice to meet you, Erica. That will be eighty cents. Goodbye! Have a nice day!"

"Bye!" Erica waved her hand up and down clutching the candies. Then it was Laura's turn.

Then - whooossshhh! - it was already time to go home.

TONY AND PETE

She went into her apartment which reeked of the morning's bacon. On the back ring of the stove the heavy iron frying pan from breakfast sat, a coating of cold fat in it. She opened her food cupboard and opened her fridge looking about for enough foodstuffs to compile something that could pass as supper. Must do a shop later, she thought. Boiled some pasta, sent the water down the sink with steam wisping soft and damp round her face making her blink, poured over it first the contents of a jar of tomato and rosemary spaghetti sauce which did not slide from the jar as in the label illustration but fell in three thick dry dollops, then a can of tuna. She stirred it all up and spooned half of it onto a plate, the other half to make do for tomorrow. She took her plate to the leather sofa which was not still warm from Steve's bottom, there was no outline of his buttocks, she wished there were! She picked up the TV remote control from the floor, where it lay half under the couch.

She clicked on the TV. A rich hammy voice announced NBC Nightly News as if current events were thrilling like 'The Lord of the Rings', and Tom Brokaw appeared. He reminded her of a Muppet newsflash. Click. Channel Thirteen had the Business Report. Boring. Click. A model swirled about in a pretty dress, but it became clear that the dress was not the focus but the necklace glittering in the studio lights, into which the camera moved close. A voice said passionately that nothing looked more like diamond than this, an incredible value at only seventy-nine ninety-nine (plus shipping and handling.) Click click click. 'The Reverend Pat Wade-Adrian's Hour of the Lord.' (A deep Southern accent, perhaps the man from NBC calling on his multi-faceted talent for dialects, multi-faceted like fake diamonds, - cried that this was the Hoouurrr of the *lorrrddd*, with your host the Reverend PAAT WAAAADE-AAAAADRIAAN, the announcer more excited about Pat than the Lord.) The accent made her think of Steve. Click. A cartoon mouse slapped a cartoon cat very hard around the face with a frying pan as heavy and enduring as the one on Sara's stove and the cat's teeth fell out slowly one by one, each tooth hitting the floor to an amused tinkle from an off-screen piano, the cat looking less appalled than disappointed, before falling forward onto the kind of fifties ironing board that pulled down from the wall. It slapped hilariously upward, squashing the poor cat. Wah-wah, said a French Horn. Click. Click. Click. Click. She clicked off in frustration. The screen went blank.

She checked her watch. I wonder if he'll show. I'm sure he will. I know men, they always go where the good times are.

She was aware as never before of the passing of time on the clock in the bookcase. She kept looking over to it. It was twenty to eight. Fifteen minutes later it was eighteen to eight. Time hadn't moved so slowly since, well, she couldn't remember when. Even a boring day in the store moved faster than this. She clicked the TV back on and surfed some more with complete indifference and then clicked it off again. The last thing she wanted was to watch junk on TV. She read a magazine which she had read before. The pages were creased where her fingers had bent them on each turn of the page the first time through. She did not remember the articles. They were the forgettable film star gossip which filled up cheap magazines like   ballast. She rarely saw films, so she knew the stars only through their wedding photographs and their divorces. One glamorous wedding photograph was much the same as another, one divorce the same as another. To add to the confusion the divorce articles were often illustrated with wedding photographs so if she was 'reading' without attention she could turn the page on a finished article without registering whether it had been about divorce or a marriage. It was always about money either way. Flicking pages, she sighed loudly, pushing her lips out so that when she expelled air it came out with a farting sound. Where was that bloody boy?

But her evening was not to be as dull as she'd feared. Sometime before nine she heard light footsteps under her open window. *It's him!* she said, almost aloud. She sprang to her feet and went to the window, to call out to him. But he was not there. He was not on the steps. Perhaps she'd heard customers going to the Mexican restaurant. What a disappointment! But then the front door downstairs opened and a voice called,

"Hey, you fuckers! Get out of there!" It was Tony. He came darting down the steps. Pete followed him. At the foot of the steps they turned towards *Boyle's Travel.* Sara ran out her apartment and down to the street.

"What the hell's going on?"

The door to *Boyle's* was open and Tony and Pete were inside. A fat black kid in a bobble hat was pinned under Tony. A willowy white kid also in a bobble hat was pressed against the wall. Pete's hands gripped his arms above the elbows. Pete turned his head to Sara.

"Call the cops!" he cried.

In the second Pete was turned away the white kid kneed him in the balls. He doubled over. The kid slid away from him snakelike and ran towards Sara. Whether he pushed her aside or whether she stepped away it was not clear, but he ran through the door.

"Fuuuuck!" said Pete. He half forgot his pain and darted out after the kid, hands cupped over genitals. Sara stood uselessly for a moment and then ran to Tony who still held the black kid captive. The kid was shaking all over, legs and arms and torso, in a kind of spastic dance as if by sheer determination he could wobble Tony off him. Head too, springing upward in a butting movement but making contact only with air. She reached out a hand, perhaps to help pinion the kid. "No, I'm fine," cried Tony. "Call the police!"

The kid reached out for her hand and grasped it. He tugged her towards him and she collapsed on top of Tony. In the confusion, the kid slipped out from under Tony while Tony grabbed Sara, thinking she was the white kid come back, so while the black kid darted out after his friend Tony pinned Sara to the ground.

Pete reappeared. He was rubbing his crotch.

"He got fucking away," he said. He was breathing hard.

"Well we've got this one."

"It's me, Antony! Me!" Sara shoved him away, furious. "My arms are all bruised," she said, not checking to see if this were so.

"Fucking little assholes," said Tony, standing up and wiping his brow. Pete put an arm on him and kissed him.

"Well, at least they didn't get anything."

This, however, was cold comfort as there wasn't anything to get. Not anything worth stealing. A cheap Formica desk was angled in the corner, probably in the same place it had been when *Boyle's* had been in business. A chair was placed behind it. A dozen or more curling posters advertised exotic vacations. On one, the back of a dark- skinned woman could be seen, gazing down a beautiful beach to a post-card sunset. In her visible hand she held a cocktail with a cherry in it. Her nails were superbly manicured. They were painted a bright red. She wore only a bikini, and her spine could be seen where she arched her back. She was gorgeous. It was unfortunate that at this moment there was no-one in the room with a sexual interest in women. Maybe that had been *Boyle's* problem. The Village was awash with queers and photographs of naked women could hardly be expected to entice them to buy vacations. Sara had a vague idea that lesbians weren't interested in women like this either.

But if he didn't fancy her, Tony did feel a connection to her.

"God," said Tony, "I wish I was her right now, a million miles from here. Are you all right?"

"A bit sore. I'll be fine."

"Jesus. Those fuckers."

"Calm down."

"I am calm. They're still fuckers."

"But what did they want?" asked Sara in Miss Marple mode.

"Who knows? Who cares?"

"I'm sorry if I messed it up," she said, still as Miss Marple, the real Sara not being adept at apologies.

"That's okay. They'd've got away anyway." Peter didn't sound as forgiving as his choice of words might suggest.

Sara wandered into the back. There was a kettle and a small empty refrigerator.

"Maybe they were after these."

"I doubt it. You don't break into a building for a kettle and a chair."

"They could've been looking for money," said Tony.

"Only if they were retards. This place looks completely closed down."

"Maybe they were planning to squat here," said Sara thoughtfully.

"What?"

"In London it's common. Kids break into an unoccupied flat and live there. Some times they even bring their furniture and stuff. They make it cosy."

"That doesn't happen here."

"The cops'd come in and blow their brains out."

"Maybe they're new at the crime game," said Sara. "They were practicing on an empty place first."

"Maybe." Tony didn't buy this for a moment, but he didn't care either. "Let's go home. Wanna come in for a beer, Sara?" This was thrown over his shoulder, not quite a sincere invitation, but Sara was fed up with her own apartment so she said,

"That would be lovely, boys. Just one."

They went out into the street.

"The little fuckers broke the lock," said Tony.

"Fuckers," said Pete.

Sara pulled *Boyle's* door shut.

"Well, at least it closes tight," she said. "No-one would know."

"Maybe we should call the police."

"But they got away. They didn't take anything," said Tony.

"But still. DNA. They may be able to trace them."

"They weren't pros," said Sara. "Not yet anyway."

"Still, we should call the police," said Tony, and Pete nodded agreement.

At the top of the steps a tiny little bald man stood nervously. He watched them come towards him.

"Hi," he said, in a thin, nasal tone. He didn't catch anyone's eye, but looked over the balustrade to *Boyle's Travel.* "I heard some noise, what happened?"

"A couple of kids broke into *Boyle's.* They didn't get anything," said Tony.

"Escaped, though," sighed Pete.

"The bastards," said Sara.

"Okay. Well, if there's nothing I can do to help…" Before anyone got a chance to say anything more he'd turned his back and was climbing the stairs to his apartment at the top.

Tony and Pete went into their own apartment. Sara followed. Tony opened the refrigerator and pulled out three bottles of Budweiser.

"Strange guy," said Pete indifferently.

"He's okay. Not very sociable," said Tony. "Harmless."

"To me," said Sara, "he's just The Man Upstairs. It's become his name, sort of. I don't think I've ever said a word to him."

Theirs was a lovely apartment, neat and clean and romantic. In a corner was the desk where Tony worked on his novel. A pile of papers sat tidily yet importantly at its left and the small laptop on which he wrote was folded shut. It was thin and unobtrusive. In the middle looking towards the window was a red suite: a couch and three armchairs. A coffee table had upscale magazines arranged on it. The walls were a muted orange which gave the room a sense of space. The lights were kept low, but the wall colour ensured the room never had that dusky greyness which Sara's had nearly all the time. The cooking area was as near as the space allowed to an expert chef's kitchen, with utensils, not all of which Sara could identify, hanging from hooks screwed onto a strip of polished mahogany. There were no crumbs to be seen. It was so clean it could have been on TV. Nice oak bookcases contained well-organized books, - not a lot, they probably kept most of their books in the bedroom, but enough to assert an air of intelligence, - interlarded with photographs and a miniature of Michelangelo's David. Sara felt she had failed to make the most of her apartment. She'd always thought that the space being so small it was hardly worth bothering to try to make it spruce. Tony and Pete would doubtless have said that because it was small it was doubly important that it be spruce in order to work as a happy living area. It was true that their apartment was packed full of things and yet did not feel cramped. Sara's was pretty empty but it seemed squeezed and oppressive. She sipped her beer and took one of the chairs. Tony sat on the sofa and Peter lay stretched out across him, head on his lap.

"You gonna call the cops?" asked Pete. He looked up at his lover. At his angle it was hard to drink beer and a little splash fell on his chin when he swigged. Tony wiped it away with the back of his hand.

"In a moment," said Tony. He brushed his fingers through Pete's hair. It was a very tender gesture. Sara wished Steve was here. She wanted to brush her hand through his hair just like that. She wanted Pete and Tony to see that she had a lover with nice hair too, a good-looking lover who liked to lie across her lap like Peter. What a tender mistress she had it in her to be! She had never called herself a 'mistress' before, even on the couple of occasions when the term would have been applicable, but she liked the idea of being Steve's 'mistress' even if it was not exactly the correct description, it had historical, royal connotations. Some distant glimmer of recalled knowledge made her think of oranges. She would have been a fabulous mistress for a king. She was born in the wrong time. She belonged in a time of grace and elegance.

The adventure over, it no longer seemed very urgent to call the police. Indeed, in the silence broken only by the sipping of beers it seemed somehow uncharitable to call them, wasting their time chasing kids they'd never find, kids who anyway had probably learned their lesson from the shock of being caught.

They finished their beers and Tony and Pete stayed put. Sara twirled her bottle. Tony did not offer her another. She didn't want to go but it was clear she was no longer welcome. Tony and Pete wanted to be alone. Perhaps they wanted to

90

fuck each other. Queens were insatiable, it was well known. They had abnormal sexual appetites. They were like black people that way.

So she stood up and said brightly, "Thanks for the beer, boys," and went to the door. "If you do decide to call the cops, you can rely on me as a witness."

"Thanks, Sair," said Tony, as though he always called her Sair, which he never had before.

Upstairs her apartment looked drearier than ever. It was twenty-five past nine. She didn't want to watch television. She didn't want to read. She didn't want to eat. She didn't want to just sit there on her lovely leather couch feeling lonely and unloved. She certainly didn't want to go to *Mulligan's* and talk about John Lennon. She might as well go to bed.

The door bell rang.

Oh my God! Could it be...?

She spoke into the intercom.

"Hello?"

"It's me." His voice was distant. It was a little ashamed. Of what it was ashamed she could not work out.

She did not want to appear grateful.

"Who's this?"

There was a beat. She interpreted the silence with pleasure: he hadn't expected to be forgotten so soon.

"Steve."

"Oh, Steve from last night. Hi." She was cool as a cucumber. Did he shuffle a bit? Good. It was a rule of one-night stands that you did not come back for a second time, even if you said you would in the heat of the moment. Did he not understand this custom? (It was a custom she had just invented but now he was here she wanted him to want her more than she wanted him.)

"Hi. Can I come in?" Haa, cane ah come iyan?

91

She paused again. She drew in a big gulp of breath in order to let out a loud sigh, but she thought this might be overdoing the matter. She didn't want to drive him away.

"I don't see why not." She buzzed him in. She put her ear to the door, listening for his footsteps. Be cool, now, ducks, don't seem grateful the little bugger's shown up.

When he rapped his knuckles on the door, even the rap having something of shyness in it, her heart beat faster. She felt like a teenager having an illicit rendezvous. Life was exciting if only you had the courage to really live it. She felt young and free and full of hope for the future. Tony brushing his hand through Pete's hair seemed old and staid to her now. They were so middle-aged, those two. They probably never even had sex any more. They probably stayed together for 'companionship' or something icky like that. They probably said to each other, I don't really mind that we don't have sex like we used to because our relationship has gone on to another plane. I feel we have a very deep connection. I love you for your soul. And the other would nod and be moved, or pretend to be moved, but he was really thinking *for Christ's sake fuck me or I'm going to leave you!* But he didn't get fucked and for some reason he didn't leave either. That was middle age for you.

She opened the door. There he was, all sweet and shy and not knowing what to say, the Band-Aid on his cheek. A strand of hair hung over one eye. He looked like Johnny Depp. Only younger and sexier.

She was so delighted to see him that any remaining mists of anger evaporated. All she wanted was for him to come right in and take off his clothes and make love to her again. But she was not so overwhelmed that she could not sustain her apparent coolness for a while longer.

"Well," she said. "What are you doing here? Couldn't keep away, ducks?" it did not come out as icy as she intended. He knew she was pleased. He relaxed.

92

"Something like that." His smile was radiant like a movie star.

He came in. He had a copy of a magazine called *Backstage* tucked into an inside pocket of his jacket, sticking out above the zip which was only halfway closed. He'd hardly come over the threshold before he pulled the magazine out and threw it nonchalantly on to the sofa.

"What's that?"

"Trade paper." He yawned. "Oh by the way I went for an audition this afternoon. Got a recall."

"What for?" She hardly cared. She wanted him naked.

He seemed a bit fuzzy about what it was for.

"Oh, a season of plays. For next year. In Pittsburgh."

"Come here, kiddo." She put her arms around him and swept him towards her. He lost his balance and fell against her breasts before regaining it. She pushed her hand down into his jeans and his shorts and touched his cock. He didn't seem to mind. She felt it hardening at the warmth of her touch, felt it fill with blood and expand, felt it press into her rounded palm. It was amazing how hard a young man's cock could be. It would never be as hard when he reached forty. Sex would never seem quite so urgent.

They ran into her bedroom and he threw himself on her bed. She pulled his clothes off him. She stripped herself as fast as possible. They kissed mightily. He sucked on her breasts, first one and then the other. She licked his balls and sucked his cock. He fingered her sex and put his mouth to it. When they fucked it was with an intensity greater than the night before, her hands against his buttocks, pulling him deeply into her. They came together. Sex had never been better, for her, for him, for anyone. This was the best it could get for the sensual human creature.

Sara was exhausted. Steve was full of life. What was that old saw about men always falling asleep after an orgasm? Sara had experienced it more than once. Eddie McGovern

93

could barely keep his eyes open for a minute. This time, it was she who wanted to drift off, Steve lay there all boyish and talkative.

"That was great," he said.

"Yeh," she said, her arm under his back," it was lovely."

"I'm all tired out," he said, though he obviously wasn't. She was worried he might want a second go. She wouldn't wish to say no because it would make her seem old and boring, but she wanted to wait at least until morning. He snuggled into her. The head of his penis was wet, she felt it against her leg.

"Saw your neighbour, he said hi to me."

"Which one? Tony? Pete?"

"Huh?" He looked thrown.

"Antony or Peter? My neighbours?"

"Bald guy. Quite old. Saw him on the stairs. He was going out."

"The Man Upstairs. Said hi? More than he does to me."

"Seemed okay."

"Grumpy."

"I guess he could be pretty negative sometimes. Seems like that."

"Pretty negative? That's a way of putting it. Moaning old sod's more like it."

He laughed his small nasal laugh very like the small nasal moan he made as he came.

"That's funny. Moaning old sod. I like that." Ah laak thyat.

"Don't use phrases like that in Memphis? Exotic to you, I   suppose? "

"Goddamn pain in the ass is how we'd say it. Fucking pain in the ass." When he used swear words he had a look slightly of apology and slightly of daring.

"Then you'll fit into New York okay."

She fell into the most contented sleep she'd had in years...

(The boy lent on his elbow and looked at her from his strange golden-brown eyes. His was not a look of love, it was a look removed from emotion. It would have been impossible for anyone to penetrate the meaning in it. Perhaps it had no meaning. Perhaps it simply was, like cliffs and mountains and the wind. He remained in that position for a long time, gazing at the blond woman with her full attractive lips, her bitterness and her need. He touched his penis and quietly, slowly, without passion, he masturbated. Not over her, either literally or metaphorically. He might not have been in her bedroom at all. He masturbated because it felt so very good. Did he think when his penis hardened, for the pleasure of someone else or just for his own pleasure, that this was his purpose? That this was the point of him? That in the spilling of his seed his very essence was contained? Not within the seed itself, but in the spilling, the orgasm, the physical sensation? His total truth?

Then he too slept.)

HUCKLEBERRY

Dawn came crisply. Sara awoke easily and fully. Steve slept on. She could hear his light breathing. She lifted the sheet, did not throw it off, she looked under it to see the gentle rising and falling of his chest. She reached out a hand. She did not touch him, but felt his bodily presence like a radiance which pricked her palm. He was warm from her sheets. This beautiful boy, naked under her sheets, naked with her. Naked with Sara. The smell of come was on him but it was not like the staleness of morning-after, it was salty and certain as the sea. She laid the sheet back on him so that he would be warm and snug.

She ran into the kitchen with the romantic idea of making him breakfast, but there was only one egg left, so she made a cup of coffee and filled her two best, oldest, daintiest coffee cups, illustrated with flowers and with a line of gold paint around the handles. She rattled the cups on their matching saucers into the bedroom. She sat down on his side of the bed. New York's light and sound filtered through the closed curtains. A church bell rang. Every hour church bells rang. She liked their chimes. They made her feel she was in some little country village of ivy-licked cottages with only a church and a corner store and a mail box.

"Wakey wakey," she whispered. He moaned and turned over to lie on his belly. "It's morning, ducks." He turned over again. "You've got work to go to." She assumed he could not afford to miss his motorcycle messenger job a second day running. He shifted again, pushing his face into the pillow. "I know you're awake, kiddo." She felt like a mother whose errant son would not get up for school. It was a nice feeling. He turned over and opened one eye.

"What?"

"It's after eight. Time to get up. Here." She shoved a cup towards him. Coffee washed over the edge.

"Notttyettt," he said, but his I'm-still-asleep merging of his words did not fool her.

"Yes, yet!" she said, sternly. "Drink up." She was annoyed that he had not sprung up at the aroma of the delicious coffee and thanked her for the gesture as she had thanked him yesterday.

"Naw," he said, batting his eyelids.

"Don't 'naw' me, like... like Tom Sawyer!"

He laughed. He opened the other eye. He wasn't pretending any more.

"Not all Southern boys are Tom Sawyer, ma'am. Besides, I like Huck Finn more. He was cool." He took the coffee.

"Oh, yes, Huck. You said. You know that stuff?" He didn't seem the reading type any more than she was. Except of course he must read plays all the time. But that was work. She sipped her coffee. It tasted excellent.

"We studied them at school. Both of them. 'Tom' when I was eight, 'Huck' when I was, uh, sixteen?"

My God, I'm sitting on a bed with a boy who remembers sixteen. Well, it was only half a decade ago for him, wasn't it? Not that even.

"Plus, we did 'Huck Finn' as a school play. Bits of it anyway. I was Huck. I was fourteen. That's what made me want to come to New York and act. I was really good as Huck."

97

"I can believe it." She felt under the bed clothes, brushed his pubes.

"Yeah, it was cool. You know the story of 'Huck Finn'?"

"Yeh, I once saw a film of it, and I think they did a TV version too when I was a kid. Whitewashing fences, Injun Joe. Injun Joe was really scary. He stalks them in a cave."

"No, that's 'Tom Sawyer'. 'Huckleberry Finn' is the sequel. It's way heavier. It's about slavery. Normally it's about slavery 'cept in our production it wasn't." He smiled cheekily. He looked just like Huck. He looked like a very free boy.

"Yours wasn't?"

"The school president let us do 'Huck Finn' because he thought it was 'Tom Sawyer.' The PTA went crazy about it. You can't do a play about slavery, they said, it's racist. So the prez goes to the teacher who's producing it, says you must cut out all references to slavery. You've got to remember, ma'am. This is Tennessee. So all mention of slavery, even Jim the slave himself, they're all cut out. They also cut out Huck's alcoholic father because they thought portrayal of drinking was unwholesome. So Huck's motive for taking the raft and going up the Mississippi is that he wants to see the world. I remember the line really well:

"'I always wanted to see the world, Miss Becky. I wanna go down to Orleans and hear some of that cool Jazz I hear is comin' up there. The black folk are makin' this cool new music which is gonna liberate them. It's real soulful, Miss Becky. '

"And Becky says, 'That sounds so beautiful! Oh, Huck, can I come too? Please let me come! I want to hear the new music of my people.' In our version Becky was black. "

"Becky was Tom Sawyer's girlfriend." Sara recalled this from the film.

"Yeah. There were a lot of black kids in the school of course, but with all the slavery bits cut out there weren't any black parts left, so they took Becky from 'Tom Sawyer' and made her African American. There was a reunion scene at the end, between Tom and Becky. It must've been the first ever interracial kiss on a Memphis school stage. Well, it was supposed to be a kiss but the girl playing Becky said Tom had bad breath so it became a sort of hug with, like, those Russian kisses they do on the air? Sort of three inches from each cheek? But the PTA were very pleased. They thought it was very progressive. And with all that Jazz in it, they got a lot of noise out of the school band too. "

"And you got rave reviews, did you?"

"I guess. And after the last night I got lucky with the girl who played Becky. I guess I didn't have bad breath. Hey, talkin' about bad breath, you wanna know something? You know how many cigars Mark Twain smoked every day?"

"You won't be surprised to know that I don't. But I expect you do as you look so smug."

"Twenty. Twenty cigars." He separated his thumb and first finger to indicate their size. "Not little ones, big fat ones."

"Yuk."

"Yeah, it sounds kind of disgusting, but kind of cool too." He looked wistful. "I like Mark Twain. He wanted freedom. Like me. I want to be free."

"Well, you are, aren't you?"

"I mean really free. Free from family and money and guilt."

"What do you have to feel guilty about?"

He made what Sara took to be a thinking face, screwing up the skin around his nose.

"Oh, nothing. Nothing actual. Just life makes you guilty, don't it?"

But Sara did not recognize this truth. She had no guilt. She was what she was, she lived for the moment. Guilt didn't come into it.

"See," continued the boy, "Mark Twain wanted to be free himself, but he couldn't because he was human. He could make characters in books be free because you can, you can send them to paradise if you want, but you can't make paradise for real people. I think Mark Twain wrote a great book because he wanted what he could not have, but Huck could have it because he was imagined. He could 'light out for the territory.' That's the phrase at the end of the book. 'Light out for the territory.' I think that's why Huck is so important to Americans. They all, we all, came here to be free. I guess our ancestors stood on those crowded boats thinking it was gonna be paradise at the end. And, well it was good I guess for some of them and maybe better than what they came from, but it ain't paradise. Freedom is something you can really really want but you can't never have it, not really. 'Cos the territory…you can't ever get to it. It's why Mark Twain's stuff is so sad even when it seems happy and funny."

"This is too heavy for eight in the morning. Get up." But she didn't want him to get up, she wanted him to keep talking so she could bathe in his lovely accent and his sweet, melancholy reflections. "You've thought this over deeply, haven't you?"

He was sipping his coffee and when he laughed he had to spit some back into his cup to keep it from running down his chin.

"Naw, I'm just saying what our teacher told us. But it seems kinda true. 'Light out for the territory'. Cool… Lighting out…" He rolled over onto his stomach, carefully propping the coffee cup between both hands. But he turned around immediately again. He was very fidgety. "Plus, I'm an actor." She was leaning in to him so his head was very near her, looking up at her. He smiled. His eyes twinkled. Those eyes with stars in them, fainter in the distilled morning light. It was as if right then and there in her bed, not before with the *Backstage* and the auditions, it was there that suddenly he realised he was an actor. He had defined himself and it was a revelation. "So I can appear cleverer than I am. I can appear stupider too." I can appear to be a lot of things, he did not say and possibly did not think. He finished his coffee and gave her the cup. It was an odd moment, she on the edge of her own bed holding a half full cup of coffee in one hand and an empty cup in the other. It took a beat for him to see his mistake.

"Sorry!" He took it back and got out of bed and walked through into the kitchen area, where he put the cup down. She followed him. When he turned towards her she saw that yet again he was half aroused.

"What's your name, by the way, Steve? Your last name? I still don't know it."

He grinned toothily.

"Smith. I'm Steven Smith."

The very name of her husband. It was a coincidence beyond belief.

"Are you kidding me?"

"No. Why would I? That's my name. Steve Smith."

Steve Smith was a perfectly common name. There were probably thousands of Steve Smiths in New York alone. It's not like she'd once married a Steve Plonk-Ericcson and suddenly found herself in bed with another Steve Plonk-Ericcson. Now that really would have been weird. But even Steve Smith… it was strange enough. It was coincidence enough. Steve Smith Two, and yet so unlike Steve Smith One.

"I better shower," he said.

She listened to the running of the water. She wanted to go in and watch him. She did not want to share the shower, but rather to stand back and watch the water shaping itself around his body. She pictured the water somehow frozen so that when he stepped out of it his form as it was in that

101

particular moment would remain forever like a glass sculpture. In the very second she pictured this image she was overcome with terrible fear, a fear that he would not come back a third time, that the adventure was over, that she would never see him again. She did not want it to be over. She did not want it to be over! She identified with Alice in the pink shoes who wanted something and stomped and stomped her feet until she got it. Sara's London Mother would have commented disapprovingly on the pout that curled Sara's lips. I do not want him to go! She looked down into her coffee cup. She saw her face in the muddy liquid. Reflected, it looked fat and spoilt and she knew he would not want to see her again because she was not beautiful and he was. Why would he have a middle-aged woman when he could have all the girls he wanted? He wanted freedom. She could not give him freedom; she was trapped herself. She had forgotten the superior sexual skill which she had believed her secret power. She finished the remains of her coffee. When he emerged, wiping himself down, she looked at him and an emotion not unlike hatred crept over her. It was not Sara herself, not her, who stalked up to him, it was her limbs, they took control and her legs walked, walked, walked, the few paces to him and her hand darted out and her thumb and first finger gripped the edge of the Band-Aid which the steam had loosened and she pulled it off, viciously, viciously, her lips withdrawing above and below her teeth, exposing them. She looked like a crazed animal.

"Take that, Steve Smith!"

"Fuck!" He slapped a hand to the exposed wound. "Whatcha do that for?"

What might she have said and done if she had not managed to recover herself? Who could know? Not even her.

"We should put some fresh on that, duck," she said softly. "I see it's beginning to heal nicely."

"Oh. Yeah."

She put another strip on the graze, gave it a motherly pat. Then he dressed and went to her door.

"Don't want another little, you know, like yesterday?" She looked down to his genitals covered in denim.

"Oh, I gotta be somewhere. I can't skip another day."

Why not, she wanted to say, why not, you can get another job, can't you, anything else would be better than riding around New York delivering stupid mail to awful corporations? Oh, and where's your motorcycle by the way? But he had opened the door and was on the landing.

"It's been great," he said.

"'It's been great'? You say it like there won't be another time." She wanted to beg him to promise to come back tonight and make love to her again.

"Oh, I didn't mean it that way. You know I love being with you, Sara." Yes you do, she thought, remembering his little groan as he came in her.

"So, tonight?"

He pinked.

"I can't tonight. I've got a date."

"Fucking someone else, are you?"

"Sara!" He looked appalled at her impropriety. She had offended his Southern courtliness.

"I had no right to say that, I'm sorry." Sara felt she had every right, but she did not want to lose him. And she knew he was indeed going to fuck someone else. She knew it so that the knowledge burned in the back of her skull.

"Got a number?"

"Sara, I don't have time, I'm running late. See ya!"

"See you, kiddo." She lifted a hand and waved to him, but she looked only at his knees. "Soon, I hope." She sighed deeply. She heard his sneakers on the stairs going down. She stepped through the door and watched him in the stairwell: He cocked a head to Pete and Tony's door, running past it, and soon she heard the front door open. She went to her window. He turned up Minetta Lane, heading for Bleecker. She looked back into her dusty living room and loathed it. There was something on the sofa.

She called out to him running up the street.

"Oy! Oy!" He did not look back. "Oy! You forgot something!" This time he turned, looked up, saw her. She threw out his copy of *Backstage*. It opened on the air and flew like a paper butterfly over her balcony and down to the ground. He ran to it and picked it up.

"Thanks." He smiled wonderfully to her, his cheek lifting the fresh bandage into a quarter-moon curve. He ran away. She watched him. There being no sun the black leather jacket did not shine. Foreshortened as he was, she could not see his bottom and his legs were sawn off. She could see his sneakers. The lace on the left one had worked free. It hit the ground as he ran, rising and falling like a miniature whip.

She wandered back into her apartment and fell onto the sofa.

What was to happen now? Was she having an affair with him, or had it been a one-night stand which became two nights but meant nothing? She wished she'd asked for his number earlier. It was a big mistake to leave all the running to him.

If only he'd stayed. For just half an hour more! She had more to offer him. She would have cupped his balls. She would have kissed the head of his cock. She would have sucked him off. She remembered how he'd shaken yesterday at the orgasm, how all of him, body and spirit, had been concentrated in sensation.

She wept. She wept so that her body too shook with sensation. It had never before struck her how near weeping was to sexual climax. You lost control of yourself when you

104

wept just as when you came. Was it a sample of the bitter humour of God, or the gods, or whatever, that the greatest pleasure should be so closely allied with the physical expression of despair?

She wept until there were no tears left to drain, until her bones were weary and her head throbbing. She looked like a bag lady. But she was not a bag lady, she was a business woman and she had work to go to. Like Steve, she had a job. Like Steve, she would do her job well and come home and he, of course, would be here waiting. No man turned away pleasure. He would be here when she got home or if not then, before night fell. He would. He would.

She dried her eyes. She showered. She dressed. She put on make-up. She looked in the mirror. She did not look sad, she looked efficient and competent. She was an attractive woman. Steve would be back tonight.

She said this over and over and over on the way to *Make Someone's Day Cards and Gifts*. He'll be back, mark my words. He'll be back. Why wouldn't he? He's got other friends, of course, he's young and horny, I don't mind that. Good luck to him. But I know more than they do and that's why he'll be back.

Perhaps it was because of the greyness of the morning or the roar of roadwork, but today these self-assurances sounded hollow in her head. She was hardly conscious of the passing day. She thought over the previous night from every angle, as if it were a globe you could turn in your hand to see the details on the underside. But look as she might she could not make out the future, could not perceive in the mists of the globe the threads leading from last night into the future. Occasionally she felt ready to spill tears again though her eyes remained dry. More often she felt that baggy-eyed exhaustion which comes after tears. So little aware was she of the outer world that leaving *Make Someone's Day* that afternoon she felt strangely disoriented, as if she were not sure what she was

105

doing on this street in the vicinity of St. Vincent's Hospital at four thirty in the afternoon.

When she got to her apartment and there was no-one waiting for her, she swept her curtains closed, which she never did. She opened a box of Tuna Helper and stirred the contents into a pan. She felt as if she had not left her apartment all day. Though she could not get Steve and his eyes out of her head, he impressed her rather as the haunting residue of a heavy dream than as an earthly reality. The shadow of the fire escape lay against her closed curtains, a strip of gray to match her mood. She sat on her sofa and ate her food and put the empty plate by her feet and sat there. She did not turn on the TV. She did not open a magazine. She sat there, arms folded, looking sometimes down at her breasts and sometimes at her feet. She heard more than once the sound of bandage being torn from skin and saw hurt eyes which did not understand the sudden viciousness of it, and knew that in this one act she, or her dream self, had made a terrible mistake which would change the course of things, not for the better.

STRANGERS

The only instances of coincidence's operations being remarked upon, of course, are those occasions when they come to light. "I was just thinking of you when the phone rang and who should it be! What a coincidence!" "I was on vacation in St. Lucia, me and my wife, and guess who was sitting by the pool on our very first afternoon! Our dentist!" "What a coincidence!" "The lights went up and there, three seats down from us, was my ex." "What a coincidence." But it may be that coincidence's strangest and subtlest workings remain unknown to all who are shadowed by them. That evening Sara walked past the *Village Vanguard* jazz club. She walked past it every day to and from work, but rarely in the evening on a purposeless stroll. Why did she take the stroll? She did not remember deciding, (having watched, or rather felt, dusk fall to night, having heard people on the street going to the Mexican restaurant, their laughter distant from her and alien, having smelt the acidic congealed paste that remained of her dinner,) that she needed to get some air. She was on her sofa pouting, arms over breasts, and then she was on the street walking. A recollection that once, very long ago, she had frequented an Irish bar near here did not draw her to it. She was drawn elsewhere, why and how she could not tell. Why take the familiar route, the route to work, (work? Did she go to work? She had a sense that no, her work was to sit on her sofa with her arms folded waiting for she knew not what) when there were so many other routes to choose from?

Sphere Masters the superb saxophonist had a week-long engagement at the *Vanguard*. He blew like an angel, everybody who knew his work said so. Sara had never heard of him, and she was hardly alone in that loss. She didn't look at the club, didn't notice that she was passing the legendary *Village Vanguard* even as she went under its awning. Two guys went to hear Sphere Masters that night, Daniel Dawson and Gene Simon. It was Daniel who really liked and knew jazz; Gene went along for the ride. They stood outside the door a few moments and entered the club. Just as the door sighed closed Sara went by. If she had looked around then she would have seen Gene's back or Daniel's back descending the stairs, though she might not have recognized either. But then she might have done. Gene with a little graze on his cheek. If she had, the outcome of this story would have been different. It's impossible to say that it would have been happier, but it could hardly have been worse.

Then she was back in her apartment. She was in bed. She did not know why she had gone to bed. It wasn't her bedtime. But when there was nothing else to do bed seemed the right place for her, in the dark, waiting for what was to come, whatever that might be. Next to her the sheets were crumpled as if not too long before a warm, living body had lain upon them. Or perhaps that had been long, long ago? In the dark with the sounds of the City going on forever outside the sealed coffin of her bedroom it was as if, not as if time had ceased to exist exactly, but as if it had been twisted somehow, so that the long past felt very recent and the occurrences of yesterday might well have happened so long before that memory could retain no more than isolated impressions, the warmth of a thigh, a sweet small groan. Salt.

108

Into this apparent twisting of time, partly dream, partly silence, partly misery, partly a self-induced blankness, an immersion in subjectivity as palpable as a tank of warm water, came like the stroke of a sharp, cruel knife a high metallic demand. In whatever downy place between fantasy and sickness Sara was at that second, the new noise might have been no more real than the illusion of love, but it was different in kind from the soft suffocation of her state, as an electric drill is different from three muted viols. It was an abuse.

Her eyes snapped open.

The shrillness cut in again.

Time untwisted liked a string snapped straight. A siren came from somewhere. Mexican music swum up to her. These were not the blades which had cut her awake. A blade sliced again.

It was her doorbell. It rang a third time.

With nothing left of her floating state except the implication of a headache, she pulled herself from her bed and went to the intercom. A voice said,

" Hi." Tiny and apologetic.

"Steven."

"Hi. Sorry."

"What do you want, Steven Smith?"

"Can I come up?"

She was not in the mood to play games. She neither wanted him nor did not want him. She pressed her buzzer.

He was at her door and he was beautiful. He was young and it meant nothing to him that it was four in the morning. He smelt of smoke. Did he smell of music too? She was not angry with him. She was not pleased to see him either. She vaguely noticed that his Band-Aid was gone. He came to her and pressed himself against her. He said nothing. She did not want him to fuck her but she felt his erection against the denim and she didn't mind if he did. He went into her

109

bedroom and stripped in a flowing, silent movement of his limbs. Was he really here? The screwing insinuated itself into her earlier state, only the hardness of his penis in her was utterly of the material plane. His rhythm in her was slow and sweet. He did not moan as he came this time, but expelled air from his lungs. She felt it on her ear. The warmth of a thigh. A sweet small outbreathing. Salt.

He was flesh and she was flesh but it might have been not so.

Until morning, with the banality of daylight and the demands, less shrill than the ring of a bell but more insistent and more persistent, of *Make Someone's Day*. Her hand reached out to where the boy was.

But he wasn't.

So it had all been a dream.

Was that how 'Alice in Wonderland' had finished? With that very statement? 'It had all been a dream'? She did not remember having read the book as a child, but that clean, simple sentence struck her as right. Or perhaps it had been the last line of the terrible Disney film version which she had been dragged to when too young to appreciate its awfulness: a chocolaty, smarmy voice over the closing of a cartoon book made of thick paper in a leather binding. "It was all a dream." One of those voices which seemed only to exist on the soundtracks of saccharine cartoons, though presumably they existed in real life too, attached to some unfortunate actor who could find no other work.

Unless! She listened for the sound of business in the kitchen, the smell of bacon. But she had no bacon left in her refrigerator. The running of a shower? No.

But in real life things that seemed real were real. That was how it was. He must have been here. She pulled the sheet away from his side of the bed. There were crumples, but they might not have been new.

110

Her eye landed on a white piece of paper lain on the pillow.

TONIGHT.

STEVE.

So he had been here! And for the first time he was actually making a date with her! She would not have to wait and wonder, he'd be here, he said so.

She sprang from the bed. Everything was marvellous now. She snatched her curtains open. The light itself was a ray of hope. Did it pour into her bedroom, or was it as muted as it had been yesterday morning? For ordinary people walking to subway stations or hailing cabs it might have been unremarkable, even a little dull. But for her it poured! It poured!

Until, Sara being Sara, it did not pour. It sputtered and guttered and was uninteresting, un-magical daylight. And Steve was an uninteresting, un-magical boy who was playing games with her. Water flowed over her lips in the shower and she spat it away. He thought he could come and go on a whim, he could fuck her whether or not she wanted him, he could tell her he'd be round tonight without so much as a moment's reflection that perhaps she bloody well did not want him to come round tonight, because, because she had other plans! She would make other plans! She would make exciting other plans which would put him in the shade!

At lunchtime she picked up a paper and telephoned the Box Office and booked a ticket to 'Les Miserables'. A single ticket. She was a gracious, elegant single woman who was not embarrassed to go the theatre by herself.

Yet she lingered longer than usual at the store, not leaving until six. Dusk was falling.

Going home she thought: It would be perfect if he was on my step waiting for me, wanting to fuck me no doubt and maybe wanting another free meal too! Little starving failing actor that he is! Well, he can bloody well starve. I'm going

111

to lovely 'Les Miserables.' I'm going to watch real actors who can actually get a job because they're actually *good*! Ha! What does he want with me? He doesn't love me, I don't think he even likes me much. What do I want with him? Nothing! Nothing at all! Absolutely nothing! I don't want him! I'll tell him so.

Turning into Minetta Lane she saw that he was not on her steps and felt disappointed, as though her thoughts themselves had somehow driven him from her. Yet as she stood at her front door pulling her key from her purse there were footsteps behind her.

"Oh," she said dryly. "Hello."

"Hi."

He looked out into the street. Was he afraid of something?

She went in and turned to push the door closed. He was still standing there.

"Oh," she said, batting her eyelashes in surprise, "do you want to come in?"

"Of course!"

"Oh... Well, you see, it's rather inconvenient. You see, I have a date."

"Oh. Well," he shrugged. "I only wanted to say hi. I've got a date too."

"Have you? How nice."

"So, can I come in?"

"Oh, I don't think it's convenient." She put weight on the word 'convenient.' She liked the feel of the word in her mouth. It was such a graceful word, somehow, so elegant and Victorian. 'That will not be convenient, Mister Rochester.'

He laughed. He looked hurt. "Oh. Okay."

"Another time."

"Yes."

But she felt guilty, as if she were breaking the wings of a tiny songbird.

"Well, you can come in for a few moments." She did not want her relenting to appear anything but unwilling. "I suppose."

"Okay."

He followed her inside. When they came to Tony and Pete's door, he made a little darting run past her and was outside her apartment before she was halfway up the flight to it. She opened her purse slowly, a prolonging of an uncomfortable moment. She did not know why she wished to prolong it. She did not know why it was uncomfortable either. It just was.

"Get yourself some juice or something, ducks." She knew she didn't have any juice. "I must get ready." She went into her bathroom and looked at her face. She washed off her makeup and felt refreshed. She went into her bedroom. She left the door open so she could hear him. He was at the window, looking out on the balcony. He was humming a rhythmic tune. She could hear movements like half-conscious dance steps. She pored through her collection of lipsticks. She chose peach. She hardly ever chose peach, but then she hardly ever went to 'Les Miserables.' Then he stepped into her bedroom and came up to her. He put a hand lightly on her shoulder.

"Not tonight, dear."

"Okay."

"I'm going out tonight."

"Yeah."

"To the theatre."

"Oh."

"To 'Les Miserables'."

"Oh."

"With an old flame. It's always nice to see an old flame, isn't it?"

"I guess."

"You seeing an old flame tonight yourself?"

"I'm too young for old flames."

"Young flames then."

"I guess." He took his hand away. He did a little spin on one foot.

She pursed her lips together.

"Like the colour?"

"I prefer the red." Was he serious or was he being mean?

"Well, it's not to please you, kiddo. As it happens it's to please someone else. There are more interesting men in New York than you, you know."

"Mmmmm." This might have been an expression of doubt. It might have been an abstract noise to cover up silence.

She had no idea she was going to pursue a new line of questioning until, suddenly, twisting the bottom of the lipstick so that it disappeared back into its holder, she said,

"I think it would be nice to meet some of your friends, Steve. I mean, we're sort of an item now, aren't we?"

He looked disconcerted at this. But then, he looked disconcerted at a lot of things. More, he seemed put out, as if she'd asked him for money. Was it that they were an 'item' and this fact was embarrassing to him, or was it that he didn't want her to meet his friends for some other reason? Was he ashamed of her?

"Oh, Sara, I thought you knew that we're not... I mean, this is just a bit of fun, isn't it?" He clicked a few beats on the roof of his mouth, spun again. He moved very nicely, she had to give him that. If he thought he could distract her from her question, he was very wrong.

"I know that." She resented it, of course, but she didn't want to get off the point. "Doesn't mean we can't meet your mates."

"Well, I'm not ready for that. I mean, I don't know that it would be the right thing to do."

"The right thing to do? It's not some kind of moral crisis, Steven. It would be nice to meet your pals, that's all."

"Maybe some day."

"Like when? The year two thousand and twenty?"

"No, like, soon."

"Soon! But not now!"

"I'm not ready for it."

"You'd be ready if I was twenty and looked like that Brittany Spears, wouldn't you?"

"Britney. No, it's not that."

She spun on her stool and looked right at him. His distracting golden-brown eyes looked right back at her, yet they did not seem really to see her. But she was not going to sway off her course!

"Then what is it, deary? What the hell is it, kiddo?"

"Whoah! Don't get like that!"

"I think you should leave, Steven."

"But…"

"Dear," she said, more tenderly, "if you think you're going to fuck me, you're not. Not tonight."

"That's fine. I don't just want to fuck you. It's not like that."

"Oh. How sweet. And what else do you want, then?"

There was a dead pause.

"I want to be friends with you."

This came out in a little whine. I want to be friends with you. Indeed!

"Well, you are. We are friends."

"Good."

But the outline of his penis told her the old familiar story.

"I'm going out. I may be able to see you tomorrow. Can't promise."

"What are you going to do?"

115

"I told you. 'Les Miserables'. You must have seen it?"

"Oh. Yeah."

"Ever auditioned for it?"

"No. But I will."

"I'm sure you'll be very good in it."

"Thanks. I guess I'll go. Is your date coming to pick you up here?" Oh, she thought in tight-lipped fury, so I can't meet your friends but you expect to meet mine!

"As it happens we are meeting at the theatre." She pronounced it 'theatuh.' "We will be taking a late dinner and then I shall be returning to his condominium overlooking the Park."

"Oh. Nice."

"Very. The Dakota building, you know." But he was too young to know about the Dakota Building. He was a theatre type. He'd probably never played a John Lennon record in his life. In her head she saw herself and her friend on Yoko's couch. "We will probably go for drinks at a musician friend's apartment. It will be a very nice evening."

"Well, have a nice time. I'll be off."

"Bye-bye, dear." She turned back to her mirror. She said, more to herself than to him, "By the way, that graze. It's not quite healed, you know. You're silly to take off the Band-Aid too soon."

She heard him go out through the front door. She heard him run down her stairs. She sprang up and went to the sitting room window.

She leaned over the balcony and saw Steve's head. He turned onto the next street.

Suddenly it came to her: I'll follow him. I'll bloody follow him. If he thinks he can come round here and screw me to his heart's content and then just waft off into the night until he decides he wants to screw me some more, he can think again!

116

Stuff 'Les Miserables'. What's the price of a ticket to a boring show which goes on too long anyway (everyone said so) over finding out about Steve?

She pulled the window closed and grabbed her thick brown coat. She reached for her handbag too, but decided it would weigh her down. So she pulled out her wallet and shoved it in her pocket and ran out her door and down the stairs. Only when she was outside did she remember caution.

She went down the steps. The metallic smell from the trash cans touched her nostrils. She had to run so as not to lose him as he went on to Bleecker Street. Once he was in her line of sight she held back. Soon he was on Christopher Street and he came to a building. He stopped outside it. Then he went in. She waited a full minute before sidling up to the door.

It was an atmospherically lit, which is to say a poorly lit, bar called *Danny's*. A long blackened window looked onto the street. You couldn't see in unless you pressed your nose close to the glass, and then you could make out shapes and hair colour and the colour of clothes but could get only the most general impression of faces. It was fairly busy.

Steve went over to a table for four people where there was one spare chair. A drink, it looked to Sara like a gin, and next to it a   bottle of tonic, was placed on the table at the empty chair. The three at the table looked pleased to see him. Everyone always looked pleased to see Steve, it seemed.

The one on Steve's left had dyed blond hair and wore loud red pants and shoes and a pink collar shirt. He was overtly gay, with a delicate physical quality which was effeminate in the way of a camp male, not actually womanly though he might have believed it was. It was rather the studied way of a movie diva, little to do with any real-life woman. Even the way he put his cocktail to his lips looked rehearsed. Perhaps it wasn't, but it looked as if it was. Perhaps in his lonely teenage years before he'd escaped small town hell for the freedom and adventure of New York City this boy had passed his empty evenings practicing his gestures, so he'd be ready for his explosion onto the New York scene, which he would already have been certain of. He sat next to Steve and kissed him on the cheek. Sara could almost hear him mark each kiss with a sound: "Moi! Moi!" A defining sound for a boy Sara imagined utterly self-absorbed, his sort of gay always was, in her opinion. He probably kissed everyone and called everyone honey.

The one opposite Steve was more likely to disappear in a crowd. Moderately good-looking, (Sara supposed from his outline,) average height, he wore a khaki shirt and blue jeans. His hair was jet black which might or might not have been the result of an application of dye. The third boy was less handsome, with a long thin face and a long thin body. His hair would be thinning too before he was twenty-five. Sara felt a pang of sympathetic affection for him - he was the necessary less attractive member of the group who got laid less often and felt grateful to be liked by the others, who however wouldn't be caught dead in his bed. His job was to appreciate his betters. His best hope was to find a nice guy equally plain and settle down with him. When he was forty he would be the happiest of the group, maybe. In a stable relationship, with a dog and perhaps an adopted child. The others would be addled, bemoaning their aging, still trying to get laid on one-night stands, bitter and unlovable. Addicted to drugs and booze.

Sara was inventing destinies for people completely unknown to her. But, she remembered, I've always been good at getting to the heart of people. I see others more clearly than most. I'm a sort of psychiatrist, I am. My mother always said so.

Which mother it was had always said so she did not think to wonder.

118

The blond boy snuggled into Steve. Sara did not know what to feel about this, or rather her melange of feelings coalesced into something she couldn't define. She felt jealous. She felt protective. She felt justly furious. She felt betrayed. She felt used. She felt naïve. Blondie put his face to Steve's and they kissed. He put his arm around Steve's waist. She felt angrier, seeing that he did not pull away, did not say, hold on I've got a girlfriend. He pushed himself closer to the blond. The blond's hand was playing with Steve's belt at the back. He was not trying to remove it but he pushed two fingers into the top of Steve's jeans. Steve's hands were on the small of the blond boy's back. Still they kissed, tongue to tongue. Across the table the boy with black hair moved in to the long-faced boy and they too clasped each other close. Sara saw that she had been wrong; the long boy was not left out. Perhaps he was supremely witty. Perhaps he had a big cock. It was always one or the other with queers.

Someone passed Sara. At the door he looked at her, eyebrow raised, mildly questioning, perhaps taking her for a nosy old woman who had no reason to be spying on the goings on in a gay bar. Sara caught his eye and smiled apologetically. He went inside. It was true that she couldn't hover out here all night. She'd probably be arrested, and anyway Steve might see her. So what should she do? Would it be safe to go into the bar? It was fairly dark inside, the music loud, and she'd probably be less noticeable there than here. But it was a big risk, and anyway she supposed she'd have to pretend to be a lesbian. She didn't like this idea; she was not fond of lesbians, at least not at that moment. She didn't even know if lesbians used this bar; perhaps it was exclusively male. Perhaps nobody would care about her, anyway. If a woman came in and didn't notice this wasn't her kind of place she was probably too dumb to notice anything. Let her park herself in a corner and drink a drink

119

or two. The queens wouldn't worry about it. Queens weren't the complaining kind. (Even before this thought completed itself she recognized its untruth.)

The alternative was to go to a nearby diner and wait for Steve to emerge, part of a quartet or not. But there was a risk she'd miss him. If she didn't, then she could confront him. She wished she'd brought her handbag with her so she could whap him round the face. Or, no, she'd act like she'd bumped into him, out for an evening stroll. Well, fancy! And who are these nice gentlemen? Or perhaps better yet, she could follow him further. Would he go home with one of these boys? Or would he go off to his apartment, wherever that may be? She could find out where he lived!

I'll go into the bar. They're too busy shoving their tongues down each others' throats to notice much of anything else anyway.

She sped through the door, but once the darkness and the noise embraced her she felt it safer to move slowly and so inconspicuously to the bar, being careful to pass behind Steve's back. The jet black boy, in embrace with the tall boy, did move his eyes in her direction. Perhaps the tall boy was a boring kisser and Jet was thinking of other things while feigning enthusiasm for his friend's lips. He didn't seem to find Sara interesting. Perhaps he thought she was a drag queen. They were probably ten to the dozen round here. She did not like the thudding dance music. She supposed it was House, which she knew of but had never knowingly heard. The voice was quite nice, a black woman's soul voice of the sort she liked herself, compromised by the need to do up-to-date material. She didn't suppose Al Green or Aretha Franklin made House records, even today.

At the bar she bought a Budweiser and found a stool, right in the corner of the room where she could survey the comings and goings throughout the bar, and most importantly the activities at Steve's table. Near her, a guy

120

leant beside the cigarette machine, nursing on a Heineken and looking at Steve's group. The group made her more irritated with each passing moment. The blond boy's head was bearing down on Steve and Steve angled his own up, so he was half lying, one leg across the blond's chair, and the blond was half lying on him. Jet and Tall were less entangled with each other but they were no doubt having an equally good time, if pushing your features against another person's features constituted a good time. Sara thought it just looked crude. Those boys could use a few lessons in love from me. She was not sure if this thought was jealousy or if the boys really were making a clumsy hash of their kissing. They were certainly having a good time. She could no longer see Steve's head at all. It looked as if the blond was eating it.

To Sara, bars were for chatter and laughter and jokes. You went to your apartment if you wanted to screw someone, to the cinema if you wanted to 'heavily pet' someone, which she supposed was the phrase for these boys' assaults. She swigged her beer and felt like a puritan. She had once said to Eddie, there's nothing wrong with a bit of nooky, is there, it's only natural, it's a part of being a person. Eddie had asked what she meant by nooky and she had sighed and refused to answer. But anyway, because she believed in nooky didn't mean she approved of dropping your drawers on Fifth Avenue! There's a place for everything and everything in its place. A bar was not the place. She looked down at her bottle, already two thirds empty, and swung around to order another.

She missed some developments, because when she turned back Jet was embracing Steve and Blondie. Tall looked on. Perhaps her first instinct about him had been right. He looked definitely left out. Steve she could not see, except for his left leg from the knee to the foot, lifted as it was above the table. His shoelace was undone. That's a bad habit, that, she thought. The tip of his shoe brushed his half-

121

full tonic bottle and it wobbled and settled. Jet was wedged between the chairs and the table, looking down on Steve. From his angle and the way his arms moved, Sara guessed that Jet's hand was on the back of Steve's thighs, rubbing up and down the top of his leg. Steve's visible leg clicked downward like the arm of an old railway signal and all that could be seen of him now from Sara's stool was the knee, folded shut. She thought of his little scar. A wave of sympathy came over her. It evaporated a moment after. The blond was still kissing him, both hands around his waist. The blond's back arched like a cat. Tall looked on, only half interested. The guy against the cigarette machine looked away. Perhaps he was a little embarrassed. But then he looked back.

Sara looked around at the other drinkers. Most of them were in groups with one or two friends, doing what bars are more usually known for, namely talking and drinking. A few were alone, leaning against a wall. Some looked through free magazines. Were they hoping to get picked up? Only two men, the one by the cigarettes and one across the room under a movie poster of 'The Wizard of Oz', looked at the show at Steve's table, and even they were not necessarily fascinated. Rather, they glanced towards it because there were only so many directions you could face, and Steve's direction gave the best overall view of the bar.

If Eddie and Bea were to lie across a couch in *Mulligan's* dry humping they'd soon be thrown out into the street, and quite right too. *Mulligan's* customers were decent folk, they wouldn't put up with this flagrant behaviour. Sara looked around to the bar itself, expecting that before too long a staff member would come round it and go up to the boys and tell them to stop it at once. But no-one did. The guy behind the bar, a short wiry Asian boy who looked like a college kid, all clean-cut and enthusiastic, leant on his elbows, one sleeve a centimetre from a puddle of beer. He was talking to an older man. He didn't care what people did at their tables. No-one cared. It was a disgrace. Sara felt her disgust manifest itself in a little screwing together of her features, a pursing of her peachy, peachy lips.

Steve's body reared up. His ears appeared above the back of the chair, red and tingly. Then he dived forward. Towards Blondie's face. Blondie dropped backward. Sara could see Steve's tongue, snakelike in the other's mouth. Doesn't he need to breathe, she wondered. Jet moved behind Steve and put two big hands around his neck. It looked as if he intended strangulation, but he began to massage the shoulders, a firm muscular kneading with fingers and palm. Steve rose to his feet. From the curvature in his jeans Sara could see that he was erect. He was always erect. It was freakish.

A new profundity of fury ascended from her fast-beating heart into her brain. She had in her imagination - naively, she now realized, foolishly, lovingly, caringly, - claimed Steve's erection as somehow her property and though she had supposed that somewhere there was a girl, on a campus or behind the glass window of a ticket booth dreaming of playing Sally Bowles, a girl who thought she owned it too, it was beyond Sara's tolerance that she should have to witness these - the word came easily to her - these perverts manhandling her lover's body. She felt assailed. They were rubbing their sweaty hands over his body specifically to get at her. They were mocking her. The blond's hand on Steve's jeans massaged the denim where the penis was enwrapped, as firmly as Jet massaged the shoulders. He had no right to. It was obscene. It was an invasion of Sara's rights. Tall came round behind the chairs, blocking Steve and the blond from her view. He put his hand on Steve's hair and mussed it with aching tenderness. He wrapped a small curl of Steve's hair around his middle finger. It was an act of unimaginable gentleness. It redoubled Sara's rage.

123

Steve withdrew his tongue and said something, and then the tongue shot back into Blondie's mouth. But Tall said something back and Jet nodded in agreement. The blond was too preoccupied to say anything.

A few moments later Steve pulled away. He patted Blondie's back and said something close to his ear. Blondie nodded. Steve spoke to Jet and Tall. Jet knocked back the last of his beer. Blondie sipped his Martini with a showgirl's vigour. Tall looked at his whiskey but did not touch it. Steve finished his Gin and Tonic. The tonic bottle was still half full. All four left the bar. Sara saw them pass by the window. They were heading in an uptown direction. She sprang from her stool and finished her Bud. She realized as she tasted the last fizzy flavourless drop that she didn't like Bud much. It was bland and commercial. It was mass-produced and tasted that way. It had no body.

She dashed out.

The boys were several hundred feet ahead of her. They were locked together arm in arm, a foursome of friends. Were they going to have group sex? They were hugging each other provocatively; occasionally one turned to the boy next to him and kissed him. Hands crawled around. It was something of an achievement that they could do all this and keep their forward momentum. What do four people do in group sex? She could understand, though she had never tried it, that three together might be different from two, but wouldn't four merely break into couples, so ending up exactly the same as usual? Wouldn't the moans of the other couple be a distraction? She tried to think an orgy could be sexy, but her imagination refused to make it so. She pictured it as a battle field after the fight is over, flesh on flesh, unmoving.

They turned left and came to a substantial apartment building. The tall man keyed in a code and the door buzzed. They went through. The door swung towards closure behind them. Inside, the boys rounded a corner. Sara ran to the

124

door to catch it. She was just too late. The buzz died. The lock clicked into place.

"Fuck!" So what was she to do now?

Across the road a round-the-clock diner threw its light onto the sidewalk. A waitress carried a plastic tray laden with plates of fries to a plastic table in the first window, the one near the door, where sat a family of four. Two adults, two young children. They were all as fat as each other. There was an empty table in the window behind them. From it Sara would be able to see anyone coming and going from the apartments. She went in. She ordered another Bud. It was better to stick with the same drink. You don't want to be too fuzzy-minded when you're a spy. She liked the feel of the word 'spy' and felt enlivened by her adventure. She had no doubt of the rightness of her actions. Steve was a liar, a very bad boy indeed. She'd give him a talking to he'd never forget. The waitress brought the beer to her, chewing gum. She asked if she was ready to order some food. Sara said just the beer was fine.

She glanced at the building. A man with a briefcase and a woman on his arm turned onto the path to the front door. With a sudden unreflective impulse, Sara leapt to her feet, pulled out her purse, dropped a generous heap of coins beside the un-drunk beer and shot out through the door. She whistled brightly, crossed the street all nonchalance as if this was her regular routine, and sped as gracefully as could be to within a few feet of the man and the woman.

"Hi," she said. The man said hi, how are you tonight? Great, she said, a lovely evening isn't it? Yes, he said, keying in his number. She followed through. Long day? she asked. Yeah, he said, yeah, the lady said. Same here, said Sara. I've seen you around but I don't think we've talked before, said Sara, I'm Kate. I'm Kate too, said the woman. They all laughed. Jack, said the man. They were at the elevator. The door opened. Jack pressed six. The top number on the

125

panel was '15' but there was no '13'. Eight, said Sara. Thanks. The elevator rose. Sara looked at her distorted body in the metal door, cut down the middle at the opening. She felt bloated and loathsome. She looked to the wall on her right. The image there was no more flattering. You're an ugly cow you are, she thought acidly. No wonder Steve strays. But Jack, who was slim in real life, looked equally grotesque in his reflection, so she felt reassured that perhaps she was not so macabre after all. They all looked up to the numbers. They were silent now. Numbers were more interesting in elevators than conversations. But how slowly they climbed. '1' became '2' and '3' and the elevator stopped. A door opened. Don't let it be Steve, prayed Sara. It was a youngish guy, but not one of hers. Oh, he said, looking at the illuminated '6' and '8' on the panel of buttons, going up? Yes, said Jack. Sorry, want to go down, said the guy. He stepped back out. The door closed. They came to '4' and '5' and '6'. Jack and Kate got out. Nice to meet you, said Kate. See you around, said Sara. She felt sweat on her forehead and under her arms, hoped they had not noticed her discomfort. She collapsed against the wall. She felt unattractive and the tension had exhausted her. '7' lit up.

Sara had acted so fast that she'd given no thought to exactly what she planned to do once she'd gained access to the building. God knows how many apartments there are in this dump. What a fool! I should have stayed in the diner.

She pressed fifteen.

I'll start at the top, work my way down. Start what? Well, I can't knock on doors. What would I say? Excuse me, madam, sir, are by any chance four youngish lads having a homosexual orgy in your apartment? No? Thanks anyway. Have a nice evening. No. I'll just have to listen.

Listen for moans.

Listen for sighs of pleasure.

And if she heard them, what would she do then?

126

For the first time she felt that perhaps she wasn't doing the right thing. Was listening outside people's doors a criminal offense? But she was a woman who had been hurt. She had a right to know if her boyfriend was betraying her. They'd never convict her. She would cry in the witness stand. She had been so appalled to find out he was cheating on her…. and not even with a woman! Her lover was a pervert! But this might be going too far, New Yorkers were liberal. They had to be; there were hardly any straight men left in the City. The jury would be all gay men! So: Her lover was gay! If only he'd told her she would have understood. He was a good man. That's why she loved him. She wanted to help him. No, not help him, that sounded too much like those religious lunatics who claimed you could become un-queer by prayer. No, she would have respected his orientation. Orientation was a good word. She would have respected his orientation. She would have let him go with love and kisses. They would have stayed the best of friends. But that night she was… she was so confused… her head would drop into her hands. They would let her go with a warning. She would nod gratefully and graciously to that row of twelve sympathetic gay men. They would smile back. She liked gay men. They were always very fair.

The elevator tinkled its silly little bell. Floor Fifteen, which was actually the fourteenth floor.

And so it began, a woman of forty-five in a long brown coat going from door to door, pressing her ear close but silent to each, listening for sounds. Frequently the burble of television leaked out to her, sometimes the crying of a baby, the clatter of plates, the revolutions of a washing machine. She heard voices, some raised in argument, others in quiet unromantic talk about something dull, work, bills, the mayor. A girl said something about "wanning to watch 'Snow White', please, please, mommy," a high spoilt voice which made Sara think of pink shoes. Surely not her? But there were plenty of others like Alice in the world. Anyway, there was no lovemaking going on anywhere, or if there was it was quiet lovemaking. Only in films did lovers as a matter of course moan in their passion. Perhaps in this apartment building people did not have bedsprings. Perhaps they all had futons or waterbeds. Waterbeds were the sort of fashionable silliness that young New Yorkers might think de rigueur. She hoped they drowned. From fully half of all the apartment doors she pressed her ear against no noise spilt at all.

Of course it was quite possible that Steve, wherever he might be, wasn't up to anything untoward. Perhaps he and his pals were watching a movie on video. Perhaps they were having dinner together. Perhaps he was the token straight lad in a circle of gays. He was an actor after all. Perhaps his friends were all gay actors. Unemployed gay actors who hung out with each other, gave each other moral support. (Until one found success, and no more moral support would be coming from him. That kind of support worked only while there was a shared struggle.) And this made sense. The blond sipped like a showbiz queen because he was a showbiz queen. Handsome Jet could be a Jet in 'West Side Story'. Tall probably specialized in snooty Englishmen and Shakespearian comedy parts. All these things were possible. But Sara's mind rolled back to the bar, to Steve's leg raised, to the spinning of his tonic bottle. Steve did not do ordinary things like watching videos and dusting his room. Steve did sex; that was his hobby, like other people collected stamps. Sex was his raison d'etre, his place on earth. If he offered moral support, it was through his body, the moral support of sex itself. It was all he knew. It was his only kindness, but it was the only kindness he thought worth giving. He understood nothing else.

Could she have touched on the truth about him? She thought over their first lovemaking. He'd said he didn't want her in a way that suggested he did; but what if he succumbed

128

because he was too polite to say no? Because he didn't want to offend? Could it be that he was such a gentleman that if you asked twice for his body he felt compelled to give it to you out of sheer compassion?

But he'd come back a second time and a third. If he was only being nice, why'd he come back? This Sara decided didn't fit in with her theory. He must have come back to her for his own pleasure, his own need. Nobody's *that* polite.

The elevator took her to floor fourteen, belled her out.

To floor twelve.

She was getting quite tired. She felt she'd been creeping along corridors for hours. Fourteen doors on each floor. Forty-two so far, one hundred and fifty-four to go. And what if she didn't trace the boys? More to the point, what if she did?

To eleven, ten, nine.

To eight.

The elevator opened. She stepped out. Just as she put a foot to the carpet, a door opened somewhere down the landing on the left.

Steve. Steve alone.

She caught just a glimpse of him. It was enough. His hair was charmingly disarrayed. Had Tall pulled on it lovingly?

Steve. He looked happy. He looked sated. She saw herself in the shiny elevator wall. She looked unhappy and frightened. She was sweating all over now. She pressed the 'door closed' button but the door did not close. Pressed the '7'. She heard the pad of his footsteps. Close, close, close! She put her hands together in prayer. She looked to the ceiling. She saw herself. Her peachy lips, her yellow hair. Her brown coat. Her black shoes, pointing out from under.

Please God, she said. She pushed herself deeply into the elevator, hoping that by squeezing herself into a corner she would make herself invisible. She pulled her coat collar up. She wished she had a hat. She wished she had a mask.

129

He called to her, his lovely Huckleberry Finn voice.

"Hey!" He'd seen her! He'd recognized her! What excuse could possibly save her now?

But he called again,

"Hold the door, please!"

No, you little fucker! No I won't!

He rounded the corner. The door sighed shut. Had he seen her? His eyes had not met her eyes.

No.

She heard him from the other side:

"Oh shucks." The elevator slid smoothly down its rails. The door opened at '7.' She pressed '1' and waited. She was safe; he'd have to wait for her to get down until the elevator could come back to him. She'd be on the street, in the darkness, before he emerged from the building.

She crossed the street and waited and shortly afterwards Steve came out and went towards Seventh, 'Fashion Avenue' as it proudly called itself, though to everybody in the City it was just Seventh, just a number. A few blocks away loomed the vast bleak edifices of Penn Station and Madison Square Garden.

The night had properly fallen now. The warmth of the day had faded, a mild chill was in the air, which was sufficient for her to pull her coat more closely around her and to do up the button at her throat. Steve was pacing at a fair rate, without hurrying but without dawdling either. He looked down at his shoes. Sara saw the drop of his head. His left laces were undone. They dragged on the sidewalk. This was a very bad habit of his. If he tripped over and bled she wouldn't be mothering him this time; he could bleed and bleed and bleed for all she cared. Little betrayer that he was. (But was he? She could not be sure. Oh, but the gently mussed hair! She knew just how that mussing had come about; she had mussed it herself in the throes of love.) He passed a small grocery store. The Latinos hanging outside didn't look like they'd rush to his rescue either. But one of the Latinos followed Steve with his eyes. Sara had never noticed before how men watched other men. She was beginning to think that all men were essentially gay. They all looked at each other with something akin to desire. But when is a look one of lust rather than of interest? Where is the line drawn between? Is there a line between at all? Men sized each other up all the time. They were competitive creatures. Was the sizing up itself covertly sexual? Was the animal competitiveness that drove the male creature stirred up with desire? Some people said big corporations fucked the whole world. If indeed such corporations were a result of masculine competitiveness, which was the redirection of lust, those people were more right than they realized. Who would have thought the Disney Corporation had come about through redirected lust? That put a new light on the matter. Fuck the world with Mickey Mouse!

Sara felt a headache coming on and she squashed her line of thinking.

Of course, the curious Latino man had probably caught a glimpse of the golden drops in Steve's eyes. Those eyes'd make anyone look twice! Not with desire, but with fascination, repulsion even.

(But was repulsion, which was negative attraction, equally a sexual experience? Stop thinking like this, girl, your brain'll explode.)

Steve's head bobbed down to his feet again and again. His cheeks puffed out. Was he whistling? Whistling a happy tune? Whistling while he worked? That would have made him a prostitute. Surely he wasn't a prostitute? The laces danced about like partying worms. He must have seen them. Perhaps he couldn't be bothered to do them up. Lazy boy.

Outside a cell phone shop he quite suddenly stopped. He put the left shoe onto the bottom of the wide low window frame. Sara was outside the grocer's shop where the Latinos

131

hovered. She pretended to be interested in tomatoes. Her eyes darted into their corners so that she could see his every movement while appearing to reflect over the cost of fruits and vegetables. She suspected that she looked a bit crazy, eyes shoved tightly towards her ear. She didn't care; this was New York. Most everyone was crazy and the few sane had mastered the fine art of ignoring them. Steve was concentrating on doing up his laces. He looked very intense. He was someone who simply wasn't very good at tying knots. It was an effort. One lace fell across the other and somehow he joined them up. It was an inept job; Sara could see that from her viewing place. No doubt a few minutes later they'd loosen themselves again. She felt the strain on her eyes and allowed her head to swivel a little to relieve it. He'd finished, as best he could. He took the leg down from the frame. He made to walk on. But then he turned back. He looked right up Seventh. Right at her? She put her hand to her face in a sudden guilty uprush of the arm, pretending to brush hair away from an eye. She rubbed her cheek thoughtfully. Were these tomatoes a little under-ripe? Were they large enough? Did they have the full rich flavour of home-grown tomatoes, or the bland watery nothingness of supermarket tomatoes? Tomartoes, she thought. Not tomaytoes. *Tomartoes*. Sara, the salt of the earth from dear old London. She tried to force herself to concentrate on this matter so that if Steve approached her she could say she was picking out tomartoes and it would be true.

But he didn't. He stood there outside the cell phone shop and looked past her. Up to Times Square and the theatre district perhaps. Up towards the Broadway of song and dance and drama. The Broadway where his name would one day flicker in an uproar of blinking red lights.

How young he looked there, hands on hips. He pulled his leather jacket closer. He zipped it up. He must be feeling the cold too. Together he and Sara had been warm. Now he was chilled. He deserved to be.

He turned away again and resumed his walk, not fast, not slow. She sprang away from the vegetable display and followed on after. But soon there was another food store. This had a large display of flowers outside, crammed into big black buckets. One of the buckets held dozens of red roses, all wrapped individually in clear plastic. Steve stopped and looked at them. He held a hand out to, first, one, lifting it an inch up so that he could see the flower itself, its size and shape. He let it fall back into the water and inspected, then, another and another. The fourth he plucked right out. A Chinese guy sat on a stool a couple of feet away. He stood, perhaps ready to lunge at Steve should he try to run off with it. Kids probably ran off with things all the time. But not on this occasion. Steve pulled a bundle of ones from his pocket. They weren't in a wallet, they were crushed into a crumpled ball. He separated three ones. The Chinese guy dropped them into the kangaroo-like pocket on his apron.

Steve headed on down Broadway. He zipped his jacket down to his chest and put the stem into an inside pocket, perhaps to keep it warm. It poked out near his ear. He zipped up the jacket again. The flower touched his nose. He unzipped a couple of inches and angled it away from his grazed cheek. The flower looked back to Sara like a third eye.

In the Village he veered off Seventh onto Waverly Place, which brought him, then Sara, to the North side of Washington Square.

He cut across the street and went into Washington Square Park. He walked with purpose now. He raised an open hand and gave a little shy wave at the level of his nipples. Sara wished she could see the look on his face. All she could see were his ears reddened in the autumnal cold, and the back of his jacket, his blue jeans, his running shoes. Laces hanging

133

loose again. The featurelessness of the human body from behind! She could tell nothing. She wanted to see his gold-splashed eyes and the softness of his lips. Then she could tell something. She stopped at the corner. Who was he waving to?

A girl sat on a bench near the fenced-off children's playing area. She could hardly have been older than eighteen. Her hair hung in front of her face. It was long and golden, like the blond boy's, like the drops in Steve's eyes. She stood up. She waved back. He approached her. She sat down again, he sat next to her. They started talking. They were closer together than just-friends. His thigh was pressed to hers. She wrapped her arms around him. He kissed her. It was a romantic kiss. It lasted for eighteen seconds. Sara counted them up in her head. Each second made her angrier until, after the twelfth there was no more anger to be felt. After the twelfth there could be only cool plans for revenge. Eighteen seconds is a long time to be locked lip to lip. He curled a finger around some yellow strands of hair near her mouth, just as Tall had curled a finger through his. In response to his fingers she put her hand, the hand that had waved, gently onto his head, tidying up the sweetly mussed waves. When they separated, she said something funny and affectionate. It was about the mess that his hair was, Sara knew this, because the girl looked up to Steve's fringe as she spoke. She patted it down. She was rearranging it fondly. He seemed to say, aw don't, its fine, like Huckleberry Finn, aw shucks, but his smile said something else. She was looking dreamily at the hair now, fingering it, fingering it, intoxicated by it but at the same time a long way away. Sara recognized these indicators of a love the girl did not doubt was too deep for words and too profound for this earth. The kind of love that made you feel religious, because surely there must be an eternity where it would continue forever. The girl was thinking of him, of Steve, of all of him. She loved him

134

very much. He was her first love. She thought they would be together forever. Sara knew this not because she had felt such a passion herself as a young woman. Who could really have loved Ted? Or Eddie? Or big Steve? They were not the sort you loved. They were the sort you resigned yourself to. Sara knew the girl's feelings precisely because she had never experienced them. She could see it all in the way the girl pushed her entire body towards him, the way her eyes dropped from his fringe to his kind, strange, mystical eyes. Who would not love those eyes? Who would not want them forever in their bed?

Sara was distracted by a sharp bolt of lightning striking the City from above. Everything was very bright for a second. Trees were silvery and skeletal. The railings were garishly rusted. It was peculiar that she was the only person who noticed this phenomenon. Steve and the girl didn't look up, didn't react at all. It was strange too that the lightning did not lead to rain.

Sara's left leg moved forward, her right leg followed. She could not control them, of their own will they were walking towards Steve and the girl. Nearly running. When they got there Sara's mouth would tell the girl the truth, not Sara herself who counselled caution, it was her mouth alone that would say, this boy will break your heart you foolish little girl, he'll break your heart and it's better you know now. He sleeps around. He sleeps with men. He sleeps with women. He sleeps with older women. He sleeps with anyone who'll let him in their beds. Has he had you, dear? Course he has. Has he whispered love to you? He's a liar, dear, he *can't* love you. He can't love anybody. He loves only himself. He lives for himself. For his own pleasure. His own perversion. Think he'll make love to you tonight? It's an illusion. He'll fuck you, yes, he's good at that, but don't you go thinking it means anything. Now you go on, girl. Back to your room,

135

back to your college dorm, or whatever it is. Forget him. He's bad. He's evil. He sells himself. He's wild.

But her mind reasserted command and her feet stopped still at the children's play ground, deserted now, and her mouth clamped shut so firmly her teeth ached. She was sweating. Her palms were sticky. She felt suffocated in this heavy close-hugging coat but when she put her fingers to the buttons to open it they were shaking, they could not get a grip on the little plastic discs. But she more than anything needed to get this coat open, she could hardly breathe, she tugged at it and four holes opened like lips to let the buttons through, but the top hole, rarely used and less pliable, refused to give, stayed closed around the button so that when she gave another firm pull the button was torn away. It fell to the ground in a cheap tinkle. It rolled. It rolled from her feet around the play area fencing. It rolled further until, at the girl's feet, it stopped. Sara pressed herself to the wire. She was grateful for a nearby tree which put her in shadow. The girl picked up the button. She looked about her.

"Funny, I wonder where that came from?" This is what she seemed to say.

Steve looked at it.

"Who cares?" he seemed to say. He took it from her, put it into his pocket. He put his face to hers again. He was pressing ever closer to her.

But not for long.

"Let's go," she seemed to say.

He smiled.

Okay," he seemed to say.

"I love you," she seemed to say.

"I love you too," he seemed to say.

"Let's go," she seemed to say again.

"Sure." He smiled delightfully, sweetly and hornily. Sara knew that smile. She loved it. She hated it. She loved it.

They stood. They were walking and hugging at the same time. Steve was a master at that.

They crossed the park, westward. They crossed the street. They came to the *NYU Hayden Residence Hall*. The girl keyed in a number. They went through. Sara crossed after them, but missed the moment of opportunity. The door was locked. Again!

She stood back and looked up. Twelve floors, packed with students studying and drinking and fucking. Even if she got inside, what would she do? Crawling around an apartment building was one thing. How could she explain her presence in a student dormitory at nine o'clock at night? She could claim to be the cleaner, perhaps. A cleaner at night? Not likely to convince.

Calm descended. Her thoughts, so stormy before, were like the gentle plashing of the sea's foam on a sandy beach.

Yet if there is calm after a storm, it is a well-known fact that there is a deceptive calm before, too.

Sara went home. She was focused. Everything was clear. She was settled inside. She felt, not happy, perhaps, but cleansed. Fresh. She climbed into bed. She wasn't hurt any more. He would be back. She knew Steve would be back. His cock would bring him back. Men!

She drifted off.

The deceptive calm lasted throughout the day. She was friendly to all. She treated herself to an expensive lunch at the *Empire Szechuan Village*. She selected a Triple Crown Chicken Platter. It was excellent and filling. Her fortune cookie brought an insightful observation. 'You are a person of depth and mystery. You are   attracted to other people of depth and mystery.' She agreed with the first half, at least. There was a lot of food left over, so she had it wrapped for supper.

He'll be back. I know he will. This was her mantra for the day. He'll be back. I know he will. He'll be back. I know he will. It had a hypnotic effect. He'll be back. I know he will. He'll be back. I know he will. So often did it recur that it became less a statement than a chant. He'll be back. I know he will. He'll be back. I know he will. By five o'clock it had taken on a sing-speak musical quality. It had become distanced from concrete meaning.

He'll be back. I know he will.

He'll
Be
Back.
I
Know
He Will.
He'll
    Be
       Back.
           I
               Know
                  He
                      Will.
                        He'll
                    Be
          Back
       I
   Know
 He
Will.
Evening came and she reheated her chicken. It was delicious. She turned on the TV and surfed while forking it into her mouth. Watching TV was like being a rat on a wheel. The same stuff over and over and over. The Reverend Pat Wade-Adrian, hell-fire preacher, still ranted about the second coming and the awfulness of homosexuals, in between promoting the thirty-eighth volume of his fictional series *The Last Days*, based on the 'prophecies' of the

138

Book of Revelations. Volume Thirty-eight was called *Sinners in Hell*. Everyone was going to hell, queers and Catholics alike, everyone except for the Reverend and a few other fundamentalist preachers. Pat couldn't wait for the end of the Earth. No doubt it would be fun to peer into the pit from his cloudly vantage point, watching those burning sodomites and those burning nuns. He was smug enough already. How unbearable he'd be once he'd been saved. Was God really that stupid? People were. Pat Wade-Adrian had a sideline as a protester. He and his two repellent daughters went to the funerals of homosexuals, carrying placards saying HELL AWAITS and SODOMITES WILL BURN. Apparently there were countless Americans who believed this. They loved it. They loved the idea of homosexuals burning forever, charred but alive. What fun it would be to see the suffering! Was there an innate difference between the Reverend Pat and those lunatics who drove planes into buildings? Were they not fundamentally - the very word! - fundamentally the same? *The Last Days* had apparently sold more copies than any other book series in American publishing history. Pat claimed this in his promotion for it. There was a volume thirty-nine still to look forward to, then a volume forty. How exciting. Sara felt sorry for Tony downstairs, who was clever and inventive and couldn't get a word published. Pat Wade-Adrian was apparently the New American Literature. She clicked to Brokaw, whom she decided she liked because at least he wasn't Pat Wade-Adrian. She moved on. Cartoons were showing as usual on various channels. Last time she'd seen a mouse clobbering a cat. This time she watched a rabbit clobber a duck. Television was an endlessly, endlessly turning wheel of sameness. A rerun of 'Star Trek' was to be found a few channels down. It was the one where Mr Spock's brain was stolen. It was rubbish. She didn't like it, though she didn't hate it the way she hated Pat.

139

She had a great capacity for love, Sara deduced of herself. Yes, she could be grumpy. She could be snappy. She had a no-nonsense personality. She hadn't been as good to her husband as she should have been. But if she was a cow who behaved badly, at least she knew (sometimes) that she was a cow. God, if he existed, would forgive her because she knew she was a cow sometimes, he would not forgive Pat because he was vile and had no awareness of his awfulness. He had no humility. Pat would burn. He would deserve to.

In fact, if I'm so bad I go to hell, I won't mind because Pat will be there too and he'll be punished more than me because he's really evil. I'm just a cow. Sometimes. Sometimes I'm not even a cow. Sometimes I'm good. I try to be. A tear came to her eye.

Her doorbell rang.

Her tear evaporated.

It must be Steve. It must be.

She clicked off the television.

Her calm was swept away before she'd even reached her intercom. Now she was angry again. Now she was frightening.

No-one plays around with Sara Smith like that boy's done! I'm going to have his guts for garters I am!

She said nothing, buzzed him in stony silence.

His soft little knuckles rapped lightly on her door.

She opened it. He had a single red rose in his hand wrapped in silver foil. He gave it to her. He had a sweet shy beam on his face. It was a very romantic gesture. Al Green threw red roses out to his audiences. She could not be angry. She was charmed.

"Hello, dear!" she said, all smiles and welcomes. She took the rose tenderly. "How nice," she said. He thought she meant the rose. She went over to the cupboard and took out a thin vase. She filled it with water. She placed it on the small table near the windows. "How lovely," she said again.

She noticed that he did not ask how she'd enjoyed last night, 'Les Miserables', dinner with an old flame.

He approached her from behind, put his arms around her waist.

"Now you hold on a moment, ducks. You're insatiable, you are!" She rearranged the rose in the vase to give a reason for his holding on. "Perhaps it should face the light. What do you think?"

"Come on, Sara." His voice cracked as though he ached, as though she'd kept him waiting for half an hour.

"Men! Horny, are you?"

He nodded boyishly. She pulled away and turned to face him. "Look," he said. "I took your advice." He pointed to his cheek. A fresh Band-Aid covered his graze.

"Good," she said. She placed her palm on his groin. "I see you are. Horny."

"Let's get naked." The sheer directness of this, its lovely crudeness, made her gasp a little. Ted of the fish and chip shop would never have said such a thing. He would say nothing, just hope at each step that she would not push him away. Even afterwards he would say nothing, go to the bathroom and wash himself down and come back to the bed. He'd say nothing the next morning even, he'd leave silently, no kiss, no acknowledgment. For Ted it was something you did and never talked about, it felt nice but it was dirty, it was shameful. They never mentioned it ever, they just sometimes did it until they didn't. Steve One wouldn't talk of it either. Steve One would move the upper part of his body over to her in the dark, put a hand on her breast more in hope than expectation, and if she did not tell him to sod off he would pull his lower half onto her, and take her in joyless silence there in the dark. But she was married to Steve One, so whereas she let Ted have his silent shame she felt entitled to say to Big Steve one evening when he sat there in Florida with the TV clicker and a beer, "I wish we did it more often,

141

dear. I really do." He looked up at her as though she'd turned into a mermaid. His eyes said *what the fuck are you talking about?* But his mouth said, "Stop complaining woman. I'm tired. I work hard. Don't get on my case." And that had been that.

"Let's get naked."

A bit of Friday night nooky with Sara, that's what he wanted.

So a swell of love drowned out all her anger. For a moment. He struggled out of his clothes. He dropped his lovely leather jacket across the threshold of the bedroom door, which was open. He stood on one leg trying to pull his pants leg over his foot but it wouldn't slide off as it usually did, maybe because this pair of jeans was new, they looked new to Sara. "Jeez," he said, hopping about for a second, his erection rocking from side to side. Then they were off and then he was naked, and she was naked too. He threw himself onto the sofa.

"Not there, in there," she said pointing to the bedroom.

"Okay." He ran before her and threw himself onto the bed in a great long-legged spring. For a short guy his legs were long. The bed creaked. She ran after him. She fell onto the bed, over his chest. She clutched his penis.

"I think," she said into his ear, "you'd best get a rubber. Safe sex and all that, don't you think?"

"Oh." He seemed to puzzle over her change of tune, but went over to his jacket near the door and pulled his wallet from his pocket. From the open pocket fell a little round plastic disc. A stabbing sensation pierced Sara. Steve picked up the disc and dropped it unthinkingly back. He opened the wallet and withdrew the package which contained a rubber. He tore open the wrapping.

"You," he said. He threw it to her. She peeled it over him.

It wasn't quite as nice with a rubber. She had never liked them. When she'd said to him, I prefer my men naked, she had meant it in every sense. It was still very good. And if there was a minimal loss of pleasure, it was worth it if it bothered Steve too. Sara did not need pleasure. Or rather, her own pleasure was heightened by the lessening of another's. When he pulled off her they lay in silence for a few minutes. Did Steve pick up on the thickness of the atmosphere, or was he too naïve? He was a sensitive person - he'd know. Too shy to say anything, too polite perhaps, that old world courtesy which found no fault and made no criticism. Sara broke the silence, but the atmosphere perceptibly thickened further.

"So it was good, was it?" she asked darkly. "Had a good time, did you?"

"I always have a good time with you, Sara." He was lying back, his head on the pillow, looking up at her ceiling. A ring of damp formed a circle above them where once The Man Upstairs had had a flood.

Steve was very relaxed, contented. Perhaps he'd like a post-coital fag, she thought. Or a pipe like Tom Sawyer. Or maybe a big fat cigar like Mark Twain.

"Do you?" This was pointed as an ice pick. "Do you always have a good time with me?"

He must have picked up on the challenge. He could no longer pretend there was nothing wrong. He propped himself on his elbows, worry fell across his open face.

"Are you okay? You sound annoyed."

"Do I?"

"Did I do something wrong?"

"I wouldn't know. Did you?" She folded her arms. They covered her breasts. She pursed her lips.

"Are you okay?" he asked again.

"I'm fine. Are you okay is more to the point?"

143

He looked upset. A little frown creased his forehead and brought his eyebrows towards each other. He was searching his mind for an answer. What had he done wrong?

You stupid child, you think it's all about sex, don't you, you're wondering if you did something to spoil it? Did you touch me wrong, did you not make me tingle as you made all your lovers tingle? What could have been wrong? Were your hands cold? Were you too aggressive or not aggressive enough? You're so stupid and naïve that you can't imagine it could be something else, can you? The only thing in the world to you is getting laid. The worst thing you could hear is that you're no good in bed, you're no damn good at it. Nothing else could hurt quite so much as that. No-one's ever faulted what I suppose you call your 'performance'. And it really worries you that I might, doesn't it?

If only it was true. That you are no good in bed. That would be human. She felt a rising of affection again, but this time it was for Ted and Big Steve and Eddie, flawed men who didn't know much about love but tried their best and were adorable because they were clumsy. Young Steve here now, with his angelic sun-spotted eyes, his libido with its intensity beyond nature, its supernatural quality, his nice sweet body which was not perfect because perfect bodies were not sexy, his superb lovemaking which was not mere accomplishment like some awful slick millionaire said to be 'good in bed', his was a different thing, some God-given natural talent. And his joy in it. His joy. If sweet angels had genitals, they'd be lovers like Steve. But she didn't want to fuck an angel any more, she wanted to fuck a human being. She wanted to fuck someone coarse and flawed like her.

"Had a good time, then?" she said.

"You know I did. You all didn't?" Yawl did'n? How disappointed he was!

144

"Oh I did, I had a lovely time." Just a beat before the self-pity was allowed to curl out like smoke. "But I'm not good enough for you, am I?"

"What?"

"I'm not good enough."

"I don't know what you mean." His mouth opened a little and stayed there. Makes you look like a moron, Steven.

"I mean, a young guy like you, you could have anyone. What would you want with a fat old cow like me?"

"You're not fat. You're sexy."

"But not sexy enough apparently."

"You're great. It's real different with you."

"Different to what? Different to those twenty-year old girls who can't keep their hands off you?"

"Oh, Sara, it's not like that."

"Different to those twenty-year old boys who can't keep their hands off you? If you even wanted them to?"

"What are you talking about?" His cheeks pinked a little.

"I'm right, aren't I?"

"What are you talking about?"

"Don't come on all innocent. I know."

"Know what?"

"I know about you, kiddo." He looked confused. "What do you know?" She wanted to say, you little creep, I followed you. But this might not make the right impression. A woman who follows cannot be blameless. Instead she said,

"Let's go out for a drink. Let's go to a bar. "If he won't introduce me to his friends I'll introduce him to mine. "Let's go to *Mulligan's*. I've mates there."

He shrugged. He was not enthusiastic.

"Okay." They dressed. She put on her brown coat. He pulled on his leather jacket.

But in the street she realized she didn't want to go to *Mulligan's*. She didn't think her friends worthy of him, somehow.

"Here," she said. She opened the door of *Wood 'n' Tap* on Jones. She'd never been in it before, and she hesitated on the threshold. It smelled cheap and beery and not much fun. It was noisy too. It drew a young crowd. But Steve would be at ease with a young crowd. So she went in.

She bought herself a Guinness but he wanted a glass of wine.

"Oh, we may as well get a bottle," she said, and ordered the cheapest paint- stripper Chardonnay. They went to a table. She sniffed the neck of the bottle. She was glad she'd got a Guinness for herself, but he seemed happy enough knocking back the wine. He was too young, she supposed, to have developed a sophisticated palate like hers.

Should she make small talk, discuss the weather and politics and life in a card store? She wanted to get to the point. Now, in public, where he could not shout back at her, she wanted to say, I know all about your playing around, ducks, because I followed you. Those boys screw you, did they, one by one? Screw the girl did you, that poor innocent who loves you? Who loves you like I do?

The problem was she could not challenge him to make a choice between her and the girl or the boys or all of them, because he knew Steve would not choose her. Hurt though she was, perhaps in fact because she was hurt, she was alert enough to her inner workings to know that she would rather continue as things were than lose him, because at least following this boy in secret, weeping over him, arguing with him, being his third - choice fuck, these were better than the tedium of cards and *Mulligan's* and more cards because they were various and therefore interesting.

"Had a good day, dear? Any auditions?"

He thought for a moment.

146

"Yes, I had a great audition. The casting director said I was terrific."

"What for?"

"A run of plays in San Juan. Mainly musicals, and 'The Glass Menagerie.'"

"Think you're going to get the job?"

"I hope I hope I hope."

"So you'd leave New York?"

"For the season. Five months."

She looked sad.

"I can't say to your face I hope you don't get it, but I'll miss you. Let's celebrate."

She splashed more wine into his glass. She sipped her stout. A few minutes later, filling his glass again, it might have been that he was already in the shows, he was catching a plane tomorrow morning, this was his farewell. They clinked their glasses. He talked about theatre, about Broadway and regional theatre and agents. He talked about Gershwin and O'Neill. She didn't know much about plays but he obviously did. He was very dedicated to his craft. He was admirable, she thought. Admirable.

"You're to be admired, kiddo."

He looked as if he was going to say, aw shucks, but he didn't, he looked shyly down to his glass and turned it around by the stem. Did a reflection from his gold-spotted eyes dance on the wine's surface?

The waitress took Sara's empty glass.

"Another?"

"And another bottle too," she whispered, hoping Steve might not catch it.

"Oh no," he protested. His speech was slurred.

"Oh yes," she said. "We're celebrating."

They talked more of theatre. With booze inside him, he could talk and talk and talk.

Finally, after her third Guinness, with only a half a glass of wine left in the second bottle, she said it was time to go. She put on her coat. He could barely stand. He fell against the table and she caught him.

"Oh dear, oh dear," she said in her best mothering tone. He laughed a little, leaning against her shoulder, nose pressed into her coat so that he could breathe in its fibres.

"Oh dear oh dear oh dear," he said, laughing. He might have been mocking her, or he might have been merely echoing her.

"You'd best come back to my apartment. You'll never get home in this state." Wherever home may be.

"Oh dear oh dear oh dear." His laugh was small and neat like the moan he made in orgasm.

But out in the street he did not need her as a prop. Perhaps the open air kicked him, not into sobriety, but into a degree of control. Still he mumbled his new chant as he walked along in front of her, swaying.

"Oh dear oh dear oh dear. Oh dear." Then his walk transformed into an ill-disciplined but rather attractive dance, his movements controlled and graceful. The "Oh dear" itself transmuted into a rhythm in sympathy with the words, duduuhh, du-duhhh, du-duuuhh, and he spun ahead of her, his dancing an inward experience for all it manifested itself in ripples along the body. He was at the top of her steps, dancing, while she was scarcely past the Mexican restaurant. She loved his swaying elegance even as it infuriated her. He was, after all, a betraying little slut. She must not allow herself to forget it. She was very angry with him and now she could have a good long talk with him when he was not in a condition to answer back. With luck, she had shrewdly decided long before, she would vent her rage and he would have only the vaguest recollection of it in the morning, muffled with a feeling not of anger at her daring to follow him but with guilt, that self-flagellating guilt which hangovers

148

always bring: Oh my God, what did I say last night, what did I do? Was I really really awful? Yes, dear, you were pretty bad. Did I make a fool of myself? Oh yes, ducks, yes. I'm afraid you did rather. What did I do? And she would never tell because it was a more delicious torture that way.

In the apartment, door slammed shut by her after he'd gone in, before she had removed her coat and before he had removed his jacket, she said,

"I know about you, dear. I know everything."

He was still vaguely dancing, like a mechanical dancer wound tight, loosening in release. He turned to her and she repeated herself.

Perhaps he said, "Huh?" or it might have been that the eyes said it so clearly it did not need voicing. "I've seen you."

Still he did not comprehend. He swayed, but this was not dance, this was alcohol and confusion.

The silence that followed was brief but terrible. She could hear cars from the road, footsteps. There were footsteps outside her front door too; The Man Upstairs must be coming in or going out.

"What do you mean you've seen me?"

"With your boys."

"Oh." For a second he looked yet more confused. Then, with a moment's clarity in his mist of drunkenness he fully understood the half-said in one swallow of realization. The confusion now was mixed with that calculation which can be observed when a guilty party is puzzling how best to wriggle free of an accusation. But perhaps because of the wine he had no resources available for such calculations. The puzzlement gave way to resignation. Then he said, hopelessly,

"I don't know what you're talking about."

"Look, ducks, don't try that on me. I saw you."

"You saw me?" On the vast, labyrinthine streets of New York, she'd seen him? Was such coincidence possible?

149

"I know about your life."

"Oh." He looked down at his hands. That he had a right to be angry at Sara's admission that she'd seen him and kept it close to her chest, that he was no longer the only guilty party, did not seem to dawn on him. He shoved his hands into his pockets. He looked like a cross between a cool kid in the neighbourhood and an earthbound angel and a found-out child. Sara undid her coat. He pulled his hands from his pockets. A little plastic disc, dragged out by a knuckle, fell to the floor. Sara saw it lying on her carpet. He didn't notice it. He undid his jacket, took it off, threw it towards the sofa. It fell short, landed in a heap on the floor. He staggered towards it and accidentally kicked the plastic disc. Still he did not notice it. Sara dropped to her knees and swept it into her palm. She sprang to her feet. He looked at her oddly, the arm of his jacket in his hand, jacket hanging limp.

He looked at her some more.

"What's that?"

"What?" She put on her most convincingly innocent look, which was insufficiently convincing.

"That. In your hand." She was quite prepared to deny that she had anything in her hand, but he reached out to her and gently unfolded her palm. The button looked up. The light caught it. Perhaps it too tried to proclaim its innocence. Because her hand was held in close to her body, the button was less than an inch from the middle one attached to her coat. That they were closely related was glaringly obvious.

"Came off my coat just now. Silly me."

"Oh."

A faint memory glided over his features.

"Hold on." He pushed his fist into one of his jacket pockets, then the other. A small downturn at the centre of the eyebrows indicated that his mind and his memory were delving as deeply as his fingers. His fingers came up with

150

nothing, but was his memory about to, so to speak, put its metaphysical finger on a truth?

Alcohol had not fogged his mind so much that he did not make the connection. On the contrary, Sara thought with bitter irony that perhaps in a narrow way he was more alert than usual. He was fascinated by that little round piece of cheap plastic lying against the flesh of her palm as he would not have been if sober. Under other circumstances he might have shrugged it off as a coincidence, but now his drunkenness pinpointed it as of elusive but enormous importance. He dropped his jacket again. It crumpled with its collar over his shoes. He stared right at the button. It might have been the Koh-I-Noor diamond. They stood like that, her hand out and his eye upon it, for an inordinately long time; or rather, an apparent extinguishing of time itself so that the moment seemed infinite, until Sara snapped her fingers shut and levered her entire arm to her, putting it to her breast in what she thought a gesture of distraught femininity.

"What was that?" His question had nothing of interrogation in its inflection.

"Oh, nothing."

"That's mine. I found it."

"Oh. Yours? Oh." But she did not offer it to him.

"It was in my pocket."

"Ah."

"Can I see it?"

She flashed it out to him and back to her again.

"No, properly."

"Honestly, Steven, it's a bit of cheap plastic."

"Sara!" He had never spoken to her like this before. He did not seem young and beautiful now. She held it out. He picked it up between thumb and forefinger and put it close to his eyes like a diamond seller weighing up an offer. It

151

wouldn't have surprised her if he had produced a magnifying glass. He put it to her coat next to her middle button.

"It's just like yours."

"Oh." She laughed. "That's why I thought it *was* mine. Quite a coincidence. But these sorts of buttons are on every brown coat in the world. Not such a coincidence really when you think about it."

He ran his eyes up the button side of her coat, from the hem up to her breasts. All her buttons were intact. He brushed a hand through his hair. He looked like Stan Laurel. He was not satisfied that Sara was telling the truth and yet he could not find the space for a missing button.

"Anyway," she said," It's very warm in here. I think I'll take this off." And she removed the coat and folded it over her arm, collar pointing downward, angled towards Steve's jacket like a dog sniffing out a confrere. It drew his attention to his flopped jacket. He picked it up. He threw it on the sofa. She balled hers up and dropped it nearby. But when she turned back to him he was looking down at the button in his hand again.

"Oh for Christ's sake, it's a bloody button!"

If only he would look up to her and smile in his boyish way! Flashing his lovely gold-splashed eyes at her lustfully! Instead, his frown deepened. He rocked a bit.

She approached him and put her hand on the back of his head, feeling the softness of his hair and the skin at his neck. She no longer wanted to have it out with him. She was cornered and more than anything she wanted to smooth things over. She regretted the whole venture, the evening in the bar, the accusation. She could bring up his playing around another time, when she was in a position of absolute strength, when she was in no danger of being found guilty of anything, when she could be, wholly and convincingly, the wounded lover who had been cheated on. The button made her a criminal. She did not want him to

152

make love to her now and doubted he would be capable of it. But she did want him in her arms. She wanted his warm flesh against hers. She wanted everything to be all right. She wanted to soothe him and he to soothe her.

"Let's go to bed, darling." She had never used that word before, to him or to anyone else. Even her husband had never been her darling.

He swayed towards her. He was near to tears, but they were as likely to be the result of alcohol as of deep distress.

"Okay." The word hardly emerged from his mouth.

He went into the bedroom, propped on her arm. He sat on the edge of the bed.

"I don't feel horny." He looked up to her apologetically.

"That's all right, dear. We've both had a bit too much to drink. We need to sleep it off. Here, let me help you with your shirt."

Her fingers went to the top button and opened it. He did the rest. He pulled off his pants and his shorts and finally his socks. She pulled the sheet on his side down and he sort of rolled into place. She put the sheets over him, right up to his neck. She kissed his nose. She brushed a finger over the Band-Aid. That silly Band-Aid.

"You go to sleep, dear. I'm going to brush my teeth. I'll only be a minute." She patted his head. She disappeared into the bathroom. The tap ran.

(He lay and looked up at the ceiling, the button wrapped in his fist. He did not close his eyes. He was deep in thought. He put his hand up to his throat and brushed a single finger around it, where the top button of his shirt had been. His frown deepened.)

In the bathroom she began to hum a tune. It was 'What's Going On', an old Marvin Gaye classic. The brush going up and down and across her teeth and the foam from the toothpaste gave her voice a more than usually wavery quality. She was very relaxed now and unafraid, everything was all

153

right again. She splashed water on her face and soaped it, hurriedly. Then she came out, ready to undress. She wanted to be in the bed with him. She wanted to hear his breathing.

He wasn't in the bed.

"Steve? Steve?"

Where the hell was he? Had he sneaked off into the night, to liaise perhaps with his college girl?

"Steve?"

She went into the lounge.

He was standing by the sofa. He held the button in one hand, the brown coat in the other by its collar. It was flopped open. He was staring at the little string of cotton at the neck.

He said, very quietly,

"This is yours."

She could not think of a reply. She spoke only to block up empty air.

"Don't be silly."

"You followed me."

"What are you on about? Of course I didn't follow you, you   stupid boy."

"You fucking followed me." He struggled to say this, but the   second time it slid out smooth and loud. "You fucking followed me, Sara!"

"Nonsense."

"You fucking followed me! I know you did! You've got no right to follow me!"

It wasn't worth trying to deny it any longer.

"Okay! Okay, I followed you! Why shouldn't I? You're my lover and I thought you were cheating on me and I had to know. And I was right! You were!" She was in full self-justifying flow now. "Who do you think you are, Steven? You come into my life and fuck me to your heart's content and then go out and fuck half of New York! Boys as well as

154

girls! What are you, some kind of prostitute? What the fuck are you??"

He looked bewildered and furious.

"Why in the name of Christ do you think you have the right to follow me? I never lied to you. I never said I was in love with you. I don't want to fucking marry you, Sara!"

"No, but you do want to fucking fuck me, don't you? You can't treat me like this, kiddo!" She was determined to prove that it was he who had behaved badly, not her.

The boy put the first two fingers of his left hand to his head, perhaps to spirit away his drunkenness. Yet he continued to sway in an alcoholic muddle and he fell forward. He slapped his right hand against the arm of the sofa, which stopped him collapsing face first onto it.

He was not so much angry when he spoke again as quietly confused.

"You don't own me, Sara. I'm a kid, I don't want no settling down, I don't want no commitments. I like fucking you, it's nice, it's different, but it doesn't mean you own me just because I've come in you. I never said I wouldn't sleep with other people."

In the millisecond's silence that followed Sara realized in a clear unambiguous way that she did indeed want to own him. That's what love is, you own each other. This kid comes into my life, seduces me, can't get enough of me, and thinks there's no price tag for his pleasure!

"You like fucking me, do you? Well, it seems you like fucking everyone else too! And not just anybody. This isn't sleeping with other people, Steve! This is sleeping with boys! It's different. You said you weren't gay!" It was not different, Sara knew. If it had been girls, it would have hurt no less. But then, it was girls too.

"I'm not gay, I'm just me. I like all sorts. I like everyone!"

155

"What kind of psychosis is it that thinks liking everyone and fucking everyone is exactly the same thing!" She was pleased with that word psychosis. It made her sound intelligent.

"Now don't you start insulting me like that! I'll do it with whoever I like. I'm a free agent, Sara. That's all I ever wanted, to be free! This is America, the whole point of America is you're free to do what you want!"

"Oh don't start that 'Huckleberry Finn' crap with me!"

This boy thinks he can swan in and swan out as he chooses and swan back again as though he has no responsibilities, he can do what he likes. That's not freedom, that's... But she couldn't think what else it was because it sounded very much like freedom to her. Then she decided, it's selfishness is what it is. But this seemed inadequate.

"You're a very selfish boy, Steven."

"Look, don't act like you don't have a good time with me. You have a good time, I have a good time, we're both happy."

A loud voice in the recesses off her head cried: WHO CARES ABOUT HAPPINESS ANYWAY? WHAT DOES IT MEAN? NOTHING! I DON'T WANT TO BE HAPPY, I WANT TO HAVE YOU TO MYSELF. I'D RATHER BE UNHAPPY AND HAVE YOU THAN HAPPILY BE YOUR WHORE!

This struck her as so blatantly unreasonable and unsustainable that instead of declaiming it she collapsed onto the leather sofa. She felt its cold on her rear. She flopped right next to that wretched brown coat. She threw her head down into her hands and began to cry. She pulled the coat to her by the collar, and rubbed her eyes against it as if it were a vast handkerchief.

"I'm sorry, Steve. It's just... I thought we had something special." She wept gently. She was irritated that he had wheedled an apology out of her, the innocent party, the

156

victim. He knelt beside her and clumsily put the hand holding the button on her head, while brushing the open palm of the other over the top of her skull and down to the nape of her neck. She might have been a wounded dog. His physical nakedness seemed like a declaration of total honesty. He repeated the stroking action while speaking.

"We do have something special, Sara. You're very special to me." But this he could have said to anyone at anytime. This was the polite Southern boy wanting not to offend. Only he had offended very much.

She pushed him away, harder than she meant to. He fell back, buttocks on heels. She reared over him like a venomous beast.

"You don't bloody believe that for a moment! You don't fucking mean it, Steve. Why even pretend you do?" She wept again, loudly, dramatically. "You're just… You're a slut, kiddo. And a user! That poor girl! How much do you think it's going to hurt her when she finds out?"

"I make her happy!"

He really believed this, he was so blinded by his own beauty he though sticking his penis in someone and giving her a nice feeling for a few moments was his duty as a male human creature? It was macabre. It was crazy.

"You monster! You monster! Are you some kind of freak? Are you even fucking human? With you weird horrible eyes!! You're a devil, Steve! A devil! You're a monster!"

She did not touch him, but from his reaction she might have pushed him with impossible power. The word slammed against his chest with a physical impact. In one movement he sprang to his feet and staggered backwards towards the balcony windows. He dropped the button. She heard its thin tinkle against the wall and saw it silent on the carpet.

"Don't you fucking talk to me like that. You've no right!! You've no right! You begged me to fuck you! I fucked you to be nice! I don't love you, never said I did. I don't like you

157

even! I hate you!" The largeness of the last words appalled him. Steve did not hate. He couldn't. The words seared his tongue. Sara saw his suffering. This boy with his endless need to fuck, his need to push himself into other human creatures in a desperate attempt to love and be loved, he did not have hate in him. Sara had a sharp insight new to her. When he put his penis into her, when a man put his penis into Steven, (she supposed they did) it was not for him an act of copulation. It was his attempt to put his very soul into someone else, to take another's soul into him, to merge with someone else so that he could love and, more important to him, so that he could be loved. His fucking was a desperate animal version of some kind of heightened, beyond-human capacity for love, which was twisted and distorted by his desire but was pure within him as it was within very few human beings. Perhaps the lust was not even distortion, but the only feasible expression to be had of the real, true, wondrous thing. He was damaged beyond words, he was loving beyond words. She liked her men damaged? Well, he was her dream come true! As if to remind her of this, the Band-Aid on his cheek loosened, so that when for a second he fell silent it flapped against him. She saw the tiny scar, not yet fully healed. Ever so quietly he said,

"I didn't mean that. I don't hate you." And she knew that he did not.

She had no idea what to say or do next. She did not want to   forgive him and didn't see why she should, but he was so lost, so pathetic, standing there with no clothes on, vulnerable and hurt and drunk and confused and beautiful and hopeless and doomed.

Her response was equally muted.

"And I don't hate you either." But she had not his capacity for forgiveness and did not believe she was necessarily telling the truth.

158

"I need some air." Ah neyd some aiyer. He pushed the window up and climbed through. She meant to say, don't you think you should put something on? But she didn't care. If he wanted to sit on a balcony in a New York night naked as the day he was born, that was his business.

She went into the kitchen and poured herself a large whiskey.

She watched him. He leant on the balcony rail, then sat on the fire escape ladder which must have been cold for his behind even if the weather was warmish. He sat and looked across the silent street. He looked down at his hands. He looked down at his cock. He looked down at his feet. He looked up again. He pressed his hands between his knees. She'd seen that movement before, the night they'd first made love. Then he stood up and she saw his left foot move in a little rhythm. He was a dancer. Always and everywhere he was a dancer and his spirit would come out in his movements, conscious or unconscious.

With a sudden impulse he sprang up the ladder, then down it again. His drunkenness had lost its darkness and its melancholy. It was a happy drunkenness again. All it took was a little fresh air to drive away the shadows!

Sara watched in envious astonishment.

There he was, dancing on the balcony, stark naked, pissed out of his mind, running up the fire escape and down it again, up it again, stretching out a hand over the street below, his whole torso over the balcony railing, clutching onto the ladder with one hand. She wanted to say, you young fool, get down from there it's dangerous - and anyway, naked he was probably committing an arrestable offense. But the rows of buildings opposite looked back, mostly dark and unlit. The Mexican restaurant was lit but quiet. Plus, this was Greenwich Village and who cared about a drunken naked boy on a wild Friday night?

She could not hear, but she saw his lips moving in his "Tch! Tch! Tch!" rhythm. And his body responding to the rhythm he gave it. His penis was half erect. All was okay now. He was back to being horny Steve who needed sex because it was all the love he had. Her semi-metaphysical reflections of earlier seemed now absurdly grandiose, sentimental, romantic. The truth of a boy was in his flesh. She looked at that half erection, that easy post-adolescent lust which knows only horniness, knows no love except the love it represents itself, only desire, no passion, only need, only physical need. She remembered his college girl. They way she'd pushed herself against him. She remembered the boys, pawing him. How many others had there been? How many were there now? Ten? Twelve? Dozens? Hundreds even? How many times a day did he fuck or get fucked? Did they give him money? Did they buy him meals? Did they pay his rent? Where did he live, anyway? Did he live anywhere? Did he sleep with her only to keep off the streets? Desire. Passion. Need. The need of the male animal manifested by a rush of blood to the genitals, a lengthening and thickening, a rising.

It was that thought - the erect penis, vulnerable yet somehow commanding - which made her see red. She knocked back her whiskey, poured another full glass and gulped it down in one fat swig, which cleared her sinuses and her head. But the fog in her mind dissipated to expose only more redness, this at the very front of her mind, rage and anger and hatred which coloured the room itself as though a sheet of red plastic were hung an inch from her. He might not have the talent for hatred. She did and she loved that power. "Tch, tch, tch," he clucked, and his arms extended, one over the balcony, the other out over the street itself, hanging over the edge without a care in the world, swaying to the rhythm he himself dictated, without a sense of danger or of consequence. Like Sara only different, he too knew no

160

consequences. Well, that's lust for you, she thought bitterly, just spilling your seed, no consequences, eh? Spilling it with Sara and your boys and who knows who?

"Fall, kiddo, why don't ya? Fall, Huck."

Then he ran up to the top of the fire escape and threw his upper body right out over the street, his spine curving outward. His hand clutched the rail, but in a moment of daring he released it, toppled forward for a split second, clutched it again. Released it again. Wobbled.

Clutched again. Safe!

His lips moved, speaking silently the thrum of rhythm. He swayed his hips in a thrust of sexual provocation. Unintentional? Unintentional, yes. Because there was no-one to be turned on by his dancing, the swinging of his hips and the sway of his cock and his balls; so drunk was he, Sara believed that to him she did not exist, no-one existed, his own body was his whole world, the only person he could excite was himself.

Again he released his hand.

Sara had always suspected she had powers of suggestion, powers to influence people. She'd felt this mysterious distinction right from childhood, but she'd never whispered a word about it to anyone, not even her mother. Once she'd cursed a girl at school in Bethnal Green who'd stolen her sweets, she'd said, "Millicent Carrier, I hope you get run over by a bus!" Millicent had not been run over by a bus, but a few days later she fell over in the playground, hard on the tarmac, and she lost two teeth. Her smile was never the same. And then Steve, Steve One as she now thought of him, or Big Steve, she remembered how she'd said to herself out of the blue one evening while he watched the television news too loud, oh I'm fed up with you, Steven, I'm fed up to the back teeth with you. Steven had swigged his beer and burped. The burp had been oniony. His paunch had curved out from his trousers like a tumour, and Sara had hated him

161

and wondered where their happy times had gone, how could her Steve have become so boring and predictable and middle aged, and not yet thirty. She decided then and there, I'm leaving you, Steven, I'll bide my time but I'm leaving you. And what was it, three weeks later, she didn't even have to leave him because she got the phone call. An accident at work... Maybe it was an accident, or maybe it was fate. Sara had pursed her lips while the man from Disney gave her the awful news. She'd pursed her lips and let him burble on sympathetically, held the receiver a few inches from her ear and brushed a finger along her lower lip - a streak of lipstick coloured the tip of her nail - and she'd looked out of their apartment at the Florida sun and thought, I never liked this State anyway. Lousy pay and all those Latins. And I'm a London girl, I'm not a sucker for a tan. She'd looked down at her arm, at the patch of burnt skin which itched and cracked. See, London girls aren't supposed to get all this sun. I'll leave. There's life insurance. Poor Steve. It must be fate. Fate saying, Sara, it's time to close the book on Florida and move on.

Now she summoned her special powers of suggestion:

Go on, kiddo! Throw yourself over!

He wobbled again, his body bending at the waist a little to his right, so that more of his body hung over the street than over the balcony. Sara looked on and felt a leap in her chest, but she did not move to him, felt her hand clutch the glass more tightly, felt its stickiness where whiskey had spilled over the rim, let him fall she thought, serve him right if he cracks his skull open, not my fault, go on kiddo throw yourself off. Go on, Huck. But he did not fall, he righted himself and danced on. Was he even aware in his condition of the danger? Did he know how near he'd come to death?

The redness inside her head flared to livid orange and she was no longer in control of herself. It was not Sara, the real Sara, who caused what happened next; of this she was

162

confident after. It was her limbs, her limbs took on a life of their own. Her left leg swept forward and her right leg swept after and her left leg swept forward again. Her arms stretched out to the open window, her hands wrapped around the sides and she pulled herself through and stood on the balcony with the boy over her head halfway up the ladder. Her eyes receiving light as they were designed to do, looked at the boy in his disgusting arrogant nudity with his innocence and his lies and his smooth Southern speech and his smooth Southern body and his need. Her eyes processed this information but did not send it to her brain. Rather it went directly to her extremities. Or perhaps not, she would never know. Perhaps her brain did receive the message and jammed on the brakes so she stood right there like a deactivated robot. Perhaps a gust of wind disturbed his rhythm, perhaps the opening of the window itself, perhaps her foot on the iron balcony caused a reverberation, perhaps his own drunken dancing misstep, perhaps something else but it wasn't her fault, she did not touch him surely? She wasn't that type, she had no violence in her. And if her hand had shot out to his flesh, she would have remembered it always, the last touch to his living warmth before he became colder and colder.

What she did remember was the second when he seemed frozen on the air, his feet off the ladder and a few inches beyond it so that should he become unstuck he wouldn't fall back to the saving metal floor but to the ground below, all the way past her balcony and Pete and Tony's balcony, past the thick bricky walls of the building to the hard stone steps far below. But for that moment he was immortalized on the air like a sculpture of opaque glass. The light from her living room threw a shadow from the fire stairs onto him, striping his pink flesh with dark lines. She thought a lot of things in that moment, and would think more later on. Later on she would not be able to separate the moment itself from the

163

subsequent reflections. Did she remember - she thought she did - the story of some old God, couldn't recall the name and never did, the one whose wings melted, the one who fell towards the sun? She thought also more prosaically of Superman. Steve's right leg was raised just like Superman's, knee pointing skyward, the leg folded on itself, the foot crooked downward balletically, and his beautiful calf was just above Sara's eye level. The flesh of his thigh put it into shadow. It was smooth and she wanted to stroke it, feel the warmth of it, the warmth of his male body which had liked her and taken such pleasure in her, as she had in him. She did not know - she realized now - that he had ever actually liked her as a person, but as a body yes, and wasn't that enough?

What are we, we human creatures, but bodies? Bodies I can understand, I can see them and feel their heat, minds I cannot understand, not even my own which I live with all the time, my mind is the least of me, my breasts I can see and feel, we hear so much about 'personalities' but do personalities even exist, does anything exist at all except the body? The head and the torso, the genitals of a man and the genitals of a woman, the legs and the feet, the mouth and the anus. Those are the facts, the rest is waffle. Up, up and away. His left arm was extended as though reaching for a star. Up, up and away. Oh my angel. My wingless melting sinking Superman angel. Why did you do it?

All these things she thought, or later thought that she had thought, and then the moment was gone and the glass sculpture was not glass but pink and fleshy and falling. He did not cry out, for which she was thankful. Perhaps, sozzled as he was, this was a thrill not a terror, like Huckleberry Finn lighting out for the territory, so that if he were to call out it would've been in a whoop of glee rather than of fear. But he did not call out. He fell in dead silence.

164

Fell past Tony and Pete's balcony, towards the stone steps that led to the front door.

She was puzzled by the trajectory of his fall; she had supposed he'd turn over and land flat on his stomach, but though he spun a little vertically so that he was facing towards her building he plummeted, looking up, up to the balustrade, to her leaning over it, then beyond her, up to the stars. A hand stretched out, palm open. He had waved to the girl on the bench in the park like that, a small shy open-handed wave. But then the hand had been held in to his body, at the level of his nipples. Now it was far out above his head. The Statue of Liberty without a torch, giving a little shy wave, greetings, America, shucks.

Did he catch her eye? Was that a cheeky grin on his face?

She saw the chocolate brown steps to the front door. Did he see them, or only feel them? He could not have seen them because still he looked upwards.

His left leg grazed the side of the run of steps, which slowed but did not break his plummet and sent his body arching over, like an acrobat or a tumbling cat. For a second he was upside down, legs in air, penis pointing to his tummy button, and his head bumped the rim of the middle trash can in the row of three, which slapped his skull and his neck to an angle and right into the black disc of the can's heart, and his shoulders went after, into the blackness. His top half crumpled into the can, folding up to fit snuggly into it so that only his legs were out. There was no clang as his flesh hit the thin echoey metal. None. Perhaps there was a black bag inside it to cushion his landing.

It's not my can, it's Tony and Pete's that one. How often do they put out their trash?

How silent had been the fall, how silent he was now.

She wanted to call to him to ask if he was all right but all she did was lean over her balcony and look down at him all folded up like that. It would not be wise to cry out; what if

165

he was not all right? She wouldn't want to draw attention to herself.

But she felt the beating of her heart and again the relief and amazement at the silence of it all, a swell of gratitude for the wonderful silence. He had not cried out! He had not betrayed her! He knew it was only an accident! He'd simply plummeted. Oh my angel, my beautiful quiet angel. Who would have thought it? In a city of eight million people someone can drop two stories from a balcony and no-one hears it. Drop to death and no-one notices.

Death? Was he dead?

But of course he is not dead, only hurt. Poor Steve. I will nurse him back to health. I will nurse him and he will get well. He will be mine. There will be no boys for him any more.

It was very, very bad of him to lie to her, very bad, she did not approve of boys who slept with boys - but she would mother him to wellness in her own bed and he would be hers. Her tongue was tart with the after-taste of whiskey, tart with words on its tip which she would not speak.

There was a stirring. *He's alive!* she thought, not entirely with pleasure. Was he moving? Was he trying to pull himself out? But still he did not call to her. The legs extended over the rim pointing at the moon. His lovely calves were dusted with the silvery gold of moonlight like his eyes, or was it the glow cast from the street lamp? He flopped backward and the can wobbled and − "Oh my God!" she said aloud, anticipating the noise which would wake the whole neighbourhood, but biting her tongue in fury at her own outcry. It toppled. As an aftermath to the perfect silence came a clang as it hit concrete, a clang that surely Pete and Tony would hear - perhaps they were out - a clang which she was certain echoed up and down the street, bounced from the walls of her townhouse to a Brownstone opposite and

166

the red walls of the restaurant and overhead to cloak the whole of Greenwich Village.

Christ, they'll hear it in Harlem! I'm in big trouble.

The can rolled a few inches, a low rumble, and came up against the third can, not Sara's, it belonged to the Man Upstairs.

Someone a few doors down opened a window. Sara squatted, tried to make herself invisible.

"I know I heard something," said a woman's voice distantly from deep inside a room. "A trash can fell over."

A man said, more clearly because his head was stuck through the window,

"I don't see anyone."

A black and white moving silence padded around a corner.

"Oh, it was a cat. That's all." The window slid down.

From somewhere a car back-fired, from somewhere else a voice called not to Sara but to an unknown person on another block, a police siren squealed. A boat on the river blew a horn. The trash can's clang flowed into what it was, just another noise in an always noisy City, a part of the fabric of sound you lived around if you lived in New York. It was still now. Steve's legs stretched out from it, pale and thin and weak but not it seemed broken.

Sara felt suddenly very sober, very practical. She moved backwards into her apartment and closed the window as quietly as she could. It lodged in place with a small woody whisper. Then she went out to the staircase, in her slippers so as to make as little noise as she could. She came to Pete and Tony's apartment, listened for stirrings. There weren't any. She went on down and tugged on the front door as gently as she could. Sometimes it stuck, so she had to pull on it quite hard, and as it opened the welcome mat caught under its lip and shuffled towards her in a rustle. She went out and pulled it shut. The mat, still caught under it, came too so that it wouldn't close and she had to push it out of the way and tug on the door. When it closed it made a very audible click.

On the steps a small pinkish oblong was attached to a step like gum. It was Steve's strip of Band-Aid, stuck by a corner to the top step's edge. She peeled it off.

She went down to the bottom and round to the row of trash cans.

No, don't get weepy, girl, think! What are you going to do? Think! You can't leave him here.

She flicked the Band-Aid into her own can.

She knelt and tugged on Steve's left leg, trying to pull him out to her. The trash can did not willingly give up its contents and itself came to her along with the body, screeching against the concrete.

Oh bloody hell!

She leant in to the can like a scavenging animal, the smell of rot mixed with blood came to her nose and she coughed in revulsion. But this time the boy came to her, bringing not the can but a flattened bag of trash folded under his shoulder blade. She put her hand on his shoulders to lift him away from the plastic, and levered his upper half forward. But he was still deep inside the can and as she lifted him his head hit the wall of the can itself, leaving a smear of blood. The sight of the blood made her emotional again, oh my angel why did you do it? But she gathered herself sternly. I must be as stern with myself as I am with others, she told herself. I can't stand easy tears, they make me furious.

Sara wrapped her hands around his perfectly shaped ankles, and his head and upper body slid out with a firm tug. But, palms against that soft/hard flesh/bone, she became aware of something softer under one hand, thought with strange invention because it was feathery and tacky that it was a bird's wing, and she pulled her hand away. It was a piece of dirty, damp tissue that had lain loose in the can. She

168

put her hand over the ankle again. People don't understand, see, she said on her breath, that it's not just the eyes or the set of the jaw or the roundness of the bottom, not even the cock that makes a man attractive. An ankle can be sexy too, the curl of an elbow, the lobe of the ear. If only people weren't dumb and so brainwashed by Hollywood they could appreciate human beauty anywhere and in all sorts of ways.

He lay exposed on the concrete as on a slab, mouth closed, sleepy and sweet as she had seen him many nights, her Steve two, her Huck, only the red-black crack on the upper left of his head, just under the hairline, spoiling the picture of contented rest. She was so glad he'd died with his eyes closed that she brushed her lips softly against his lids, her kisses like pennies.

"You're really beautiful," she said lovingly, "a really beautiful boy."

Something touched her wrist. She opened her mouth to yelp and snapped it shut so fast and hard she drew blood on the tip of her tongue.

"Sod off, Felix!" she said, and slapped the cat's nose. It drew away for a second and came back, not to her but to the body next to her. It brushed its head against the boy's thigh, making its claim of ownership. Sara let it. As long as it was quiet it couldn't do much harm. If she annoyed it, it might scratch and arch its back, it might hiss. She tasted blood on her tongue, on her teeth.

She closed her eyes to concentrate. She could feel the lower sets of eyelashes entwined with the upper. Think, woman! Think!

Now I must be very calm and sensible and think through exactly what I am to do. I have the corpse of a boy lying beside a trash can and I cannot leave him here. It's true that his death was a terrible accident and that I did not kill him, but who knows how much explaining I will have to do if I

169

call the police? It would be better to take him somewhere and, and what? Bury him? Where would I find a plot of land to bury him in? The park, perhaps? I could go up to the park and find a nice spot for him, a nice shady spot for his everlasting rest, thousands of native New Yorkers would love such a privilege, to rest forever within the lungs of the City. Ten million bucks will not buy you a grave in the park. Steve would like that, to be one with the City. I will bury him with his feet pointing towards Broadway, the symbol of all his hopes and dreams.

I cannot give him a gravestone, but perhaps I can put him near a rock, I can spray his name on the rock, STEVE, OVER THE RAINBOW 2002, and people will think it's just a bit of graffito, only Steve and I will know that it marks his life. I will visit it every day, or every week at least, frequently anyway, or perhaps it would mean more if I came only on the anniversary of, it will have to be his death as I do not know the anniversary of his birth. No, the anniversary of our meeting, the anniversary of our first making love, because I do not want to celebrate his end, but his life, his warm full life and love. Yes. Well, I can work out the details later. I must get him up to the park.

But what if he's discovered? What if someone, some early morning jogger, notices the freshly turned earth and takes a closer look? What if I do not dig a deep enough hole, and rainwater washes the soil away and someone sees, a hand? A leg? Just a toe perhaps, stiff, gray, skin flaking away. I would not want that. It would be humiliating for Steve if her were dug up naked and rotting, cut to pieces and post-mortemed. I want him when he is underground to stay there for ever. He deserves no less. Poor Steve. I loved you, you know. In my way I loved you as I have never loved another man.

But then, do I have the strength to dig a hole for him? I am not a strong woman. She coughed consumptively. I am

170

not a strong woman and I do not have a spade. Are there twenty-four hour stores near the park where I can buy one? If there are, how could I buy a spade without arousing suspicion? Who is that attractive woman with the golden hair, they'll say, who has come in to buy a spade at midnight? What does she want with it? You can tell by her graceful, thin wrists and her elegant make-up that she is not used to digging in gardens. She is the sort who hires gardeners and gives them instructions. She probably has a beautiful garden which she has designed with care, some lavender here, lilies there, a rosebush here to set the crocuses off, but she will not have done the toiling herself. She perhaps does a little pruning, that's as far as she'd go. Snip snip.

Can I trust Tony and Peter? Would they come with me and help me dig the grave? If I told them all that had happened, surely they would be sympathetic to my plight? They would lend me their car if only they had a car. We've been so close for so many years now, they love me so much just as I love them, I don't doubt they'll help me all they can.

But will they be able to keep their mouths shut? They're so gossipy, and who knows what confidences they'd spill out in some terrible gay bar after they'd had one too many? They may mean to keep their mouths shut, but queers cannot keep anything to themselves, it's well known.

So I must keep Antony and Peter out of it. I am on my own.

Not on my own exactly. Me and Steve. Secret between us. Only me and Steve will know. This thought manifested itself physically in her leaning into the body, her tapping the lips twice gently with her forefinger to say, ssshhh. She could trust Steve. At least she could trust Steve.

The park would not do.

Where else? Where else could you dispose of an unwanted body in this packed overstuffed City full of prying eyes and malice?

171

Well, the answer was obvious.

The water.

The East River or the Hudson. That was a traditional dumping ground for bodies, wasn't it? How many thousands, tens of thousands of bodies in the years since white men built New Amsterdam and then renamed it, how many had sunk to the bottom of the river?

'Take me to the river, wash me down...'

Down, down, down to Davy Jones' locker.

'Way, way on down.'

But then Steve would not have a monument! He would be one of the lost, one of the forgotten. She could hardly paint a buoy, point it to Broadway, marked for Steve: STEVE 2002 COME TO THE CABARET.

She remembered poets' corner in Westminster Abbey in London. She had not visited it but she knew of it. A series of slabs on the North side of the Church, in the wall and in the floor, commemorated distinguished poets. They were not buried there, they were buried all over the place. The slabs were meant as tributes, not as gravestones. So it was not necessary for a great person's memorial to mark the site of his remains. Why hadn't she thought of that before? She could send Steve downriver and still pay tribute to him somewhere else, in the park perhaps, near Strawberry Fields. Did Lennon fans think John was buried in the park? But he wasn't. (Was he? She wasn't quite sure. But she thought he wasn't.) Strawberry Fields was a place to reflect on John's life, and she would build a little nook for Steve where she could reflect on his life, on the greatness which had been cut short, not by an assassin but by his own crazy drunkenness. Sara alone had perceived that greatness, but it only takes one.

So it was to be the river.

But there was still the problem of getting him there. Transportation. She could hardly bundle him on her

172

shoulders. She could hardly take him on the subway. She could hardly call a cab. She had a vague memory of an old movie in which two people   transported a dead body in their car, they crossed a border and told the guard their friend was asleep and the guard bought it. Could she bundle Steve into a cab, tell the driver he was completely sozzled? Sheer gall might pull it off, because what driver would think a passenger could be dumb enough to transport a dead body in a yellow cab? A body that looked dead was more likely to be drunk than actually dead, surely? Would it work? No. That was movies, this was life. Anyway, Sara wouldn't even be able to get Steve to Fifth or Sixth Avenue to hail a cab in the first place. She'd barely been able to drag him out of the trash can.

Two people emerged talking from Panchito's Mexican restaurant. They turned right, towards Sara and her apartment building. She threw herself over Steve and tried to look like a heap of, what? A heap of laundry? Anyway, she hoped the scraggly tree would be   sufficient cover for them.

The guy was talking to his girlfriend. He was a little merry, not madly drunk like Steve had been but jolly. He was talking about getting a new motorcycle. He was talking about the pros and cons of particular brands of motorcycle. His girlfriend said,

"Kurt, you can't afford a pair of fucking roller skates, let alone a Motorcycle. Besides, where would we put it?"

"We could keep it in the hallway."

"If you think I'm having a motorcycle in the hallway for everyone to trip over and probably sue the asses off us, you can forget it."

"Oh, honey," he cooed sweetly. "I want a nice bike. A cool bike. It would be useful. Like this one. Now this is cool."

At the foot of Minetta Lane on tiny Minetta Street was a lime green building with a wrought iron gate leading to a

173

door you could not see, and a long balcony with an array of potted plants so mature and well-cared for their greenness swept over the balcony and hung low enough to block out the window below. If Greenwich Village had only been built on canals one might looking at this building have been in Venice. In front of the mysterious gate was a huge motorcycle. The couple stood there and looked at it, possibly in awed silence. Sara could not see them. Her face was pressed up to Steve's. She could feel his nakedness underneath her. She could feel his lips cold against hers. She could feel the tackiness of the wound at his temple against the wrinkles of her frowning brow. Her arms were thrown over his head. She hoped she looked like a discarded curtain. She thought *get out of here, you fuckers!* Go away go away go away! She could hear their footsteps. They were circling the bike. The guy whistled low. The girl finally said,

"Yeah, that's something. That's sure something."

IT'S A FUCKING MOTORBIKE! Sara wanted to scream. IT'S JUST A FUCKING MOTORBIKE LIKE MILLIONS OF OTHERS SO WHY DON'T YOU PISS OFF? IF YOU WANT TO LOOK AT MOTORBIKES GO TO A BLOODY SHOWROOM!

"Maybe we could take out a loan."

"Yeah, maybe we could get a loan. We could manage the payments."

"It would mean I could zip around the city. It'd make a big difference. No more subway fares. We'd save a lot."

"Yeah." But like most women with their heads together, she did not soften for long. "No way, Kurt. No fucking way. Where would we put it?"

Sara heard their voices retreat.

"In the hallway."

"And have the others sue our asses every time they walk past it? Forget it, Kurt."

"We'll let them use it too."

174

"Like hell we will. Forget it Kurt."

"Ooooh Come on, honey." In a last desperate appeal, he was snuffling her ear.

"That feels good. Forget it, Kurt."

"Sure?"

"Yeah."

"Sure?"

"Yeah."

"Absolutely sure?"

"Yeah. Keep doing that."

Sara lifted her head an inch. She tried to force her hearing into acuteness as if by sheer willpower the potency of her senses could double. There was nothing to hear now.

A motorcycle. If she stole a motorcycle she could kind of strap Steve to her back, wrap his arms around her, he could ride pillion and she could get to the water. But where would she find a motorbike whose owner had carelessly left the keys in the ignition? This was not movies, this was life.

No, not a motorcycle. A set of wheels yes, a motorcycle no. It clicked into place. Sara felt a physical sensation of satisfaction as the answer came to her.

A shopping cart. Perfect. She could fold him up neatly in a shopping cart and wheel him to the water.

But again there was the question: where would she get a shopping cart? Especially at this time of night?

She checked her watch. It was ten to twelve.

The Bleecker Street stores would all be closed by now, and anyway stores like *Murray's Cheese* and *Ottamalli's Prime Meat Market* (specialty wild game) were too small for shopping carts. What she needed was a supermarket. She checked off in her mind the large stores she passed on the way to work: *Jefferson market* and *Citarella* and *Food Emporium*. They all had shopping carts, but only *Food Emporium* would be open at this hour. She had ten minutes to get there. It was near the Greenwich Village school, a good fifteen

175

minutes away even if she moved fast. And anyway, though *Food Emporium* had pretensions to being a supermarket of the sort familiar to people who lived in suburbs, like everything in New York it was somewhat reduced: the aisles were narrower, the stock poorer, the shopping carts themselves too small: you couldn't get a body into a *Food Emporium* shopping cart. Like everything else in New York, shopping carts were too compact for comfortable human habitation. Sara felt a wave of anger. Any damn where in these United States, any damn where except this city, if you set your mind to stealing a shopping cart it could easily enough be achieved, and you'd get a decent size shopping cart which would actually be of some use. Why do I not live in nice leafy suburban Connecticut, with its lovely glassy branches of *Stop and Shop* and their large carts designed to fit countless weeks' worth of groceries, or even better *Home Depot* with their massive coffin-like carts? Ideal for moving corpses about. And sitting around in huge paper-strewn parking lots, easy to steal too. Why do I have to live here?

I must go and seek one out. I won't be long, Steve. I'll be back for you in a jiffy.

She put a hand to his head, brushed his hair back affectionately. The blood on his temple was blackening. The scar on his cheek was a faint white streak.

I can't leave you here for everyone to see.

She knelt to him and put her hands round his feet, pushed on the soles to force him back into the trash can. She pushed hard, felt her heart beat faster. He moved but so did the can. She went around to his shoulders and lifted them. His head fell backwards. He looked like Christ in a renaissance painting, taken down from the cross, head lolling back, not yet the saviour risen from the tomb. She was Mary Magdalene. Only Steve's short hair spoilt the illusion.

It was easier to pull the can to him than him to the can, so, holding his shoulders six inches from the ground, she

176

dragged the can to him - it let out its chalklike squeal - and pulled it over first his head and then down to his chest. She thought of an old-fashioned candle snuffer dousing the flame: the can was dousing the last of Steve's spirit. Her arms began to ache. Even a light boy can be very heavy in death. She let him go. The shadow of the can's rim sliced across his nipples.

She could now either continue to push him in, hoping he would fold comfortably into the space, or by standing the can up he would naturally curl deeper into its mouth. She decided to raise the can. But when she lifted it a couple of inches at the rim, his back arched and his feet dragged and she could feel the corpse slip not into the can but to the ground. She put the rim back down and pushed him further in. His neck crooked against the pressure, curving into the bottom of the can. (She remembered Eddie's weighty, aroused body on hers, her head angled uncomfortably, un-erotically, against the arm of her old sofa.) It was as if sleepily he was looking up at her, and as with the half-waking of an affectionate lover the eyelids lifted, slowly, dreamily, somewhere on the verge between sleep and waking, aware perhaps only of the warmth: of the bed, of the person who shared it. Cosy, snug. But Steve was aware of nothing. The pupils, half exposed now, were not focused. They could no longer express anything. All their subtlety had been extinguished. They expressed not happiness, not horror either. Nothing. Even the flecks of gold expressed nothing. They were light bulbs switched off.

Still, those eyes appalled Sara and she leaned in to the can, the smell of stale waste notwithstanding, and she reached out first to one eyelid, and she drew it down with a gentle touch of the ball of her first finger, and then the other. Now he was asleep again. Now he did not look so very very dead. Now he was a lovely sexy snoozing lad.

177

Then, in one great lunge, a shooting pain running through her back as she made it, she uprighted the can and the boy with it, his back sliding downward and the head moving across the bottom. The knees drew in to his chest. His feet faced the moon. He did not fit into it as well as she would have hoped, but when she placed the lid on top so that it rested on his soles, hooked over the toes to keep it from sliding off, it looked simply like a full-to-bursting trash can, which it was.

She headed up Minetta Lane to Bleecker Street. She meant to go towards the Hudson River in her search for a cart. It seemed as good enough a place to start as any. Yet a cart proved easier to find than she had imagined: as she came to Father Demo Square she saw exactly what she was looking for.

Stretched out on one of the benches was a man with a long thick knotty gray beard and knotty lank hair. He wore a grubby raincoat. His shoes were cracked and split. A toe peeped through the left one. It was not a clean, shapely, well-manicured toe like Steve's. It had been beaten on by wind and rain. It was scabby and misshapen. It was the colour of cigarette tar.

Parked next to the man's bench was an ample shopping cart, filled with soiled plastic bags containing, presumably, the detritus of his disastrous life. She reached out for a bag. Occasionally someone crossed the square, and people were coming out onto Seventh and going up it or down it; at least some of them must have noticed the wreck on the bench and the plump, attractive woman leaning over him with her blond hair, her full body which pulled the eye. Perhaps they thought she was a nurse come to take him to shelter, or a distributor of food to the poor. Perhaps they thought the bags she clutched were full of sustaining balanced meals which she was placing in his cart so that he would find them when he awoke as children find Santa's gifts on Christmas

178

morning. In fact she was removing the bags, very slowly and gingerly, so as not to disturb the sleeping man with the scrunching sound carrier bags make when the handles are gathered up. She dropped her hand into the cart and lifted a bag out and moved it at breast level through the air and lowered it to the ground. She was like one of those coin machines with arms which are supposed to give you a stuffed bear but however many times you try they never give you anything, somehow always manage to drop the bear just before the arm can deliver it to the chute. Sara was better than those machines. When her arm dipped into the cart she actually picked up a bag and successfully manoeuvred it to the ground. She placed each bag beside the bench. Soon there was a long row of them. You couldn't see under the bench, it was all blocked up with bags. How many bags can one man have, especially a man without a home? Even Sara could not fill so many bags with the things from her apartment she would wish to keep if she were suddenly to become homeless. She wanted to look inside them, see what he treasured so that he would happily (happily?) push it around all and everywhere forever, but she had to keep rustles to a minimum so she resisted the temptation.

In time the cart was empty. It smelt dirty. She didn't like the idea of delivering Steve to his watery resting place in so filthy a transport but what choice did she have?

The man on the bench stirred, and without properly waking tried rolling himself around. He yawned and she saw into his mouth. He only had two teeth. His gums were black. It was like staring into an empty trash can. He settled again, back to her, his nose poking through the slats.

She felt guilty. Here she was, taking his cart away from him. If you were homeless your cart was the nearest thing you had to a home; she was, to all intents and purposes, stealing his very house. She put her hand into her pocket and withdrew a five dollar note. That would pay for the cart. He

179

would be able to steal another one in time; two, even, of the smaller sort at the *Food Emporium*. It would be more complicated she supposed to push along two small carts than one large one, it would take a more calculated choreography, but it wasn't as if he didn't have plenty of time on his hands.

She experimentally pushed the cart a few inches forward, a few back. The front left wheel squeaked a bit. The man on the bench moved again, turned onto his back looking in the direction of the stars, though all he saw, Sara guessed, was the red behind his eyelids. Sara put a hand to her chest. Her heart was racing. How ironic it would be if she were to keel over now, have a massive heart attack and die in the arms not of her beautiful boy but of a smelly vagrant with two teeth. Could you in your very moment of death flare your nostrils at the bad smell beside you, which was an augury to come if you went to hell? Did hell smell? There was no biblical tradition she knew of which mentioned the fate of the olfactory sense, but eternally burning skin must undoubtedly smell of something horrible? Yet roasting meat was one of her favourite smells. Who knew?

But Sara didn't believe in hell; to the extent at least that she had never given any thought to it. It could at least smell no worse than this combination of rotten teeth and urine on the bench. If it did exist - just if - would she be doomed to burn forever, or would she be one of the saved? She had always been a giver, a worrier after other people. God would welcome her into his domain, which she pictured as a garden; lilies here, crocuses there, gladioli over there, a smooth lawn ideal for croquet. Steve would be waiting, croquet mallet in hand, wearing a white cap to keep the cool sun from his sympathetically golden eyes. Behind him would be a big old English country house, long French doors open to a wide stone balcony, looking down onto the lawn. A bottle of wine in its ice bucket glittered next to a table covered in pristine cloth which was a white of such purity it was not for earthly eyes to look upon. A butler came through the door carrying a silver salver laden with cucumber sandwiches with the crusts cut off. Steve approached her and kissed her and threw his hand to the balcony and around the garden, as if to say all this was hers now.

All this was hers now. All this. Is this yours? Yes, it's all mine. Hey, is this yours?

"Hey! Is this yours?"

A deep rough-edged male voice, aggressive and surly. She looked to find the speaker. There wasn't anyone near her except the sleeping vagrant. At the other end of Father Demo Square near the cigar store a man held out a little pocketbook to a young woman.

"Oh my God!" said the woman. She patted her jacket pockets. "I must've dropped it! Thank you so much! My God!" And she took it. "Thank you so much!"

"You're welcome, lady," said the surly man, making a little saluting gesture with his first three fingers before moving on.

So, back in the quotidian surroundings of the Village, Sara pushed the cart forward, each squeak of the wheel setting her teeth on edge, moving slowly, slowly, and waited for the traffic on Sixth to ease.

It should have been easy enough to get across; it was after midnight, there were intervals between cars. But standing there looking at the headlights, waiting for a break, Sara felt oddly powerless and when a break came still she looked up the avenue, she didn't budge. Her hands were pressed on the cart's handle. She didn't know what she was doing, why she was there with an empty shopping cart , why she wasn't in *Mulligan's* with her dull friends drinking Guinness and jawing about nothing much.

Again it was a voice that brought her back into place.

"Hey!"

181

Another lost purse?

She looked over her shoulder.

It was the toothless vagrant. He was standing, looking down at all his bags and across to her.

"Hey!"

A long arm pointed straight to her, a long thin finger unfolded to its fullest extent. The legs apart, rooted to the ground, the body under the raincoat curved forward. This was not so much a man pointing to her as the performance of a man pointing to her, a Shakespearean actor's version of pointing. When he lifted his arm to the sky (like Liberty, like Steve) and let out a roar that too was Shakespearean in quality. His roar could fill a theatre. Just as a classical actor can rage and roar and roar every night as King Lear and not damage his voice because he has been trained to make his full round cry from the diaphragm, so the tramp produced a roar which he must have rehearsed many times in order to summon such considerable power without straining his vocal chords. He roared so effectively that everyone in the Square and on Bleecker Street and on Sixth looked right at him and then followed his sightline to the woman at the edge of the Square. Sara felt eyes on her from all corners.

What to do? An inspiration came.

She turned to the vagrant and said, as loudly as she could but less skilfully so that she felt the strain on her throat,

"You're a monster, Terry, a monster! When you can sober up, then I'll think of taking you back! Not till then!" And she ran, she hoped tearfully, onto Sixth. The tramp stalked after her. A car screeched to a halt. It nearly touched the shopping cart. She looked around, saw a furious face the other side of the windshield, and behind her that other furious face, approaching her, not fast but relentlessly.

From within the car - it was a yellow cab - a voice called, harshly, "Out of my fucking way you fucking crazy bitch!" This was not well articulated, might well have torn a chord.

182

Lear was on the sidewalk's edge. He stepped off it. Sara darted onto the opposite sidewalk, ran as fast as she could past the basketball court, squeak squeak squeak went the front left wheel, oh my god, she thought, he's going to kill me, and fear gave wings to her feet. Lear ran in front of the cab, but the driver, a split second earlier had put his foot angrily on the gas and his cab sprang forward. There was a muffled thud, and Lear let out a huge rather lovely cry and the harsh voice said, "Oh my fuck! Oh my fucking Christ!" People all around them looked towards them, just as Sara swept left into the comparative quiet of Minetta Street and down to the Venetian building and the motorcycle, then left again into Minetta Lane. Another couple came out of Panchito's. They went up to Bleecker, away from her. Her wrists were tiring and her legs moved impossibly fast, she was not so much controlling the cart as hanging onto it. She nearly collided into the building next to hers, at the last moment swinging the cart away and pointing it up the street. But the sharp turn toppled the cart so that it ran for a second on two wheels, then fell to its side and lay there. The wheels spun. Sara collapsed on top of it. Her heart beat faster than ever, she could scarcely breathe.

(The couple up near Banana Republic at the top of Minetta Lane, round the bend so they couldn't see Sara, stopped and looked back to Panchito's, wondering about the sudden metallic crash. They did not come to explore. Perhaps they decided the chef had dropped a couple of pans. If they said something, Sara could not hear it. They went onto Bleecker, into the heart of Village life.)

Minetta Lane was awesomely quiet. Noises could be heard of course, but they all seemed a long way away, as if heard through a blanket. The yowl of a siren nearby seemed distant, removed. It could have come from over the river. Sara felt very alone. She sat up, breathing heavily. She put her hand under her breast and felt her heart. She was glad to

183

be alone. She sat like that for some time. She closed her eyes and let herself feel the places of her body, not through touch, not sight, but through the connections inside her linking one part to the next: Her head, fair and well-shaped with her full lips and delicate eyelids, pert nostrils. The soft skin over her lips, dewy with sweat. Her tongue against her teeth. There remained a lingering taste of blood. Her neck: she tautened the skin around it, felt the tension in the tendons. Her generous breasts with the large nipples. She pushed her shoulder blades together and her breasts lifted. Men had loved her breasts. Steve had loved them. She felt the shallow arc of her back. She pictured the run of her spine down to the small of her back. She felt her buttocks pressed flat on the ground, she dilated her anus. She felt the depth of her sex and almost the sensation of Steve's penis inside it. Her thighs which were smooth; men liked to brush their palms gently up and down her thighs. She pictured Jet rubbing Steve's thighs and an uprising of jealousy nearly spoilt the moment. Think of your body, girl, not his, not anyone's. She managed to crush the image. She felt the skin tight at her folded knees, and the firmness of her calves, her ankles, her feet. First, her left foot, the heel curving round to the soft ball in front and the toes. One, two, three, four, five. The nail of her big toe against her stocking: it needed clipping. And the right foot.

And so, all of her; the whole Sara. There was no hell, no heaven either, because Sara like all human creatures was the sum of her physical construction. All of her was encased within this frame. This - and she pinched her thigh - this is me.

A great calm descended and she was ready to do what she had to do.

She rose and went to the middle of the row of trash cans at   number 33, the one with the lid on it.

184

Steve lay in the can, if he could be said to be lying which did not seem quite the right word, folded in half as he was, toes hooking the lid. She took it off and looked down at him and felt an outpouring not of emotion this time but of profound detached human sympathy, a sympathy she imagined she had a more than generous endowment of. Steve was just like her with his feet and legs, his genitals, his anus, his back curving uncomfortably, his head, the features. Soft lips. Nice eyes, half open again. He did not look happy. But he did not look unhappy either, because unhappiness is a living state. Steve did not live any more. He simply was, as the cart on its side simply was and the street lamp was and the siren was which shrieked   somewhere for room to pass.

She put the lid back and righted the cart and went up the steps, hand running up the black railing, feeling its chill. She unlocked and went inside and climbed the staircase and went straight to her closet and pulled out her worst clothes, a woollen bobble hat which had once been Big Steve's: it could make anyone look dowdy, even Sara. A shapeless navy blue sweater, a pair of very old, worn slippers, a depressing gray skirt. She stripped off her dress and, regretting the losing for now of her beauty, she pulled on the raggedy clothes. She washed away her lipstick and her makeup, she pulled her hair into an untidy straggly mess. She put on the flat slippers and the hat. The hat over her eyebrows made her look sad and worn out. She let her cheeks sag. She knelt to the piles of sheets and blankets. She pulled out the thickest, richest straw-coloured blanket and bundled it under her arm. In her slippers she descended the stairs light as a ghost. She moved the mat away from the door so that it would not catch in it, and she closed and locked the door as quietly as possible. Pete and Tony might be in. Or the Man Upstairs. She must not disturb them. She angled the cart onto three wheels to keep it from squeaking and she pushed it under the ailing tree. She looked about her for signs of life from the other

185

buildings. The Venetian gate was black and silent. No-one emerged from Panchito's. The window of her own building's basement was grimy and filmy and there was no life behind it. The sign for *Boyle's Travel* looked hopelessly optimistic. Even the cat had lost interest.

Poor Steve had somehow to be transferred from the trash can to the shopping trolley. She removed the lid and looked down at him, like a witch inspecting her cauldron. She laid the can on its side and, his body relaxing, he slipped forward so that his feet were over the rim again. She knelt down and wrapped her hands around his ankles again and prepared to pull him out.

But she had no heart for the job. Pulling him out and lifting him up in her arms as if she were Frankenstein's monster and he a girl in a faint, laying him into the cart. No, there must be another way. She lay the cart on the ground, mouth to the can's mouth like hesitant lovers, and she pushed the can towards the cart, over the edge, until Steve's feet touched the wiry mesh. She pushed the can still a little further, his feet disappearing under the rim. The rim pressed on the mesh. She tensed her muscles and shoved the cart and can upright. She pulled the can over his head and he slid out like a perfectly done steamed pudding slipping from its bowl onto a plate. But he was not quite perfectly done. A steamed pudding would have kept the shape of the bowl, whereas Steve did not stay compactly folded: as the can passed over him, his head fell back against the cart's plastic handle with a dull, dry smack. She could not pretend any more, looking at him blue and cold, that he was merely sleeping. He looked alien and strange and not remotely of the living world. His legs stayed tucked into him. She pulled him a couple of inches towards the front of the cart and his head bounced off the handle and onto the mesh at the back. His toes touched the front end. She threw the blanket over her shoulder onto him. It fell on his face and over the

186

handle. She pulled it down across his body. It reached right to his toes and she wrapped it around them. She laid it out as flat as she could, patting it. She tucked it around his sides. As best she could she pushed it under him as well. She lifted his head, folding the blanket over the ears and round to the nape of the neck, but pulled tight it shaped the outline of the skull and a little triangle formed at the nose, so she loosened it to misshape it as best she could, to make it an innocent amorphous lump. He was entirely wrapped in the blanket. She could not see any of him. He was just as likely to be a pile of books or a large gathering of Coke cans to be taken to a recycling point, (5 cents a can, worth the effort if you didn't have any money,) as a human body. Yet Sara was not quite satisfied that the cart looked sufficiently like a homeless person's home-from-no-home. She had an inspiration. She went upstairs. She pulled out a dozen old empty carrier bags. She found some more old clothes, an old pair of shoes. A pile of the 'New York Post.' She filled the bags up and staggered down with them and pushed them into the cart, around his sides and his feet, one at his head like a pillow and another pressed to his face, some on top of his chest. Now the cart looked authentic, now it looked like the property of a gentleman - or a lady - of no fixed address.

So now that she had perfected the cart her next task was to perfect herself.

LOTTIE

Yes, now she had to perfect herself. She had to turn from elegant Sara Smith who pulled men's eyes, into - the name came out of the blue - into Lottie Fairfax, who had been beaten by her husband and taken to an asylum by a wicked psychiatrist in cahoots with him. But she had escaped and she lived on the streets now, a hard life of quietly suffering dignity. She was free, was Lottie. I want to be free, Steve had said to Sara, that's all I want. He'd said Huckleberry Finn had wanted only to be free. Lottie was free! But oh, those cold winter nights. Whoever said freedom was easy?

Sara's belly loosened and rounded against the jumper so that attractively full Sara Smith was, could it possible be so?, overweight.

Fat! Fat!

Lottie wouldn't fear the directness of the word. She had not been smoothed and cramped by the lies of political correctness. If you were fat you were fat, and Lottie would willingly have called herself fat. She would have called herself plain, too.

As Sara's features collapsed into jowly dowdiness so - she felt it - her skin reddened and dried as if battered by years of wind and rain. Her sight lost some of its sharpness, her focus fogged. She was nearly cross-eyed; not that she saw double but when she looked up nothing quite formed, so for example she could not distinguish individual leaves hanging from the Venetian building, the plant life was one solid blur, a long hanging tongue of greenery.

Her fingers fattened and roughened. Her left hand ached dully, an ever-present familiar ache (though she had never felt it before), an ache wearily and uncomplainingly tolerated. Her arm and leg muscles were strong from pushing the cart all these years. The skin under the soles of her feet was hard and flaky and whitened and unsightly from years of treading, treading, treading these streets. Her legs were slightly bowed from all the walking. When she experimentally walked the cart a few yards forward she noticed that her feet were splayed. She waddled like a duck. She could not stand up straight; always she leaned a little, even when she stood still, even when she sat down exhaustedly on a park bench.

What an amazing creation Lottie Fairfax was. Studied and realized in perfect detail.

What an actress I could have been. I could've been Dame Sara Smith by now if my life had taken a different turn! (She felt a new bitterness against Big Steve her husband, who by marrying her had prevented her discovery of her true talents.) What an actress I would have been! One of the great character players! I would not have been doing the starring roles, and I would not have been a dumb beauty like 'Huck' Steve in the cart, a good-looking boy who had no range and would have found work only because he was so easy on the eye. A shallow kind of actor for a shallow kind of role. No, I would have been quite different - a true character actress, one of those actresses who only get one scene in any particular play or movie. But that scene becomes my own. It would have taken many years for my true greatness to have become apparent to dull-witted critics, of course. When it did...

'Depp does some wonderful work, but in the scenes with Dame Sara Smith he is undoubtedly outshone.'

'Smith's greatness is unmatched, but Miss Redgrave is fairly effective too.'

'The pairing of Smith and Brando is inspired.'

'I had not realized before that the brilliant Sara Smith, so hilarious yet so subtly touching in her comedic performances, could summon such a perfectly judged, indeed profound, illumination of the tragic. Does her talent have no limitations? It would appear it does not.'

Sara lifted her head to an angle and, even in those gray and depressing clothes, those flat slippers, somehow she felt herself royal and commanding. And with just a swing of her hips to the left and the right her complexion cleared up and she was sassy and ready to take Broadway. Or with a puzzled squeezing of her eyelids and a shrinking shyness she was Miss Marple.

These were parts for another time. Now she had to play Lottie.

Lottie Fairfax pushed the cart and it rolled forward, squeak, squeak, squeak. She tried to angle it onto two wheels to silence the squeaks, but the weight it contained made an unbearable strain on her wrists. A stab ran up her aching hand.

She thought it safer to avoid Bleecker Street, so she turned left out of Minetta Lane onto Minetta Street, right past Venice, and up to McDougall. A store on the corner announced WE SALE BALLONS, YELLOW ROSES 2 FOR - but a white label had been stuck over the price. Perhaps all the yellow roses had died. WE OPEN 24 HOURS. This was useless to Lottie who had no money. She stopped at a municipal trash can and peered searchingly into it. There were no recyclable bottles to add to the stash she already had. Up she plodded to 3rd, where buildings owned by New York University ran in all directions. She turned left.

The *Village Psychic* was open for business. Her basement was painted red, red like - red like whose lips? Lottie had not worn makeup in more years than she could count.

She made a point of stopping at each trash can until the frequency of them meant that if she made a show of interest in every single one she'd never get to the water before dawn. So she became selective. A promisingly full one would draw her eyes, or the glitter of crumpled metal against the street light or the green flash of a beer bottle. If a passing stranger looked towards her - they didn't often - she would head straight for the nearest can and thrust her hand greedily into it. She would pluck out, say, a Pepsi can or a Budweiser can and inspect it for a refund. If it promised cash, however little, she would shake it over the sidewalk to spill out the last remaining drops and place it in the cart. She'd waddle on, squeak squeak squeak. The relentless monotony of the un-oiled wheel would have driven Sara Smith crazy, but Lottie had lived with it so long that it hardly broke into her consciousness. She took a right on 6th and passed the Waverly Cinema, then sidled up to West 4th.

Lottie was oddly alert to her surroundings tonight, which she usually was not. She was on edge, she was overly sensitive. Even years on the street could not kill your feelings; you could suppress them for a while, but there were always times when they reminded you how susceptible you were, how vulnerable. Why otherwise would a card store called *Birthday Suite* give her a little chill? She did not know; only Sara knew about the boy in his birthday suit under the blanket. And why was she seized with horror at the name of a bar on the corner of Jones, *The Slaughtered Lamb*? She ran past the bar as fast as her splayed feet and stiffly bent legs would let her. Squeak squeak squeak to the corner of Barrow Street, to the corner of Christopher Park, where two ghostly chalk-white men stood beside a bench apparently talking to each other, almost touching, frozen into utter stillness. Two

191

ghostly chalk-white women sat nearby. Was it the lights that made them look dead as marble, cold as ice? Lottie stopped and looked right at them. They did not move. She tried to focus but they would not solidify. At least they were not looking at her, they were unaware of her it seemed, and yet she felt obliquely that in their frozen stillness they were talking about her, giving away her secrets, giving away secrets indeed that she did not know herself so very secret were they, but which she knew were about her and damning of her. When she ran on again it was with a fear focused enough to bring sweat to her brow and a beating to her heart. She did not look for traffic as she swept her trolley over Christopher Street to continue up 4th, blindly ran, oblivious to a call on her left, a hoot from somewhere. Had she heard a call earlier in the evening, a hoot, a cry? She felt a wash of déjà vu over the front of her brain, the sensation of repeating something she knew had not happened before, and to underlay that a siren shrieked from somewhere not far. Lottie was over the street now, relieved to have her back to the four ghosts who knew too much. The cart shook its contents about as she ran on up 4th, the Coke cans rattled against the mesh.

The pile under the blanket must have shifted a bit, working the tucks loose, because a toe could be seen and the roundness of a buttock.

Lottie stopped the cart outside *Beach Bum Tanning* and covered the boy's bottom, which she did not recognize as such. To her it was a carrier bag stuffed with warm clothes. The toe was a little porcelain squirrel from her childhood. The paint had rubbed away with the years. The figurine caught the street light and glistened freshly. She pulled the blanket over it to keep it warm. Someone walked towards her and looked right at her. Did he know something? Did he spot something in the cart? Or was he looking because the homeless and suffering were interesting to see, like exotic creatures in the wild? He did not slow down, and was

192

soon past her. She froze and listened to his steps and counted them, one *two* three *four* five *six* seven *eight* nine *ten*. He walked with a limp. She turned and watched him. He'd stopped to wait for the light to change. His body was weighted to his right. He must have felt her eyes because he looked back at her and he held her gaze just as she held his. He had a thin, pock-marked face with a small moustache. Lottie smiled kindly, felt the spaces with her tongue where teeth had once been and mourned their loss. He smiled back at her, more edgy than friendly. He had gaps too. The light changed. He crossed. He was very thin, his jeans hung floppy at his narrow rear.

Lottie pushed on into Charles Street. A Townhouse was for sale on the corner, an authentic Brownstone with thick slabs, now paled to a milky coffee colour. Buying a house was so far from Lottie's reality that she did not think to speculate on the price that was being asked. But she stopped the cart and looked up. The higher slabs maintained their chocolaty darkness as the lower had not. Coffee and chocolate. A chocolate cookie dipped into coffee, the chocolate melting enough for the surface to run a little. How delicious chocolate tasted when it was beginning to melt but was still firm, how soft and warm on the tongue. When there was a generous bite of chocolate cookie in the mouth it was lovely to sip some coffee, let it swim over it, let the flavours coalesce, feel the hot liquid soften the chocolate some more. Swallow the coffee and let the cookie sit on the tongue for a moment more, sticky, before it too was swallowed. There were uneven footsteps somewhere near her but her ears were closed to the sound of the street, she was in her childhood home eating a chocolate cookie and drinking coffee. She was sitting by the fire. The only sound was an un-oiled bicycle being ridden past her window. She could not see the bicycle but she could see the boy on top of it, a general shape through the thin white nylon curtains. Squeak squeak squeak.

193

Her brother had a bicycle, she seemed to remember. But this bike did not stop at her house so it couldn't be her brother's, it went on past, squeak squeak squeak past the next house and the next. Her brother kept his bicycle pristine, he oiled it twice a week, he would have been ashamed of a squeaking bicycle. Some people had no standards.

Lottie returned gradually to Charles Street and the Brownstone and reached out to her cart. Her hand clutched air. She reached again and clutched air. She tried to focus on the space where it had been.

It made no sense to her that it should be gone; it was no more logical or plausible than if the brownstone itself had vaporized under her gaze.

The squeak of the bicycle wheels were a long way away; on the corner of 4th and West 11th. She could see a very thin man pushing something. He was trotting. He looked rather silly, he had an inelegant way of running. His jeans flopped loose at his bottom. He was unattractive. But that was not a bicycle he pushed, it had four wheels. Squeak squeak squeak.

When she realized the truth Lottie felt a great crashing plummet of despair in her heart. He had stolen her home, he had stolen all her worldly possessions. She stood there uselessly, wanting to cry. She did not run after him. She stood still and felt the water in her eyes.

She wanted to say to the man, no she wanted to shout it, WHY STEAL OFF ME?? I HAVE NOTHING TO GIVE! THAT IS MY WHOLE LIFE YOU HAVE THERE! SOME WARM CLOTHES AND A PORCELAIN SQUIRREL AND SOME CRACKED SHOES AND BOOTS! Then she wanted to appeal to his humanity. WE ARE BOTH THE SAME, WE ARE BOTH THE LOST, WHY WOULD ONE LOST PERSON TAKE FROM ANOTHER LOST PERSON THEIR EVERYTHING? WHICH IS NOTHING, NOTHING AT ALL! How many women in Greenwich Village had big thick wallets full of

194

dollar bills which would pay for some food, some shelter. Why steal off the only person who doesn't have any bills, doesn't have any shelter. Why me?

Maybe the man took pity, because he stopped the cart stone still. He was shaking. He seemed to be shocked. Perhaps it was the realisation that he had done something terrible, perhaps it was guilt and shame which made him shake so. He shook, but for a while he did not step forward. His head was bowed, he was looking right into the trolley. Finally he did move, a slow uneven stepping backward, hands held out to the trolley as if to push something away, though all he pushed was air. Back he went, a dozen slow paces; then he turned around and looked right across the street at Lottie. He looked at her first with a kind of horror, then -she could not quite read his features, the distance and her poor sight meant she could only make sense of the simplest of expressions, - he seemed to smile at her, not pleasantly, the smile was humourless and stretched, demonic even. When he moved again it was in a spurt, at first it was towards her but when he'd crossed the street he ran up West 10th, away from Lottie, his thin legs flapping one after the other, his legs and feet below the knees angled outward. He looked silly. He had a comic way of running. He had no ass. His jeans could have been stuffed with straw, he could have been a scarecrow.

Lottie was relieved that her cart was safe and sound, also that she had not needed to chase after him, because with her bow legs and her stiff joints she could never have caught him.

(Sara on the other hand was furious. If the cart had been stolen and that repellent creature had been landed with the body it would have been perfect. She would have been Scott free. Even if he'd gone to the police, which she doubted, his description of Lottie Fairfax would never have led them to Sara Smith. More likely, a policeman would have spotted the

195

strange shape in the cart and unveiled poor Steve and looked right into the eyes of the bottomless madman who was his killer. She would have loved him to go to jail for the murder of Steve. It would have served him right. Did they have a death row in New York State? Whatever he'd got, he'd have deserved it for stealing from a defenceless homeless woman.

(Perhaps the cart could be left where he'd dumped it, under the little half-oval balcony of an apartment building. In the morning it'd be found. She'd be snugly in bed by then, catching an extra hour's sleep before preparing for *Make Someone's Day*. It was only the feeling that she'd made a promise to Steve to give him a decent send-off that made her go across to the cart and retrieve it.)

Lottie was relieved to have her home back. She wanted to be sure the man hadn't stolen anything. She put her hand on the blanket and squeezed. The clothes were still there. She pulled back the lower edge to see that her squirrel, too, was still there. It had not been broken. It looked out to her. She covered it up to keep it warm. All was right with the world. She went on down the street, squeak squeak squeak. The squeaks were comforting now, they sang of childhood and an uncomplicated life.

Lottie pushing her cart further down Fourth was not privy to any specific purpose in her choice of direction; she was heading for the river because, well, because she was, she might just as easily have headed uptown (after the gap-toothed man?) or down to the business district and perhaps tomorrow or the next night she would choose one of those. Tonight, no. The river. Why not?

She found herself in a mainly residential district now. A silence unusual for this City was about her. She looked up and down and behind her and in front and did not see a single human being. Some of the apartments had lights on in them, most did not. There were no stirrings in the lighted rooms. She passed a second-hand bookstore, and a

196

Laundromat - 'wash, dry and fold' - which drew her eye because it was brightly lit even at this time and because she would have liked to wash and dry and fold her own clothes. As if in compensation, she leant to the blanket and smoothed away the little wave-like folds, which reminded her of a painting of a storm-tossed, white-foamed sea. Just as she did so, she smelt for the first time the richness of the Hudson itself. She was on the corner of 8th Avenue and Jane Street. She looked down Jane. Manhattan was falling gradually to the water and she could see the river in its blackness, out beyond it the unlovely outline of New Jersey. The street she crossed was itself called Hudson, as if it were a gateway to the water itself. The eighteen forbidding stories of 61 Jane Street shadowed her. Surely someone in there, looking through one of the dozens of windows, would see her below? But would they think twice about a batty bow-legged woman and her shopping cart full of clothes? If they did think twice, then they wouldn't think a third time: There was nothing to think beyond the stark fact that a homeless person was passing.

The surface of Jane Street ceased to be asphalt, was transformed into row upon row of bricks laid right into the road, perhaps to slow drivers down. Lottie passed onto this new, uneven surface. The squeak of one wheel was chorused by the clonk-clonk-clonk of the others. She felt a pinch of fear, the clonk-clonk bouncing off the walls, announcing her coming. After a few hundred yards she became aware of staring eyes. From a first floor window a pale but shadowed face, long and distinguished, looked right at her harshly, with full comprehension of her guilt. It was a haughty face. It was patrician. It was a face which was used to giving instructions and having them obeyed. She had the urge to push her cart on as fast as she could but something in the face made her stop. There was an unlit candle to one side of it, and on the other side a small American flag, which she saw

197

was propped against the face. The eyes were completely blind; more, they were completely blank. It was a bust which Lottie did not recognize as the head of Jefferson, though the flag told her it was a figure of patriotism from the past. With the candle and the flag it looked prepared for some strange ritual. Perhaps it was a sort of private ritual of the house's resident, the flame lighting the face in a cleansing ritual, a post-September 11th ritual of strength, of pride, a ceremony ensuring that, as America had not fallen before, so it would not crumble now. Lottie wished the candle was lit so she could see the face better. It would be rather beautiful. She felt a small uplift of love for her country somewhere in her chest. She wanted to hum the National Anthem.

Where had Lottie been on that terrible morning? She could not remember clearly. It was over a year ago. She did remember the palpable adjustment in the City's atmosphere. She did remember the way people were different afterwards, sadder, politer. They were more generous with their spare change. She did remember her own mounting horror when somehow - an overheard conversation? A page in a newspaper left on a bench? - she found out that something evil had taken place. She did remember not going further down the island than Penn Station for weeks afterwards. She gave Jefferson a small bow and moved on. She felt a deep connection with her fellow beings. She hoped they felt a connection with her.

She rolled on, clonk-clonk-clonk-squeak.

Outside an apartment house, behind a half-built wall, a small pile of bricks awaited the return of the builder and the finishing of his work. Lottie stopped her trolley and admired the bricks. They were a deep, rich red. She went around the wall and picked up one of the loose bricks. It was heavy. She felt the strain on her wrist. It was a beautiful brick. She turned it around in her hand. She placed it in her cart. Why? It was a pleasing object. It would provide company for the

198

squirrel. Then she took another. Now there were three friends sitting next to each other in the corner of her cart.

Rattle rattle rattle went her cart down Jane. How it shook. Squeak squeak squeak went the wheel. Tink tink tink went the cans against the mesh. Not far to go now. There was a smell of salt. An odd smell of salt. Why should a river smell so strongly of salt? Rattle rattle rattle. Clonk clonk clonk. Squeak squeak squeak. Tink tink tink. The squeaking wheel cut through a pile of dog droppings on the corner of Greenwich. No more than a yard from it a sign on a trash can said,

KEEP NEW YORK CITY CLEAN
DOG LITTER
PUT IT HERE

Well, the droppings were in the general vicinity she supposed. Over Greenwich, the surface of Jane Street continued, inlaid with brickwork. Clonk clonk clonk. The properties got nicer and nicer. Everything was sleepy. Who would have thought it in New York? One would almost have called it a leafy suburb had there been any actual leaves. Spiritually at least it was leafy.

She squeaked-tinked-rattled over Washington. Had the bust been of General Washington, she wondered? But in that famous painting had his face not been fuller, rounder? But who else would it be, here near Washington Street? Yes, it must have been Washington: who could not tell a lie.

She was on the final stretch now. The leafy suburban quiet fell into the arms of New York noise. Traffic sped across the highway at the foot of Jane where suddenly she was. A twenty-four hour parking lot was on her left, the *Hotel Riverview* with its *Jane Street Theatre*, a plaque proudly announcing the date of its construction: AD 1907. Pride comes before a fall, and the *Hotel Riverview* was empty and

199

silent. All those windows with their wonderful views of the water were blank as dead eyes. No doubt soon it would be razed to the ground or turned into hair-raisingly pricey apartments, but for the moment it was allowed to stay uselessly there, twenties flappers now phantoms of its decline.

She went to the curb and waited for a break in the traffic on West 12th. A large green sign hung across the Highway: *Meat Market exit 4*. Meat. Somehow this word disturbed her. She looked back at the blank windows of the *Riverview* and to the *Meat Market* sign and these seemed to be saying something. She experienced as a definite sensation a softening in her mind. *No!* said Lottie firmly to herself as if the hardness of the thought would stop the softening, no, they are saying nothing. A green sign cannot speak, a building cannot be dead, it can only be empty. Of course, the callous and ignorant think anyone who lives out of a shopping trolley must be crazy, must hear voices all and everywhere, but I am not crazy, I'm sane, and I do not delude myself that a building can tell me stuff.

Yet she did think some obscure message was being given to her, so she turned back to the road with a sharp switch of the head which made her neck creak. She did not want to stand here with the *Riverview* right behind her, it unnerved her. She ran a few yards down West away from the hotel and the *Meat Market* sign.

There was a traffic light and she pressed the button and waited for the WALK signal. She darted across.

She was at the river. Jersey looked over at her.

It was not threatening. It was indifferent. The night felt colder. She was tired.

Five wooden benches sat facing not out to the water but inland to Jane and the *Superior Ink Company* with its oddly out-of-place thick high-reaching smokestack. An industrial chimney in Manhattan seemed as strange as a skyscraper in the Sahara, but there it was, solid and real. (Was it? Yes.) And here were five benches arranged so that it could be viewed by admiring passers-by! Why? Why would anyone want to view it when there was the water behind them? It made no sense to Lottie, who however dropped onto one of the benches. Her bones ached. She felt so very tired that the cold would not keep her from sleep. Nothing would keep her awake. She pulled the cart towards her and parked it right beside the bench so that she could reach out to it for reassurance at any time. Why would there be an industrial chimney at the, the what the superior meat company perhaps they roasted meat in it for sale in uptown delicatessens do I smell roasting meat I think I do and why is it salted I'm sure it is I can smell salt yes salt beef I like salt beef it's a pity cows had to die but the cycle of nature means we all have to die but not yet I want a hot salt beef sandwich please with pickles we all have to die but not yet I still have a few good years in me yet - and she reached out for reassurance to her cart - with all my worldly goods my clothes my bottles and cans to get me a little money I do not need much just enough for some food a hot salt beef sandwich with pickle my but its smoky in here...

Her head fell forward and her eyes closed.

BOB

Sara was delighted to let Lottie sleep. The poor woman would not have to see what was to happen next. Sara rose, with great caution so as not to disturb her by her side and she put her hands around the handle of the cart and wheeled it away from the sleeping woman, slowly slowly, the duff wheel squeaking a little, through the break in the semi-circle of benches past some raised flower beds to the railing overlooking the river. Benches positioned for taking in a more obviously appealing view than the Ink Company ran in a long row away from her. Lottie did not stir.

Sara wished Lear had not stirred, because then things would have been all right for him. She would have returned the cart to him as soon as she'd finished with it. She breathed in deeply to feel her lungs pressed against her rib cage and to lift her breasts into their dignified ample presence.

You're still a looker, you are Sara, you're still a bloody attractive woman.

She stopped the cart, handle touching the railings. Behind her the road buzzed with traffic.

On the water broken discs of light thrown by tall green street lamps rose and fell lapping against the stone walls. The greenness of the lamps tossed her back into deep-past time for a second, to memories of the lamps of Brighton on the coast of England, where she had spent childhood vacations.

The circles of light lay on a sheet of inky blackness, black as the ink the factory had made. The water was far down, the wall high. A cluster of wooden posts broke the surface on her left. Perhaps once they'd been the struts of a pier. Further down new piers thrust into the river like sharp tongues. A rich smell of salt came from somewhere. On her right was an enclosed children's play area with, at its rim, the pretend deck of a pretend ship, wheel and all; beyond it, a vast brightly lit warehouse projected onto the water. Trucks were parked in its driveway.

Over the water, New Jersey shone like a depressed gin palace. Lights, lights, lights, all around her, lights. At least no people, no witnesses.

A black shapeless form far down the sidewalk floating here and there like a cloak on the wind coalesced into three, no four, very loud and drunken men. She stood quite still and clutched the cart, waiting for them to pass. The drunk men stopped at the nearest pier and sat on benches and made remarks to each other which elicited snorty laughter no doubt out of all proportion to the quality of the jokes. Eventually they moved towards Sara. One of them waved and said, "Hi, honey," with lewd intent, which came out as hiii, unna, almost 'hyena' so the fat ugly laugh that came after it was appropriate. His eyes were drunkenly heavy-lidded. How very much like Steve in his death sleep he looked, his eyes scarcely able to focus, his effort to meet her own stopping in the vicinity of her nose without quite reaching it. His friends let out gasps of appreciation at his wit through their nostrils. A small clump of snot came out from one of them with the laughter, landing on the arm of a friend's jacket. The snot-maker thought this uproarious, and so did his friend, unaware that his jacket had been soiled.

They turned at the crossing and pressed the button.

Sara hoped they would not wake Lottie.

203

They didn't wait for the light to change in their favour, but with the luck of the undeserving they staggered safely across and went up Jane in a spray of giggles.

Now Sara was alone.

She looked up and down. The bright light from the warehouse disturbed her.

She flipped back the blanket, exposing Steve's feet. Sara was not prepared to allow feelings to interfere with her necessary task. She flicked her head away from what she could see of the body, squeezed her eyes closed and pursed her lips far forward, and thus steeled she looked back and drew the blanket right off him and, just as cool as if she were taking a hunk of meat from the freezer, she went round to the handle and reached out towards his head. His eyes had opened again, but just as the drunken man had been unable to focus on her, neither could Steve. His head was inclined towards stars.

She tucked her hands under his armpits and pulled. He moved an inch. The cart rolled. The handle pressed heavily into her chest. She p-u-l-l-e-d. Steve rose towards her. She veered him over her left shoulder. His nose brushed her ear, which she would once have found sexy. His body was not as pliable as it had been. His weight forced her left side down, her right lifting in compensation. Then his back slid smoothly over her. As if out of modesty he turned over, rolling down her arm, so she could not see his penis. She folded her elbow into a cradle and caught him. His torso craned downward, his feet still in the cart. His knees hooked into the space between the back of the cart and the handle so when she pulled on him again the cart came too. She cursed his knobbly knees.

Then she saw how they could be useful. She let the cart come with him. She lifted him up. He stretched out horizontally, level with the railing. She drew his head and neck over it. She rested him on the railing just below his nipples. He formed a bridge between the river and the cart.

She stood away from the boy and breathed in. Steve's head gazed down into a halo of light on the Hudson, his torso angled towards the water. She saw with distaste that little squares had been pressed into his side where his flesh had lain against the trolley's mesh.

He slid forward and the front wheels lifted, but his knees, locked into the space under the handle, stopped him sliding out.

She picked up first one brick and then the other, and knotted a corner of the blanket around them. She tugged the knot three times. She twisted another corner of the blanket and wrapped it tightly around Steve's right ankle. She pulled on it and his foot lifted and dropped and lifted like a responsive marionette. She tugged again but she used more strength than she meant, so his right knee unhooked. He slid to an angle like a gliding plane: he lay on the railing at a diagonal, one shoulder, a nipple, his chest, pressed on cool iron.

She sprang around the carriage and, cradling him, she pushed him with the flat of her spare hand, hard. He slid towards the water. His arms flopped over the railings. He looked like a slow-motion diver He did not plummet, just slid slowly forward until his torso went over the railing and his bottom followed and then his thighs.

And he stopped, absolutely still, in a pyramidal shape, not at all beautiful. Sad and humiliated.

He slid again and his lower legs and feet passed across the railing. All of him, over the railing, swinging. His tummy rubbed against the wall. She hoped it was not grazing him. Poor grazed boy! It was a graze that had brought them together all those many years ago as it now seemed to Sara, who in the pitch of night with the sleeping woman a few feet away and the sound of traffic had lost all sense of time.

205

But he did not fall. Sara looked back to the cart. The bricks had lodged in the space under the handle. There was a period of near stillness, broken only by his pendulum swing.

But for the first time the drag of the boy's weight had the advantage over the cart and the front wheels lifted high like a bucking horse, the bricks dislodged, flew over the rail and the boy fell. After the slowness came the speed of his final descent. A hand scraped against the river wall but the wrapped bricks, flying over his head out to the blackness, jerked him over and spun him. The blanket tautened. It looked like an alien seabird flying to the moon with its prey. It's unwrapping, thought Sara with a terrible shock. But the knots at both ends tightened, Steve's hands and legs splayed until he hit the river flat and displaced a fountain of water all around him which formed an outline of his body like a ginger bread man. The water fell back onto him and he was submerged. The bricks dropped under him, pulling him upright. The top half of his body rose over the water, his reflection falling in a yellow disc of light. He looked like a royal playing card. Then he followed the bricks swiftly downward, his head was engulfed by river water and he disappeared into the deep.

A series of expanding circles were the only clue that the river had taken a victim.

'Take me to the river, wash me down,

Cleanse my soul, put my feet on the ground.'

Goodbye, Steven. I will pray for you.

She noticed the strong smell of salt again. Had his body dislodged salt far below, sending it to the surface like a shaken snow globe? Was that possible? How deep was the Hudson anyway? The saltiness worried her. It reminded her of sex which reminded her of life. It reminded her of condiments, the shaking of salt and pepper over her Sunday roast when she had been a girl. She missed Sunday roasts. They were a great English tradition. Roast beef and horseradish sauce, Yorkshire pudding and roast potatoes. Thick rich gravy and just two shakes of salt and two of pepper.

She pulled herself back to the river. She felt a terrible emptiness beneath her heart. Like hunger but not precisely a physical thing, something abstract and unpleasant which could not so easily be sated as a craving for food.

For Christ's sake, girl! None of this nonsense! You should be pleased! You've given him a decent send-off. You've got yourself out of a hole. Everything is finished now, you can get back to normal. None of these silly adventures with randy untrustworthy boys. You were a fool, and you've been given a second chance so take it, girl, take it! Back to *Make Someone's Day* in the morning, back to *Mulligan's* tomorrow night.

Her boring ordinary life no longer seemed quite so awful as it very recently had. There was something to be said for boring and ordinary after all. Perhaps she would make a pass at Eddie one night when his wife was away, just for old times' sake. She longed to feel his heaviness on her, his moustache itchy against her cheek.

She turned away from the river and looked first across West 12th, then South down the sidewalk. A shape emerged from the blackness and under a street lamp it was clearly distinguishable as a couple, a man and a woman, hand in hand. They were talking. They came past the nearest pier and at the underwater forest of wooden pillars they stopped and looked out to - not to the water but across to New Jersey. They leaned against the railing. The man put his arm around the woman's waist. She put her arm around his. It was a beautiful image of love. Sara felt jealous. With his free hand the man pointed to a building on the horizon, perhaps the office building where he worked. The woman nodded and pointed somewhere else. He nodded in his turn. They fell silent. They were as close to each other as it was possible

207

to be. They were madly in love, it was obvious. Sara followed their sightline. New Jersey looked attractive to her now as it never had before.

A disturbance in the water pulled her eyes down.

At the edge of a yellow disc the dark night water was lightened by a different glow, pinkish like rose petals. At first it was just a vague colouring of the water, expanding and thickening until it was a clear bright island bobbing on the surface.

She could see the tracery of Steve's spine.

Then his hair surfaced, the nape of his neck, arms and hands stretched beyond.

Then his legs and feet.

He looked very relaxed.

You silly cow, Sara! If you'd only tied it tighter! Oh my God! What am I going to do?

Waves swirled Steve around to her, towards the wall, and his head brushed, softly, the sheer solidity ten feet below her.

Sara snapped her head to the couple. They were gazing out to New Jersey. She snapped her head to the warehouse. No sign of life there.

Away! Away! I must get away!

She ran from the sight of the boy. She did not wobble as Lottie had done, but then she was not bow-legged as Lottie was. Still, her fastest was not very fast and she'd barely started when she felt pressure in her lungs. She cursed her lack of regular exercise. She ran up to the warehouse. She noticed but paid no attention to the sign on the gate leading to it:

NYC SALT STORAGE FACILITY

She swept into the road, across all four lanes. Perhaps, like those drunken men, she was lucky because she was an undeserving case.

208

She ran north and, meaning to swerve into Jane which was actually behind her she turned instead into Horatio. She felt the beating of her heart. Her legs wanted to give under her. When had she last moved faster than a quick walk? She was ashamed of her lack of fitness. She felt old and useless. She was forty-five. She might as well have been seventy. Her knees did not want to rise above her thighs. They complained each time they shot up. All the oxygen in her body rushed to her heart and limbs, leaving none for her mind. A sensation of wishy-washiness came to her both inside and out. She felt her brain knock against her skull and saw the road itself flow up and down like the river. When she stood, nearly fell, against a wall to catch her breath she scraped a knuckle. At least Steve was not conscious to feel his body knocking on stone, less like a boy than a buoy. She could feel everything. The hardness at her back, the up-and-down movement of the road which could not be happening but which made her lose her balance so it must be, the blood pumping as fast as it could which was not fast enough. She had always imagined a heart attack would feel this way; perhaps she was experiencing a heart attack. She slid down, and landed hard on her bottom. Pressed to the wall like that, failing to find a focal point, she could have been, to a passer-by, the wretched old vagrant she had tried to become. And there were footsteps: so someone was near her. She spotted a shadow diving across Horatio and disappearing into the city. Why would a shadow come to her, after all, a useless broken old meths drinker like her?

She could not focus. No-one in New York could focus, it seemed, everyone was cross-eyed. The whole world was out of focus. Was it because of September 11th? The big wide world had lost its focus and the individual human creature in some metaphysical act of sympathy could not focus either, chose perhaps not to focus because to see too clearly the streets of the city or the negotiations of the wide world, to focus was to see only horror. Better the world be blurred. Did people drink more after September 11th? Had someone done a survey that showed everyone was depressed and wanted to be drunk to shake away the truth, whatever the truth might be? It was like the whole world was drunk. Not happily drunk. Not party drunk. Mean drunk. Sweaty three-in-the-morning I-hate-my-parents I-hate-my-life throwing-stones-at-stranger's-windows-God-it's-too-fucking-dark-in-here-let-me-out-let-me-out-let-me-out drunk. The world was intoxicated with some powerful lethal drug which brought out all its bitterness and hatred, which made it rage at all and everything. Sara wandered if she herself had become more bitter after that day. Would Steve be alive today if September 11th had not occurred? Why had this beautiful boy had to die? Was there some malevolent fate that decided all innocence, all beauty, all goodness, must now be embittered or smashed? These spinning thoughts were like the circles of black water on the river. In and out they swirled. Bigger and smaller.

Did she fall unconscious for a moment? Certainly she was aware, while simultaneously unaware, of a total, eerie silence impossible to find on the streets of New York anywhere at any time. No traffic, no footsteps, no calls, not even the soughing of wind. Not even the lapping of water. Not even the bobbing of a floating body touching stone and touching stone and touching stone, a brush with the hair, a run of limp fingers, the back of a heel. Touching so lightly and then not touching and touching so exquisitely lightly again. Touching with that aching tenderness of first time lovers before the fucking turned them animal. As one can be touched by the gaze of beautiful eyes, as Sara had been touched by those eyes which were like the sky looking down. As dead eyelids can be brushed by lips that mourn their deadness but are gentle too so as not to awaken. Sssshhhh…. Like a butterfly on petals. Ssshhh… like the lashes of a sleeping child the lower and the upper gossamer-webbed together. Sssshhh... the ashes in the grate sooty and silent lifted by a breeze and twirling a fairy dance and dropping to place once more. Sssshhhh... An old woman on a bench who has given up her ghost with such perfect ease you could not doubt she'd wake again... but not yet... let her rest awhile...

Old women. Lonely old women. Lonely women who were not old. Lonely men. All the loneliness of the human creature. The human creature in her quiet abandonment like the woman in the wedding dress whose cake had long since been eaten by rats but who still believed that her man would some day return and if he didn't, which he wouldn't because that would break the loneliness which as if by some supernatural directive was not ever to be broken, if he didn't then the loneliness itself in its festering and its bitterness would take the place of comfort as a parasite which fed off it but kept it alive and gave it a reason to exist, eventually the only good reason perhaps for any existence. Loneliness told you you were alive. Bitterness was palpable like meat.

How long did she sit there squatting against the wall? Did she lose consciousness and drift away? She knew she was lodged somewhere between sleep and waking, but not how far into sleep itself she went: that she knew something suggests she did not go all the way. And as always in that strange space she did not know of the passing of time. She couldn't distinguish between the passing of a minute and the passing of an hour. She did not recognize such concepts. All she knew was the eerie silence and then the breaking of it with what at first sounded like the beating of a heart and then the beating of a thousand hearts and then like footsteps in rhythm, marching footsteps from somewhere, (she looked about her which suggests she was somewhat awake,) somewhere out of sight, behind her perhaps but she could not twist her neck around because it ached. Lying against the wall had made it ache maybe. And when she put her hand to the wall to help her stand up pain shot through the small of her back. She had been sitting, legs pulled into her body so that her knees touched her breasts, at a funny angle and her back had passively accepted it until asked to shift. Then it let out a silent scream. Ow! She rubbed her back with the flat of her palm. My God, she felt she was a hundred.

She was at the corner of the meat packing district. She looked down towards the dealers' outlets. They were dark and silent; the ground was slick where it had been hosed down. There was a strong smell of meat. A big sign over one of the warehouses said

Imaggio Beef Corp.
Wholesale beef, lamb
Pork Poultry Provisions
Variety Meats

What was variety meat, she wondered? Was it cheap bits of meat, all pressed together to make sausages and franks and cat foods and dog foods?

It was very cold. She might have been in a freezer room. She wrapped her arms around her for warmth. She took one step forward, then another, then another, slippers slapping click on the ground, their echoes fuzzing against the walls and countless metal doors.

Did she hear a sound, like distant castanets? Trucks sat silently around. Meat businesses surrounded her, wherever she turned. *Bell and Evans* sold 'the excellent chicken.' *New York's Complete restaurant Supplier* served, it insisted, 'the finest restaurants'. *Royal Corp.* Had its specialties too. It sold

VEAL	LAMB
NATURE VEAL	IMPORTED LAMB
CHOICE VEAL	BOXED LAMB
BOB VEAL	FRESH LAMB

212

And it reassured its customers that it had COMPLETE PORTION CONTROL – FABRICATED CUTS.

Looking up at this sign Sara realized that though she ate meat of one sort or another every day the language of the butchery business was alien to her, like the language of computers. She was in a strange, cold, alien, violent world. What was Nature Veal, and was there an Un-nature Veal? What, or who, was Bob Veal? Was he a cartoon calf used as cartoon chickens were used to encourage the eating of more chicken? Did Bob have big cute eyelashes like that wretched Minnie Mouse, those sweet appealing eyes intended to send you to the butcher to buy the bodies of Bob's own brethren? "I'm delicious! Eat me!" "More! I'm cute *and* delicious! Eat me! Taste my flesh! Taste my blood! " And as cows were all girls why had they chosen a boy as their mascot? Perhaps because the girls had all been slaughtered, only the boys were available for promotional purposes.

The sound like drumming heartbeats re-emerged from behind her. She spun but there was nothing to see except blank-faced buildings. She spun again. Nothing. But the heartbeats continued, they intensified, they drew nearer, or were there more of them? She turned around and around, making four complete circles. She felt dizzy and wanted to collapse but she firmed her leg muscles. Perhaps the heartbeats were overhead? But there was nothing but darkness overhead, darkness and little yellow discs which the lights of the city made faint. Perhaps the heartbeats were underground. She looked down. There was nothing to see but the paving and the trickles of liquid from hosing.

But the trickles were not water. They were reddish. The hose had not successfully washed away all the blood.

If the sounds had been under her feet, they would have had a bounced, bulbous quality like laugher in a bath house. No, these sounds were at street level. But they weren't floating on the open air. They weren't lifted to her from over roofs, they were issuing from an enclosure, tinny and muffled in their beat, beat, beat. They grew so loud you'd have thought they'd wake the neighbourhood, you'd have thought all of Manhattan would be opening windows, wondering what in hell that loud rhythmic pulse was, was it another invasion? Sara clapped her hands over her ears. This did not mute the noise, it was as if it were inside her own head and could not be muffled, though her ears told her it was outside, her eardrums hurt, she felt a painful electric buzz. Beat beat beat beat. Imagined sounds do not cause earache.

Several of the buildings had huge metal doors like fire stations, for letting trucks in and out, and one of these doors began to open, rolling upward. Its bottom lip lifted away from the ground, the beating sound escaped under it, redoubling its loudness. Sara saw row upon row of booted feet waiting in line as the door rose, very slowly. The boots were rising and falling in perfect unity like soldiers, up and down and up and down, marching on the spot. Up and down and up and down, big black boots hitting the ground. Thirty of them right at the front, fifteen pairs of feet, and fifteen more pairs behind, and behind fifteen more. She squatted and the rows went as far back into the building as she could see. Up and down and up and down and up and down went the countless feet. Up up up went the door, rising painfully slowly as if for heightened dramatic impact.

There were countless men in ordered rows in army uniforms. They did not have guns. Their arms were held stiffly to their sides. Their legs lifted and dropped in the marching rhythm. The door rose over their heads. They stayed on the spot, marching, marching, marching, not going anywhere.

Marching, marching.

Sara looked right into the face of a man at the front.

It was not human.

It was animal.

214

It was like a young cow. The body was human and (as far as she could tell) male, but the head was more cow-like than bull-like. It made no sense. Sara's eyes flowed across the front row. All of them had calves' heads. They weren't masks, they didn't have that plastery look, but nor did they seem quite real. It might have been the long cute eyelashes that gave them so artificial an expression. Like Minnie. Like Mickey. Like a sentimentalized projection of animal life. Their big eyes designed to be appealing. They weren't merely painted on as on some cheap Halloween mask, they were convincingly deep and 'realistic' but they seemed neither to receive nor to give out any light. Perhaps they were blind. Perhaps they were false, made of glass or something. None of those eyes rolled towards her, though she was directly in their sight line.

She looked down to their chests. The words BOB VEAL ran under a cartoon drawing of a calf - a cow or bull calf, whatever it was - which smiled out into the world. Then the sound of marching like beating hearts was joined by some other noise.

Music. Cheap music.

A tinkly tune.

It came from behind her and she swung around. Bang in the middle of the district sat a carousel, unmoving. It was colourful and brightly lit, with a dark red painted base. White wooden horses ran into circular eternity on it, black staffs running vertically through their bodies. They were oddly thin horses. Their front legs were lifted up. Their back legs were attached to the carousel floor. A Bob stood in the middle of the carousel and switched it on. It began to spin, slowly at first and then faster. Several Bobs leapt onto it, regardless of the danger, and clambered onto the white-painted horses. The carousel spun and spun, the horses ran into circular eternity, it spun and spun faster and faster, impossibly fast, until there were strips of colour on the air, reds and yellows

215

and golds and whites. It was like a circular rainbow. It tinkled out a tune which became faster and faster with the spin of carousel until it was a single high tinny shriek.

At the bottom of the carousel a thick scarf of red spinning and spinning and spinning flew off its axis and unfurled in Sara's direction. She ducked. It went over her head and hit the ground near the open doorway. Further red scarves unfolded after it, for a moment like thick wool and then thinner like cotton and then sheer like silk. Each scarf sprayed into strands, flowering like gushes from a fountain. Wetness. Splashed to the ground, flowed in rivulets, into the open building, towards Horatio Street, floods of deep dark red. Floods.

The little rivers had the consistency of beef blood. The rich smell of meat thickened in Sara's nostrils. Gushes spurted over her, splashing the ground and walls and trucks and Sara herself. The meat district was a shallow sticky pool of - blood? Sara dipped a finger into the flood running over her shoes and smelt it.

Yes, it was blood.

Blood. Blood.

She did not scream. No, she did not feel any particular horror. More a fascination, she was quite calm and scientific. Blood, how interesting.

The carousel slowed. Before it had stopped, the Bobs were climbing off their horses and jumping onto solid ground. They made quiet mooing noises to each other, indicating enjoyment. As they moved away there was a sucking sound, boots on sticky fluid. Until only the controller Bob was at the carousel. The machine spun very slowly now. The music had slowed too, a normal merry tinkle. The carousel stopped. The music tinkled happily on. Tinkle tinkle tinkle like an ice cream van.

Sara looked up at the horse nearest her.

It was not a horse at all. Not quite.

216

It was not a cow either, or a bull.

It was a kind of twisted human being.

A naked, white-painted twisted human being with blank eyes which did not have corneas, were outlines like on a marble sculpture. Above and below the eyes ran long thin strips of black, six above each eye and six below, the stylized eyelashes of the Bobs, of Minnie Mouse, of Daisy Duck.

It was Steve's face. His narrow, boyish, beautiful face. A drop of sculpted hair hung over one eye. His body impaled on the black shaft. Angled as he had been between the shopping trolley and the river wall, frozen, falling but never hitting the ground.

Still Sara did not feel anything as clear and clean as fear. The horror she felt was not at the impaled boy himself. Or the impaled boys themselves, each of the horses being the same representation of Steve. No, it was not this that bothered her. It was the long cute lashes. It clarified what she had always felt, that the cuteness was an insult to real, lived life, that just as the figures on the carousel were an insult to Steve, so Bambi was an insult to the real living feeding rutting shitting deer of the forest, so Pluto was an insult to the smelly needful subservience of an actual dog, that in these images there was something reductive of life. It was the neutralizing of experience, the turning of blood and flesh and sex and death into nothing, neutral, heart-warming deadness. Even death itself, the warmth turning cold, was knotted up with actual lovely dirty life. These bloodless pencil-made creations were not death. They were nothingness. They were limbo. They were un-livingness. They were barrenness.

The controller Bob joined his brothers in the open warehouse where they resorted to their on-the-spot marching. This continued for a moment before the front row pealed off and headed towards one of the trucks. Controller Bob opened the back doors. Several Bobs

217

climbed aboard. There was a scuffling sound, then they re-emerged, huge joints of frozen meat wrapped in plastic, carried over their shoulders like guns.

They marched back to the warehouse. Rows of thick lethal hooks hung from the ceiling. Controller Bob pressed his joint of meat onto the hook over his head. The hook pierced it and it hung, waving from side to side until it settled. The others hooked their own joints. They gathered into marching formation and went into the back of the warehouse. All the other Bobs stepped forward to give them room to reform their row at the back. The joints rose into the ceiling, out of Sara's sight.

The next row of Bobs marched out and went to the truck and shortly came out with meat on their shoulders, which they hooked as the first row had done. They took their positions at the back and the Bobs stepped forward a place to accommodate them. The third group marched to the truck. The fourth, the fifth, the sixth. All the time the crass music-box tinkling continued behind the kneeling woman. Not once in their back and forth did any of them look to Sara or discern her presence in any way.

The seventh row. Any ordinary freezer truck would long before have been emptied of its stock but this one contained it seemed an infinite supply of joints. The seventh formation didn't have to go deeper into the truck than the first. Perhaps the joints hung from a circular conveyer system, each new batch being moved mechanically to the front. But how many batches could one truck hold? Not this many.

Sara gradually became aware of a stickiness on her left knee. She looked down. She was kneeling in a rivulet of blood. Her knee was a sort of island round which the river parted, flowing back together on the other side just as the Mississippi parted to pass an encumbrance, an island, a sunken river boat, a floating house, to merge then back into one. The Mississippi which Steve had perceived as an escape to freedom, a metaphysical Mississippi which brought you to the territory, to paradise. Sara had a sharp sudden insight: life was the Mississippi rolling into the blackness; the head of the river was death, that was the freedom, the paradise to which you came. The stream at her knee was Steve's river away from the constraints and rules of civilization.

Sara wanted to escape too. She wanted to find her own steamship to take her away from New York, away from the meat district and the Bobs, away from the Disney Corporation and her boring life in a card shop. Away from memories of Steve who at the same time she knew she did not want to forget. She wanted to be with him. But she wouldn't be with him, not at the end of any river to anywhere.

The eighth line of Bobs went to the trucks, like robotic labourers. They were like slaves. But they did not mean her any harm and she decided she did not mean them any harm. There was not even fear to keep her there.

She stood. Her left knee was damp. She turned away from the warehouse.

The carousel had vanished.

But still the music played.

Turning a corner she came to more warehouses and, located between two of them, an art gallery. Who while buying their meat also buys art? She knew, and Lottie had seen, that the surrounding area was being spruced up for wealthy residents, and yet she did not think wealthy residents would select their artworks within sniffing reach of butchery. Perhaps the butchers themselves used the galleries. Somewhere they must have homes of their own with bare white walls. But how many paintings would they buy, and how much would they spend on them? You could buy nice paintings in Ikea for forty dollars. You did not need to go to a posh art gallery. Perhaps they were super sensitive, those butchers, passed their lunch hours weeping over the beauty

219

of a perfectly captured sculpture of the human form, an accurate still life of a lily.

Yet would not the rich scents of meat infiltrate and linger in the canvasses? Would it not cause the frames to curl just as excessive heat was supposed to do? Perhaps they would get used to the smell, not notice it any more, as Germans, it was said, had once got used to great amounts of dust in their curtains.

She gazed into the art gallery. There were a number of paintings on easels, and in the window the white sculpted figure of a male ballet dancer, one hand over the head, one leg standing on point, the other up and out, foot in its ballet shoe inclining gracefully to the ground, the other leg. It was a lovely sculpture. The outlines of the torso were perfectly delineated; the legs were in close-fitting tights that outlined their musculature.

The face.

She looked closer into it.

The face was... no, it wasn't, not quite. It wasn't quite Steve. That would have been an impossible coincidence, the stuff of dreams and Sara was not dreaming. She shook her head to confirm this, felt her hair brush her cheek, felt the ache at her knee, these things of physical earth-bound reality which dream states could not reproduce. The sculpted face was wider, the nose was a bit longer, the hair a bit shorter. The body was better developed. And for all Steve's love of dance and his ambition for it he could not have been a ballet dancer in a million years.

The figure began to spin very slowly as if it were the dancer atop a music box, and she put her ear to the glass and realized that it was from here the tinkle-tinkle music was now issuing. Perhaps it always had been. Could such a small, mean sound muffled by a sheet of glass have passed so forcefully around the meat district? Now she could scarcely hear it, she had to press her ear against the glass to distinguish the individual notes.

One of the paintings was of the Jersey shore, from Manhattan. It was a good painting. The reflections from the street lamps were perfectly realised, the blackness of the water, the outline of the buildings opposite. The effect was spoilt by a pinkish blur on the water near the foreground. It was as if the artist had spilt some pink paint onto his canvas, and though he had painted it over a faint discolouration had seeped through.

She stepped away from the gallery.

I must go home. I feel very tired. I need to sleep. I need a long, long sleep. She walked with stately purpose past more warehouses until the meat market with its Bobs and its smells was at her back, and before she was aware of it she was on the corner of Ninth and everything was familiar, not because she knew this particular place, familiar in kind. She felt her heels, sore, rubbed with all that walking. She looked down and did not recognize her outfit. Why would she who took such pride in her looks have put on these appalling, dowdy clothes? Why was she wearing these uncomfortable flat slippers and not an elegant pair of shoes? No wonder her feet hurt.

Traffic passed. Three yellow cabs sped past one after the other. She crossed the street. She was back in safe territory.

So why, now, back in this world of normalcy, should she suddenly feel a monstrous, gut-wrenching terror? It ran right through her. It plummeted from the top of her brain to her sore feet, an onrush of wind through all the caverns of her mind and her body, like falling a hundred stories. Then it rose, as if her fear itself had taken physical form and was being shot out of a cannon, it rose so far that she thought it would burst through the bone of her skull, but it didn't, it slapped against the casing and fell back down again, equally fast.

221

She toppled backward. Did she fall against a wall? Or did she land on the sidewalk? She didn't know. But now her elbows ached too. And the bottom of her spine. Soon all of her would be one huge ache!

SARA

She awoke to the ordinary sounds of the City, breaking, muffled, through her thick curtains which made her room for a second or two before her eyes adjusted as black as Guinness and then as murky gray as a headache. She reached out to her alarm clock. It was ten fifty-eight. A motorbike set off from somewhere not far from her. Perhaps from Venice. A quantity of children's voices came from over some roofs, playground noises. A church clock rang the hour in deep rich chimes and when it fell quiet another chimed from another direction, higher and less authoritative, as if ashamed to be a few seconds from the dead-on truth.

The previous night came back to her with crystal clarity. Steve. There was no more Steve.

She had hardly slept. She wanted to spend the whole day lying where she was, in her own quiet room where no-one would disturb her.

Christ, she thought, I can't face *Make Someone's Day*. I'll have to call in. She called so rarely that though she part-owned the business she could not recall its number; she had to check her address book. The answering machine clicked on. Christ, I was supposed to be there alone this morning. Well, stuff it.

She tried to make herself sound unwell and deepened her voice a little, but it came across more like a hangover than illness.

"Hi, guys. It's me. I'm not going to make it today. Sorry. A sudden flu. Hopefully I'll be right as rain if I take it easy today." To make it clear she did not expect to be incapacitated for more than twenty-four hours she added brightly, "See you both tomorrow!"

She flopped back onto the pillow. The pillow had not been washed in two weeks and it was greasy. The room smelt enclosed, airless. She felt trapped. She became aware of a dull ache at her left knee and she threw the covers off and stretched a hand to it. She scratched it. A flake of dried blood fell away from the scab. She would have to wash it down.

She put her hand gently on the sheet in the place where Steve had slept, would and should have slept last night if he had not been such a fool and so unlucky. She imagined when her palm touched the cool cotton that it was warm, that a rising of heat still trapped within the threads was the last of his own body heat, the last of his living warmth now that his blood was cold. There was no such heat until Sara's hand itself warmed the sheet a little, and it was this she managed to tell herself with the delusion of despair was his.

She drifted back off.

In her sleep he came to her. A thick dark gash discoloured his temple and the strip of Band-Aid was peeling from his cheek, hanging loosely at both ends revealing the edges of his graze. Did he smile? She could not see his mouth. His eyes were not angry. They looked a touch worried, like a child who has lost his homework. She said to him that she hoped he was healed. He did not reply but turned. Light fell from somewhere, from an impossibly bright full moon perhaps, it touched his nipples and chest as he turned to walk away, touched the curves of his buttocks and fell across his shoulders, laid like a robe of gold. She threw his clothes in a bundle to him. He watched them fall with big sad eyes but did not move to claim them. He was happier naked.

Sara owned to nothing one might call a religious conviction, but like everyone she occasionally mused on life after death and what heaven would be like if there were a heaven to go to. She hoped if there were that men would be men and women women, not dreamy ethereal spirits who played harps and chanted. She had never been to a church service ever in her life. Her marriage had taken place in a registry office. Churches were buildings you went into on vacation, like old castles and historic houses, so her negative vision of heaven, the heaven in which she took it many people believed and which she hoped it was not, was coloured more by the cards she sold in her shop - angels with trumpets, fat cherubs, a thin weak clean-toothed Christ who held out his hand with sappy benevolence like a social worker, pious rhyming doggerel about footprints in the sand - more by these things than by any deeply wrought theology. Perhaps in heaven there were no zips to keep lovers from each other. This was what she wanted heaven to be, an unleashing of physical energy, a perpetual orgy in which all were welcome to join and from which only joy could come. Bodies she understood. When Steve had climbed on her it was his full being she had felt against her skin, when Steve One with beery breath had taken her as was his right, when Eddie's heavy weight had pressed her down, she had felt these weights as the complete men. She sensed no other, separate pieces to them, lighter than the sun's heat and invisible, which some called the 'soul' or the 'spirit' , which would float away to somewhere over her head when the flesh and blood and sinew had turned gray: the sinew was all. She had observed this in her card shop over many years, bored silly and the days passing oh so slowly, so always-the-same.

225

When customers came in they were mere variations on each other, a few faces repeated over and over again, a few limited reactions, mostly predictable. Behind the eyes there was not soul but electronic impulse throbbing mechanically, ineffectually, thinly, through the brain to no more depth or richness than the calculations of a hungry cat stalking a mouse; The cat, indeed, with its arched back and its silent pad, more alive and alert than the seekers after cards, their poring through racks as selections were made then discarded for a preferred one; the revolting Alice of the pink shoes obsessing stupidly about Disney cards, the husbands hurriedly, guiltily picking up romantic photographic images, candles and sunsets, for birthdays and anniversaries, office workers choosing a vaguely tasteless cartoon for a fellow worker's farewell, the young opting for garish pictures with COOL and FUN and SEX in big bold letters, the plump black women with their taste for religiosity no less cloying than Minnie Mouse's coy desperate eyelashes, the little old ladies with sticks seeking yet one more *Get Well Soon* card. Sara's heaven of nudity and lust seemed to her resonant of life, of energy, of animal need. Animal need she could like. Dreamy cloudlands, these were the bloodless wishes of those who had hopelessly failed in the human skins which encased everything they were.

Drifting in and out of dream, she surfaced every so often into a half-awake condition. Perhaps, she thought while hovering somewhere not exactly asleep, perhaps Steve is the lucky one, he died while he was still really alive, driven by the impulses of his body which to him were everything and enough. Later he would have grown out of his beauty, his easy erections, his easy satiety, into, what? Disappointment? The flaccid computations of her customers? The flaccid computations of the regulars at *Mulligan's*? Her own flaccid computations, trapped in a cycle of *Make Someone's Day* and pints of dark stout?

226

Mulligan's.

Tonight she would return to *Mulligan's.* She would reintroduce herself to her old life. She would put on red lipstick and she would go to *Mulligan's* and they would all be please to see her and she would drink her Guinnesses and make amusing, acerbic remarks. Steve would be a part of the past, a weird episode which would seem as time went by more and more like an illusion, an imagined encounter. Steve was a dream. Reality was *Mulligan's.*

SARA AFTER MULLIGAN'S

The lights of Fifth Avenue spangled shinily. To Sara the stars of the headlights blurred and lost their points, became a series of expanding discs laid one on the next like a set of translucent plates.

No tears girl! Enough of this rubbish! Get back home this instant, get into bed, get some sleep, get on with your life. You've got to be at *Make Someone's Day* at eight-thirty tomorrow. Pull yourself together!

Standing there in Washington Square she felt rather unwell. She regretted again all those ribs and wings and legs.

A weird, hilarious cloud of paranoia came upon her, which made her laugh out loud with happiness.

All that meat in your stomach, girl! Wouldn't it be ironic if you collapsed right here and now of food poisoning! An ambulance had to come and take you to hospital! But too late! You died, you died! Oh, the workings of fate! The lovely, perfectly working mechanisms of fate!

Fate working in its own mysterious way, it was like Justice, it balanced the scales!

Steve was gone. Now she would have to go too, soon!

Fate had decided!

How perfect, yes! How too, too perfect!

Of course, she did not rush home. She did not call a Doctor. She just laughed delightedly for a long time.

In her spirit, the spirit in which she did not believe, a stillness formed hard and real as a pebble.

It might be that the creature who went by the name of Sara Smith would not have very much longer to live! Hahahaha. She'd already had longer than Steve. She didn't mind if she did not go on and on and on. If this was to be it, this was to be it. She did not think long lives heroic or desirable. Fate would decide and that was that. She felt a painful tightening in her stomach.

GENE AND OTHERS

She went home. She went to bed. She woke up. She felt well. Perhaps she did not have food poisoning after all? She went to *Make Someone's Day*. Routine was swiftly and painlessly re-established. It was a pleasant Sunday morning. She rarely worked Sundays but she was determined to recapture her old routine as fast as possible, so today she worked until lunchtime. She had a nice lunch in *The Empire Szechuan Village*. Not once did she think of Steve. All was calm. She was renewed. She was a considerate and caring person.

Back home again she went past Tony and Pete's apartment, as always. Romantic classical music spilled delicately under their door. Tony played classical music only when he was upset about something. When he and Pete had argued, or when he'd received another rejection slip, or when a friend had died. Poor Tony. He was an emotional person. In her kitchen, she had a friendly inspiration. She'd take him a cup of tea. He liked tea. He liked honey stirred into deep brown tea.

(Tony was lying stretched out on his sofa, looking out of his windows. The apartment smelt of fresh flowers. He heard the rap on the door. He knew it wasn't Pete, Pete had been called to the office on an emergency, and Tony didn't want other company, so he stayed lying there. He hoped the visitor would go away. It must be Sara because the Man Upstairs never called and outsiders had to be buzzed in. There was another knock on the door. Another. Another. Which confirmed that it was Sara because only she would be so insistent. Tony could quite happily have stayed put and let her knock and knock until she gave up, but he had to be her neighbour so he had to get along with her. He sprang up from the cushions and opened the door.)

"Hi, Sara."

She held a cup of tea in one hand and a jar of honey in the other.

"I thought you might like some company," she said.

"Oh. That's sweet." He looked at the jar, and she thought he meant the flavour of honey. He opened his door wider to let her in. The music spilled onto the stairs.

"That's pretty," she said. "What is it?"

"Delius. 'The Walk to the Paradise Garden.'."

"You seem down," she said caringly, sitting in an armchair.

"Yeah," he said, opening the sticky jar and spooning a fat slow-moving slide of honey into the cup.

Another rejection slip in yesterday's mail, its impact only now taking full effect? She wanted to ask him about it. But she held back and let him talk.

"It's just a friend. A friend of ours died." He laughed, not happily.

"Oh, I'm so sorry."

"Not even a friend, really, an acquaintance."

If it wasn't somebody close, that's a blessing at least."

He shrugged.

"It's weird. I don't even know if it *is* our friend. The name's wrong. But he had a peculiar, characteristic I suppose you'd call it, which I can't believe he shared with anyone else."

He threw her a scrunched copy of the 'New York Post.'

231

The main headline was a political story and next to it ran a bold statement:

T.V. PREACHER'S 'ABANDONED' SON
DROWNS IN HUDSON

The son of TV hellfire preacher and best-selling author of the *Last Days* novels The Reverend Pat Wade-Adrian apparently fell into the Hudson River to his death last night, the police said. Foul play has not been ruled out. Russell Wade-Adrian was easily identified due to the distinctive yellow spots on his eyes, the result of a childhood illness.

The body of a homeless woman was found on a bench at the river's edge, near an empty shopping cart with a streak of blood on the handle. The woman had apparently died in her sleep.

"It's too early to say, but there may be a link," a police spokesperson said.

Russell Wade-Adrian, nineteen, had been estranged from his father since coming out as bisexual when he was fifteen years old. The Reverend has denied the existence of a son on many occasions since. Attendance at his massive Golden Cathedral in Tennessee, from which his show is broadcast, runs into tens of thousands. He was unavailable for comment last night.

"I do not have a perverted son," he has said in the past, "I have two lovely Christian daughters who help me do the work of the Lord." Russell was brought up subsequently by an Aunt, Merrilee Prentiss, in Memphis, Tennessee. Mrs Prentiss said last night, "Russ was a great kid. He was kind and compassionate. I'd hoped that his father would make up with him. That will never happen now. His father abandoned him."

Russell had been residing in Manhattan for ten months. His Aunt gave him money to live on. He regularly received death threats purporting to be from members of his father's church.

"He was in New York to find a profession right for his talents," noted Mrs. Prentiss. "He was a troubled kid, but he would have found his niche. He couldn't stay in Tennessee. He lived in constant fear."

His father is widely known for his fundamentalist views, expressed frequently on his *Hour of the Lord* TV show. He has been quoted as saying "Homosexuals deserve Old Testament punishment for their appalling sins. They will burn in hell when Christ returns." He has continued to campaign for the outlawing of homosexual practices.

His series *Last Days* has sold over two hundred million copies.

*

Next to the article there was a little photograph of the boy, about the size of a passport picture.

The hair was combed differently. The picture must have been a year or more old. But it was Steve. It was her Steve. She rubbed a hand across her forehead and felt sweat. Was she sweating for him, or for herself? The room spun and she squeezed her eyes tight shut to let it settle.

"Well," she said when she'd caught her breath. "Well!"

She threw the paper back to Tony. He unfolded it and stared at the picture (as he had stared most of the afternoon.)

"Yeah," he said. "I'd swear it was him. It's got to be. "

"Knew him well, did you?" asked Sara brusquely. Had they screwed him as she had?

"Well, we knew a guy who looked a lot like him, but he wasn't called Russell."

"What was he called? Steve? Tom? Dave?" She was fishing.

Peter came in. He dropped his briefcase near the door. He saw Tony's drawn face. He saw Sara. Something was wrong. He had an inkling what it was. He took his lover in his arms and said, very simply and very tenderly,

"What?"

"Something awful." He pointed to the 'New York Post.'

"Yeah," he said. "Yeah, I know. It was in the 'Times.' I thought of calling you. But I thought, maybe it's not him."

"It's him."

"I know." But he wanted not to know.

"What was his name?" asked Sara. "Jim? Ted?"

"No, it wasn't that... I don't remember. It was an unusual name." Tony looked sad. "Isn't that awful? I can't remember his name. He threw himself into a river or someone pushed him or something, and I can't even remember his name."

"It was Winston," said Peter.

Tony snapped his fingers.

"Yeah, that's right. Winston. Never knew his last name." He looked at the picture and said with genuine feeling, "poor kid."

Steve Smith? Winston Smith?

"Smith, was he?"

(Tony thought she was making a clever literary allusion. He doubted the good taste of jokes at a time like this but he smirked to say he'd got it. But for Sara there was no joke.)

"I don't think he said his last name."

"So just how well did you know him, then?"

"It must be someone else," said Peter.

"Peter," said Tony, "if it's someone else it's an identical twin."

"Well, the hair's a bit different."

"Your hair was a bit different yesterday. It's him."

"Then why did he make up a name?" "Does it matter?"

Peter gave up. "I guess not."

"He was a sweet kid." Tony ran a hand gently over the picture as though he were brushing Steve's face. Winston's face. Russell's face, whoever it was. "Very sweet. Very needy."

"How well did you know this boy who didn't give you his last name?"

"Not very. Spent a day with him."

"Do you mean a night?" asked Sara in her Judge Judy voice.

Tony shrugged. "A night and a day as it turned out. Pete and me got lucky on - when was it? Last Sunday night. A week ago."

"Yeah, he came back here for the night. He came on to us, not us to him. He came on big time."

"Yeah. And of course we were safe, we didn't do anything stupid. But it was a good night." (For an instant Tony's face went blank as the night came back to him.) "And the next day Pete went off to work. I gave the kid breakfast and thought he'd go. He didn't want to go. He wanted to stay and make love again. And again."

"Which you didn't refuse," said Peter, not minding. One thing about gays, thought Sara, they're not jealous and possessive, not like straights. My Steve One, he thought he owned me.

"Not the first time. But he was insatiable. I guess I must be getting middle aged because I couldn't keep up with him. Fact is, I don't think I was as horny as him even when I was twenty. Finally I said, Winston, you're gorgeous and I like you and it's been fun but I've got a deadline for a book - this was a lie - and anyway you've worn me out. He was a bit hurt, I think. He sat around the apartment most of the day. At six I said, Winston, bye-bye. He was still naked, he hadn't worn a thing all day, and I had to watch him get dressed. He looked as if he wanted to cry. I've never felt so guilty throwing a guy out. He put on his sun glasses to try and be

235

cool but he looked, like, really vulnerable, you know. He didn't tie his laces. I remember that. As he went through the door I called to him, your laces Winston, but he didn't turn back. He was trying to be dignified." Tony put both hands to his face and covered it. "He was really hurt. I don't know why. Did he think he was gonna move in with us? A cute kid who pretty much begs you to fuck him and then acts like you should want to be his friend for life. "

Peter patted his lover's knee.

"Some people just are really hurt. Really damaged. They just are." He looked at the paper. "And now we know why."

Sara had thought a bit of damage would've made him sexier, but that wasn't how she'd meant it.

"What kind of creep is this man, this Rev Wade-Adrian? What kind of psycho is it who treats his kid like that? It's fucking horrible. It's fucking evil." Tony screwed up the paper in frustration.

"The kind of creep who gets rich selling the idea of eternal punishment for everyone except, by coincidence, the viewers of his show and the buyers of his books. They apparently are all saved."

Tony turned back to his tea.

"Well," said Sara, wanting very much to be alone, "I just thought I'd drop by and say hi. I'm really sorry about the news. Take care." She patted Tony's arm, then Peter's.

"Thanks for coming in, Sara. I appreciate it." Tony seemed perfectly sincere. He made to hand her the half-full cup.

"Later. Finish it." She went up.

She sat on her sofa and folded her arms and thought very hard.

There was no way the body of this Russell person could be linked to her. They'd never been seen together by anyone. Except the odd waiter. Would the waiters remember him? Did they notice his eyes?

236

What would she do if someone made the connection, if the doorbell rang and it was the police? She had not committed a crime. Had she? She wasn't sure. The poor boy fell, it wasn't her fault. Perhaps a day or two before now she would have panicked. She would have been frightened of discovery. Not now.

She felt a pain in her stomach.

Not now. Fate would decide now. Her body would decide. No-one could reach her now. She had nothing to lose. She felt very free. Having nothing to lose was the essence of freedom. Having nothing to live for was the essence of freedom.

Somewhere under her heart she felt a sensation like the shifting of salt, the dropping in a whisper from an upper bulb to a lower, not moving fast but moving relentlessly, until the salt would all be at the bottom and she was over, she had run out like the salt through the thin space of the neck between the bulbs. This is how she would picture her life from now on, however long she had left. When there was no salt to slide through, then it was, mm, over, easy as shutting off a switch. It would be over, as it would be over in time for everyone, as it was already over for Steve. It was really very easy when you thought about it like that. You come from darkness and spend a little time in the light. If you enjoy your time, good, then you go back into the darkness grateful for the life. And if it's a disaster? If you are a failure, if you are a bad human being, if you have not led a good life? Then, too, it will soon be over and you will slip back into the darkness grateful for an end, without having to worry any more, without guilt any more. The world was full of foolish people who were terrified of their mortality, but mortality was a good thing. She felt the salt slipping. Mortality was a good thing. Thank you, God, for not existing. Thank you for that great beneficent non-existence.

237

Until she joined God in his heaven of blank nothingness, she would try her best to be a good person. I have not been good, she told herself without surprise and without the slightest pang of remorse, I have not been good but I will be good from now on. I will take Tony honey in his tea. Is that enough compensation for the past? It is something, and something is all I can do.

Steve. Steve Smith. Winston. Russell Wade-Adrian.

She would remember only her Steve with the constant erection and the love of dance, the Steve who knew theatre, the Steve who was trying to get his equity card so he could burst onto a Broadway stage. Fuck this Winston with his love for men, I didn't know him, I don't want to know anything about him. Fuck this Russell Wade-Adrian, this ruined preacher's son rolling in money from his Aunt and living a lie, living all sorts of lies. I don't know him either, don't want to. So he drowned. Probably killed himself. Poor lad. But I didn't know him. It was Steve I knew, it was Steve who stayed in my bed and fried bacon and shifted from leg to leg, his slim waist, his love of dance, his balls which shook sometimes as he spun. Circling around my lounge to his own rhythm, Steve Steve Steve. The Steve with one leg swinging over the other as he perused *Backstage*, a hand playing with the head of his penis quite without knowing, turning the page, marking suitable auditions.

Did he ever, ever, ever, go to any?

Well, Steve did, Winston no but then Winston knew nothing about theatre and cared less, probably read nothing but gay porno mags. Russell : no. Russell, no, he was troubled by the hellfire curses of his awful father. Sara felt that because she was not the very worst of people she was therefore okay. She did not drive planes through buildings in the name of a God that could not be known. She didn't ruin her kids in the name of a saviour who would never come. If there was a God - there was not - he would be weeping,

238

wouldn't he? Weeping with hatred for Pat Wade-Adrian and Osama Bin-Laden, weeping with love for sinful uncorrupted damaged Russell Wade-Adrian, and Winston, and especially for horny Steve whose body was his all. If there was a God-there was not – his special love would have been for the romantic and their spilling of seed, their need to touch and feel and fuck other human beings because how else could you get really close to a creature just like you? God's love would be for those who lived in a world of flesh and did not think of him. Perhaps God, if he existed - he did not - loved most those who never thought of him, saw in those who never thought of him more nearly his own image.

Perhaps he even loves me.

Except that he doesn't exist.

Steve. Steve trying for his Equity card. Gifted Steve who could've lit up the Great White Way. He was on the verge of his break, Steve was.

*

In her dorm at NYU, overlooking Washington Square, Martine Fatio wept for her boy from Columbia. She had at first believed it could not be him, that picture, not her Tom Parker, her gifted chemistry student lover, her lover for six glorious months, (her first, he'd taken her virginity, and she had had the conviction all this time that he was to be her only one, her husband, eventually the father of her children.) She had tried to call his cell- phone seven, eight times that afternoon after seeing the 'Daily News' and it had been off every time. Of course, for hours she had told herself it was not Tom Parker at all. Tom's hair was different, and there was no graze on the cheek of this Russell Wade- Adrian. But then there had been no graze on Tom's cheek three days ago. No graze on his knee. And the picture was very crisp, there could be no doubt that either this was Tom or Tom had an

239

identical twin. An identical twin with the same eyes of deep brown flecked with tiny dots like drops of gold. Once more she rolled from her bed and reached for her cell-phone. Dialed the number. A voice said it was off.

She had never seen Tom's dorm room at Columbia, but they had strict rules about off-campus visits. That's what he'd said, why should it not be true? They'd often met up just a block or two away from it, he'd pointed out his building. Once he'd kissed her neck on a bench. My pals could see us if they looked out their windows now, he'd said in his delicious Southern sing-song. She lay again on the bed, on her chest, looking at the folded paper on the floor, Tom looking up to her sweetly and faithfully. She couldn't believe it but she had to believe it. She reached her hand and flipped the paper over so now all she could see was his shirt collar on the fold. She wept again for Tom but soon it was for herself she wept.

Sphere Masters did not read the 'Daily News', did not read the 'New York Times', did not read the 'Post', even when he was in the City, and now he wasn't. Sphere did not need the outside world. He needed his instrument, he needed his music, and that was all. It was Jules the pianist who had the 'Tribune', who left it on one of the   tables in the Chicago club they were playing while they did a soundcheck. Sphere was trying out different mouthpieces. He cradled the saxophone just like a lover. He had cradled Gene Simon a few times like that, but Gene was soft and warm and pliant and the saxophone was shiny and harsh and demanding. He saw the picture out of the corner of his eye.

Shit, that looks just like Gene.

Sphere did not dwell long on it. Not that he didn't like Gene and hope he was well and happy and that this was not him and he was not dead. It had only been supposed to be a one-night fuck, that was all. But Gene kept coming round. Sphere let him, because he looked good. He'd had strange eyes, that boy, dark brown flecked with gold. Also he liked Jazz, seemed really interested in it, Sphere had never found a boy who actually liked his music. The first time they'd met he didn't mention jazz at all; he was with another guy, a guy who thought he knew it all, but Gene had said next to nothing, had sat and listened, and looked at Sphere with such openness, such innocence, real intelligence too. Later, at three in the morning, Sphere had come out of the *Village Vanguard* and there Gene was, leaning against the awning's pillar. He said nothing but he held out his hand and Sphere took it. It was easy. There was no need of surreptitious signals. He wanted to go to Sphere's bed and Sphere wanted him to come. In bed he had been silent. He had a sweet body, he was sexually alert, his fingers touched the right parts of Sphere at the right time. Not many men had this talent.

But the second time, suddenly he'd known Sphere's work really well, he could talk thoughtfully about his recordings. Gene had those sensitive lips, those distinctive sensitive eyes, and it was cool to watch his lips move as he talked, to watch his eyes glitter.

But hell, he'd been getting clingy so if he was gone he was gone. Once, Gene had whispered as he came, "I love you, Sphere," and Sphere had said, "Hey, baby, I don't love no-one. I love my sax, that's what I love. I don't love nothin' but my horn." Sphere had felt the need to say this precisely because he did feel something for Gene he had not felt for his other boys. It was not love exactly, but it was something other than lust, or lust heightened into something greater than itself. Few things can kill a romantic moment more thoroughly than telling your lover he comes second to your music, but that was how it was. His instrument was his life, his lovers were a diversion. That was how it had to be. Sphere cradled the sax, felt it jab his chest, cold unforgiving, and knew that though his instrument was not all

241

he wanted it was all he really needed. He blew into it again and it wailed ecstatically.

Still, there'd been something about Gene. Sphere could not quite forget him. He always forgot everyone, but Gene would not go out of his head. His unique eyes sometimes came to him in dreams, and if not the eyes, even more strangely the colours of the eyes; a brownish sky dotted with stars so that the dreaming Sphere thought, "that sky's just like that kid's eyes." Or a field with daffodils growing here and there: "Like Gene's eyes." Or gold coins in the bottom of an old trunk. "Man, it's like that boy's staring up at me." It was like Gene was everywhere he wanted to be, not a person at all but an essence. A presence.

*

There were those for whom the boy had been a dark secret. Daniel Dawson was married with three kids and after failing to suppress his homosexual side had lived his gay life in secret. He loved his wife and his kids in his way, truly he did, but he wanted more. So he'd had the beautiful Greg Swift in hotel rooms, he'd treated him to dinner and once given him a huge wad of cash. They'd once been to the *Village Vanguard* where Greg had seemed fascinated by the music, by the sax especially. They'd talked to the great Sphere Masters, who'd come near their table on a break. Daniel had said how much he loved his playing. What a great musician he was. Sphere had seemed pleased. He was not crabby as many musicians were, did not dismiss a compliment - "I love your work" - with an indifferent "do ya?" and a turning of the back. He'd joined their table and talked. Greg was silent, but then what did he care about jazz?

That night as on other nights they'd gone back to a hotel and made love. In the morning light Greg's side of the bed

242

had been empty. That was usual. But he was not a prostitute, did not ask for money.

It was spooky how much like Greg the picture in the 'New York Times' looked. At first Daniel said to himself it's someone else, but soon he accepted that this Russell was his Greg. It was the eyes. No-one else had those eyes. Daniel felt disappointed that Greg, Russell, had lied to him. No, he had not lied, he hadn't said anything at all. He had simply been the boy Greg who liked sex and was fun to hang out with.

Of course Daniel could not discuss this with his wife, which made his mourning harder to bear. He supposed it was mourning, this bleakness which lodged in him for weeks. That night she commented on Russell, the death was big news because of who he was. She hated those fundamentalist preachers, she said. Daniel agreed, and thought more about Greg and Russell, in the deep of the night. He dreamt of him. He felt an ill-defined sense that he was somehow guilty of something, and his wife noticed how quiet he was for the next few weeks. But long after Daniel did not seem quiet any more Greg still came to him in the shadows of his head, Greg loomed as he had not loomed even in life.

*

Make Someone's Day Cards and Gifts was quiet and Sara was alone, Dave and Ruth gone for the nearest they could get in walking distance of the store to a lovey-dovey lunch. (Not the *Empire Szechuan Village*, because they did not care for Asian food.) No customers in forty minutes.

A little man in a thick woollen hat walked past the door and looked in at the window. He hovered for a second, then walked on and out of sight. Less than a minute later he was back at the window, looking in. His fists in their gloves

243

opened and closed. He had a very round face, a large round nose.

She said aloud,

"Oh my God! The Man Upstairs!"

She hadn't recognized him with the hat over his shiny bald head and his ears.

What could he want? He'd never come to the store ever before. He caught her eye. *What do you bloody want?* she mouthed, making a shooing gesture at the same time. He looked discomfited but still hovered, rocking from his left foot to his right and back again, doing a frightened little dance on the spot. She was fed up with people in this City doing little dances on the spot. The Man Upstairs was no Steve Smith, no Russell Wade-Adrian who could really dance. He had a paper folded under his arm. He went off. Then he came back again, walking faster, determined, purposeful. He pushed on the door urgently and ran through it as if to stop himself changing his mind. He looked about suspiciously and approached the counter.

"Sara Smith?" he said. His voice was shaking.

"You know bloody well it is."

"Sara Smith, I think we have to talk." He raised his chin in a muster of authority which only made him appear weak and sinister.

"Well there's a first. What about?"

He unfolded the paper. Yesterday's 'New York Post.' The picture of Russell Wade-Adrian looked out at her, wide-eyed, innocent, sexy. A liar. A bloody liar and a fraudster who deserved what he got. The Man Upstairs pointed his gloved hand to the picture, tapping it twice. His hand was shaking.

"So?" She felt a wobble at the back of her throat.

He narrowed his eyes. Was he making his best effort at being threatening?

"I know."

244

"What?"

"I know. About you. We must talk."

Sara couldn't think of anything to say, so she laughed. The Man Upstairs looked offended.

"We must talk," he hissed again. He turned his back and left the store.

So he knew! All Sara's indifference, all her new calm, was blown away in an instant by the reality of imminent blackmail. What was she to do? What did he know? How much? He couldn't have seen her with the body. Could he? Perhaps he was guessing, making a stab in the dark in hopes of a little money. He'd met Steve on the stairs one time; Steve had mentioned it. Was that all he knew? A face on the stairs and the photograph in the paper? An easily explainable coincidence, surely?

There was no point in guessing about what he knew and what he didn't know. She'd find out soon enough. For now, she would go on as if nothing had happened. She would whistle a tune. She would be happy. She would be nice to customers. She would not allow that horrible little man to upset her in any way!

It was remarkable - Sara herself thought so - how equable she managed to be for the rest of the day. Dave and Ruth didn't notice anything wrong. On the contrary, later that evening they remarked to each other what a good mood she was in.

"She's okay when she's like that," said Dave.

"Yeah, she can be sweet. If only she wasn't such a downer half the time."

"So what do we do?"

"I know we've been talking for months about getting rid of her, but she's a character."

"Ruth, she's nice when she's nice, but she's not nice all that often. She offends customers."

"Well, if anyone is going to tell her we don't want her, it's you. Give me half an hour's warning so I can get far away first."

Dave wagged a finger.

"If we fire her we fire her together. We give her the money for her part of the business, with a big fat extra, and we say don't come back. We do it together or not at all."

"I don't like the idea of just, you know, telling her to go away like that. When she's nice she's very nice."

"You're copping out?"

"No!! I'm not copping out! I'm just saying we might want to think twice about it."

"Ruth, we've already thought twice about it. We've thought ninety-eight times about it! Decision time. Yes or no?"

"No." A long pause. "Yes. Yes yes yes! I can't stand having her around."

"So it's yes."

"Yes."

"Together we tell her. Tomorrow."

"Tomorrow."

"It'll be much nicer without her."

"Yeah."

"Tomorrow we sack her."

"Yup."

They slept extremely well that night. They could not know that even as they discussed the matter things were happening which would take the decision out of their hands.

*

When Sara came up the stairs he was standing at her door, holding the paper. If he had let the matter go, if he had left the card shop and forgotten the whole thing, ignored her when they passed in the street or at the mailboxes as he

246

always had, everything would have been all right and both of them might have gotten on with their lives. But he was there. He was very frightened, moving about from foot to foot in another little nervous dance. Steve had danced well, his movements had made him look more beautiful even than his stillness. His body in motion had been lighter than air. The Man Upstairs, small and bald and inept and weasely, was hopeless in his movements, terrified and cowardly. His movements like his face were strangely incomplete. He was less like a living being than a stylized sketch.

If you're going to blackmail me, Sara said to herself, you could at least be forthright about it.

She gave him a friendly grin.

"Good afternoon," she said, with a tiny formal nod of the head.

"Good afternoon," said The Man Upstairs. His voice was very thin and rather high. It came from the back of the throat, somewhat strangulated. He returned her nod.

"I suppose you want to come in?" She was giving him a chance to say no. A chance to return to the old ways.

He coughed apologetically into his hand. A little splash of phlegm hit his palm. He wiped it on his coat.

"We do have matters to discuss, madam."

Madam. Like Steve. Ma'am. But different.

"Call me Sara."

"Call me Manny." She would not call him Manny. She would not call him anything. She would think of him only as The Man Upstairs. (Not The Manny Upstairs, even.) He could try to extort every penny she had from her, but to her he would have no name. He could force her to sell her apartment if it came to that. He would remain a blank, a nothing. Names were human. She would not credit him with humanity.

"I suppose you want to come in?" She delved into her purse for her key, making a show of a search even after she'd wrapped the key in her hand.

"I suppose I do," he said. Was he beginning to doubt?

"Well, then you must." She could say: Damn, I left my key in the shop, I'll have to go back. That might buy time. He could then suggest they go up to his apartment, couldn't he, where she'd be on alien ground, less sure of herself. What was the point of delaying the inevitable? It was better to know what he wanted, then she could deal with it.

He doesn't know about my nest egg. I don't think he knows I part-own the shop. He probably thinks I'm hired help for seven dollars an hour. Less. He might think I'm an illegal immigrant. Maybe I can get rid of him with a couple of thousand dollars. Five thousand dollars.

But blackmailers come back. They spend their couple of thousand dollars and come back for more. And more and more and more. For ever. They have you over a barrel. If I give in to him once I'm in his power.

But if I give in to him once, that'll buy me time. I could sell up, move uptown. Even Harlem is supposed to have nice bits nowadays. Or I could go back to London. (A big red bus drove through her mind.) It would be nice, a little flat in Canary Wharf. A flat in Fulham. Maybe I could try Brighton. I'd be near the sea. I bet I could afford a flat with a sea view. That would be a nice kind of retirement. But all those queers! Brighton, England's gay mecca, there aren't any straight men in the whole town, it's a well-known fact. I'd have to be a bloody fag hag if I wanted any friends at all! But, hang on, as my only friends in this big cold city are the queens downstairs I'm already a fag hag, so I may as well get used to it.

She put the key in the lock and turned the handle. The Man Upstairs stepped forward to the open crack as aggressively as he could.

"Hold on, no hurry," she said.

He looked about the hallway. No-one ever climbed these stairs except her and him, so why was he so on edge?

Perhaps he thinks I'm going to push him down the stairwell. These stairs could do a good bit of damage. But he might fight me off. Then I would be in big trouble. Maybe he'd throw me down them. Don't fancy that.

Anyway I'm not that sort. I don't have to do anything to anyone to exact my revenge. I have powers of suggestion. So Steve One gets squashed at Disneyworld. Steve Two falls head over heels to his death. If this Man Upstairs only knew what kind of person he was dealing with he'd be gone faster than a rat from a sinking ship. I have powers over fate, I do.

With a glimmer of pleasure at this remembrance, she went into the apartment and held the door open to receive her blackmailer. He stepped through. He did not look happy. Why, as he was about to squeeze money out of her, did he not look happy?

Sara had never before prepared for the negotiations of blackmail. Should she stand arms on hips in intimidating silence while he sputtered out his charge? Should she sit at her little table and say, "spit it out"? Should she offer him a place on her leather sofa and say, "So you've something you want to ask me"? She felt the enclosedness of her apartment and smelt the still lingering scents of bacon. The pan from which Steve had fried her breakfast sat on the stove, coated with a rim of fat. She went to the windows and threw them open. The sounds of the street lightened the hermetic stuffiness. The Man Upstairs sidled over to the sofa and sat in it, on the very cushion Steve had used. This offended her, it seemed rude. Next to him was the 'New York Post' sitting on its own cushion like the Queen of Sheba, Russell Wade-Adrian staring up. His face was fattened at the curve of the fold which was not pressed down. He didn't look like Steve at all. The Man Upstairs pressed his hands between his knees as Steve had done. How few are the variations of the human creature, in his movements as in the range of his expressions and the range of his thoughts. All businessmen knew that. She knew it. She was in business too. You calculated what most of the human creatures would desire and you gave it to them. That's how Disney got rich, how Ray Kroc got rich. That's why her card store did well. You picked out all the sickliest sentimentalities you could find in all the card catalogues you got sent, and you watched as all those creatures came into your shop and handed over two dollars fifty for a bit of thick cheap paper with some colours swirled across it.

"I'm sorry about the smell," she said, meaning the bacon.

"That's all right," he said, pathetically. He was rubbing his hands together. One finger wrapped around the ring finger on the opposite hand, where a ring would have been if he'd had a ring. Possibly once he had. It would have been a cheap ring, not because he had no money but because he was mean and austere. Why else would he try to extort money out of a widow who worked for seven dollars an hour?

"I'm going to make some coffee," she said.

"Thanks," he said, as though she were making an offer rather than a plain statement. His pale eyes glanced up to her. He looked lost. But her pity was not aroused as it had been for Steve. At his age, The Man Upstairs had no right to look lost. It was weakness to be lost when you were an old man.

She scooped coffee into her cafetiere and poured in water. It hissed and was soon making bubbling noises. The Man Upstairs stared out of the window. He played with his hands some more. The newspaper sat folded next to him. She wondered if he felt more than she the onrush of shame and guilt. He flipped it over to the back cover, flattening it at the fold. Only Sports News looked up at the ceiling now, a big football player, arm in air triumphantly.

250

"So what is it you want?"

He looked round to her where she watched the coffee drip.

"I think it would be better if you sat down, madam."

This made her firm.

"You can say what you've got to say and then leave. I've got to go out. I haven't got all day."

He stood up, took the paper with him. He stopped near the fridge, a few feet from her. He watched the coffee drip drip drip. The coffee was the focus of the room, the black liquid and the little splashes and the aroma. Everything else fell into the distance. Only the coffee mattered. Drip drip drip. Thick and rich and black. Evocative of far countries. Far from New York and sordid blackmail and poor damaged boys and greedy men.

They stood there until the drips of liquid slowed. A last bubble gathered roundly under the filter and dropped, rippled over the surface and became one with the generous unmoving darkness below.

"Done!" she said loudly, breaking the spell. He batted his eyelids as though the cut of her voice had given him a shock. He looked like Minnie Mouse. She got out a cup and poured to the rim. She took her coffee black. She went to her table and smoothed her dress before sitting in the chair. He went back to the sofa. The light caught his face and made it sallow. Was he insulted that he hadn't been offered a cup? Who did he think she was, Little Miss Starbuck? He could drink his own bloody coffee in his own bloody apartment.

"So what is it you want?"

He turned the paper right side up, unfolded it. He pressed it down so that Russell looked out in all his glory, the roundness at the fold reduced to a crease which crinkled his chin.

"This boy... You know him, don't you? Knew him?"

"Never seen him in my life."

251

"You have."

"What would I be doing with the son of some dreadful Southern preacher?"

"I know you did. I met him on the stairs. He knocked on your door."

"Dunno what you're on about."

"Don't play games, Miss." Miss, is it? You condescending rat! "I met him on the stairs."

"What if you did? What if he was on my stairs? What of it? "

"No, it's not just the stairs. I saw him on your balcony."

"So? So he was on my balcony you say, if he was here at all, which I'm not saying he was. Anyway I don't know this Russell-"
 She leant over to the paper as if to remind herself of the name - "Wade-Adrian."

"Please, madam, let's not play around." He batted his eyelids together again. "He was here and I know it and you know I know it."

"So?"

"So I saw him dancing on your balcony. Naked. I was upset, madam. This is a respectable neighbourhood. You shouldn't have allowed him to do that. I was going to call the police but…"

Since when had Greenwich Village been a respectable neighbourhood anyway, she wanted to say; she'd been drawn to it   because it wasn't boring or respectable. This is New York! She wanted to admonish him. It's all unrespectable, that's the point. If it's not nudity on a balcony it's greed on Wall Street. If you want respectable move to Boston!

"But?"

"I didn't wanna get you into trouble, lady. You're a good neighbour. Quiet. Respectable, as I say. But you shouldn't have let that wild boy into your apartment." "Well it's a bit late for me to apologize, isn't it?"

"Madam, I saw him fall."

"Did you indeed?"

"I don't get why you didn't call the police or an ambulance?"

She squinted. This was not the turn of conversation she had expected.

"How do you know I didn't call them? If what you say happened happened at all."

"It happened. Why didn't you call an ambulance? Why did you take it into your own hands?"

"Hang on, Mister, what are you trying to say? Are you accusing me of..." She flapped her arms about in despair, "of murder? You think I killed him?" I don't think he could have seen me on the balcony, she calculated. She couldn't see much of Tony and Pete's balcony below hers, and she doubted The Man Upstairs could any more clearly see hers. He would have seen Steve only when he was on the fire escape. Did he see my hand on his flesh?

Hang on, Sara, your hand never touched his flesh. He fell, a terrible accident. She pushed her eyelids tightly together, trying to squeeze out water.

"It was a terrible accident."

He held his hands palms outward before him, appalled.

"Oh no, madam, I don't think you're a murderer. Not at all! I'm not saying that."

"You're not?"

"Oh no, I wouldn't be talking to you now if I thought that! It seemed odd that you didn't call the police."

"I was so confused..." She ran her hand through her hair, deliberately mussing it to represent distress. She wished her make-up would run. She shook her head. "I mean, a naked boy in my apartment. It would look so bad. I didn't know what to do." What the hell does he want? She sipped her coffee which tasted harsh. She pulled her cheeks together, let

253

her jaw sag, a vision of wretched melancholy. "What came over me? I'm a respectable woman."

He said, very quietly, "Madam, I know you are."

"Thank you." She wanted to reach out to his hand and pat it gratefully, felt a surge of anger that she had placed herself so far from him.

"But why the shopping cart? Why didn't you call an ambulance?"

Her brain fizzed in its search for explanations. Well you see I took him to the hospital. I put him in the cart, poor boy, and pushed him all the way to the emergency room all wrapped up warm and snug in a blanket. You know how slow ambulances can be!

For a second she thought she might get away with this, but if she pushed him to the hospital how did he end up in the Hudson?

I pushed him to the hospital but he died on the way. What could I do? I was stuck with a dead body in a shopping cart. I didn't know what to do. I walked around for hours in a terrible state. I thought if I pushed him for long enough he might recover, a bump on the road might jolt his heart back to beating. And then... I was so tired... so tired. I sat down on a bench. The cart rolled away. Rolled towards the water. I ran after it, it was too late. It hit the railing, it threw the boy out. It threw him into the river! His body floated off. It was awful.

No. I was pushing the cart to the hospital, and a horrid old homeless woman - she's mentioned in the article - she grabbed it from me. She ran away. She was cackling crazily. She was completely mad!

This felt like a betrayal of poor Lottie, who had had enough betrayal in her life. It was a betrayal of Sara herself, of her brilliant creation. It was like a novelist betraying his own characters. She couldn't do it.

254

No. I was so tired I sat on a bench to recover and these drunks... I don't know if they were homeless or not but they smelt terrible. They grabbed my cart from me and ran away whooping and hollering.

No, I was so tired I sat on a bench to recover and these drunks... They wore expensive suits and they must have come from a late party, four drunken men, and they grabbed my cart and ran off with it hollering and whooping. Perhaps they thought I was homeless. I must have looked very tired. They were loud and arrogant and cruel and drunk. They probably worked on Wall Street.

Sara's sense of her mortality had faded. She had something to lose. She sighed deeply.

"What can I do for you?" This was packed with ache and regret. She couldn't read the situation any more. His big stupid cartoon eyes looked at her so full of softness and caring she wanted to scream. When's he going to ask for money?

"Madam, I'm not a rich man."

Now. Now he was getting to his mean little point. Blackmailing a distraught widow. How repellent.

"Nor am I," she said, looking at her purse as if to support her point, "a rich woman."

"I had not imagined you were. Money doesn't matter to me."

Then why are you trying to get it out of me? The room seemed to move a little in her confusion. When he spoke again it was with the air of a rehearsed speech. It came out stilted, like a bad actor who can remember his lines but cannot make them seem ideas of the   moment.

"Madam, you don't know me well. We have been neighbours all these years and said very little to each other. But I've admired you. For a long time." He looked at his hands. "A long time. And I've noticed that when we've passed you've smiled at me with sympathy. Friendliness.

255

You are a very friendly woman, I know. What other sort would sell greetings cards? I know you're a kindly person. It has always seemed so to me."

He picked up the paper and looked at the photograph. He breathed in deeply. She heard the intake, she heard the air running through his clumps of nose hair.

"I would like you to marry me."

Sara mussed her hair some more, this time unconsciously. Her jaw fell wide open. She looked like Marley's ghost. He saw the expression on her face.

"Does the idea appall you so very much? I'm a good man."

She tried to picture him in her bed, reaching out to her, making his demands. The sheets warm from his body.

"I won't ask anything… you know… of you. It would be a marriage of companionship. Sometimes you must get lonely as I do."

"This has come as a bit of a surprise." There was nothing else she could say.

"Of course it has. I know it has. All I ask is you give it some thought. I'm a lonely man, and I'm not getting any younger. You are a lonely lady." She noticed how in a second he had turned her from someone who may occasionally be lonely into a full-time 'lonely lady'. She hated him for this. How dare you call me lonely! You know nothing about me! He was playing with his fingers and did not look into her face. He looked at those fingers, one pulling on another. His head was down to them, she saw the sheen on his scalp, the contours of his nose which was squat and wide. His eyebrows were bushy. There were tufts of hair coming from his right ear, which was cocked slightly towards her. He pulled on his fingers, pulled and pulled.

What if she said no? Would demands for money start to trickle then? Was he saying that if she said no, I don't want to marry you, you dreadful ugly little man, or some politer

256

version of the same sentiment, then things would return to normal, he would go back to being The Man Upstairs and they'd pass on the stairs and nod fondly to each other? She supposed she would at least have to learn the art of nodding fondly. But surely it was unimaginable that things could be as they were. There he was all pathetic and lonely on her lovely leather sofa asking for her hand as if he were a complete innocent who wanted nothing more than her happiness; yet the reality was he was blackmailing her as surely as if he'd asked for a million bucks. It would have been preferable if he'd asked for money in fact, which was at least clean and clear. She might even have given him some. But this! This he seemed to imagine was somehow not so awful, so corrupt. But this was the worst blackmail of all. He wanted all of her! He wanted her very life!

She drank a big gulp of her coffee. It bit her. She wished she'd added milk.

She could feel no pity for him, and so she could see him with utter clarity. He was a nasty blackmailer, no two ways about it. She stood up and went towards him. She towered over him. The light from the balcony windows threw her shadow onto him like a blanket. He looked up to her in his new place of darkness and blinked like Bambi. Did he think she was going to threaten him?

She leaned down to him. She exposed her teeth not in a snarl but in a lovely warm sunny smile. For him, she imagined, it was a light brighter than any coming through glass. It was the light of hope.

"Ducks," she said, "this has come, as I know you understand, as a bit of a shock."

He nodded sharply four times.

"I know it has, madam. I'm sure you will want some time to think it over. I think we could make each other happy." Why??? She wanted to yell like a trial lawyer. Why do you think YOU, of all people, can make ME happy??? On what

257

evidence??? What makes you think I would not rather be miserable and homeless on the street in the heart of a New York winter than snuggled up with you in your warm smelly little bed? I bet he farts in his sleep, she reflected. I bet he snores. I'd rather die of exposure than go anywhere near him!

"Yes. It sounds really great. It will take me a few days to think things over. It would be a big step. "

"And then we can start to make plans."

How fast he was moving! He pretended to be patient but he wanted everything signed, sealed and delivered as soon as possible. ASAP. From someone who had lonely moments to a little lonesome old lady to 'making plans' in, what, three minutes?

He stood up. He reached out to one of her hands, which she found had itself reached out to his without her brain knowing. He put one hand on top of hers and the other underneath in a sweaty, desperate clasp. He was shaking, she could feel his fear run up her arm.

"Plans? Yes."

"If you say yes, of course. As I hope you will. " His eyes widened so that he looked if possible even more innocent and unformed and cartoonish. But she saw through him. 'As I hope you will.' That was a threat. A veiled threat. And if I say no? She wanted to grab him by the neck and throttle him.

"Of course."

"Like if you sold your apartment or I sold mine if you prefer, we'd get quite a lot for it. That would give us a nice little pot of money. We could go on vacations. We could go on cruises."

"That would be nice! Cruises!" She supposed she looked as if she was already lying on the deck in her imagination. She was dining at the captain's table. She was leaning on a rail watching the sunset. She was wearing her best evening dress.

"And we could go to shows. I never go to shows. It's not the same by yourself. Have you ever seen 'Phantom'?"

"I haven't."

"But you would like to?"

"Oh yes. Broadway! Lights! I knew a kid once, had dreams of Broadway."

"'The Lion King'."

"Oh, 'The Lion King'. Yes. Lovely."

"'Aida'."

"Marvellous."

He had moved to the door. His hands held hers so she was pulled towards the door with him. She thought that he did not really want to leave, perhaps he was hoping she would pull him back to the sofa. He wanted her to agree now, she could see this. He wanted to start making those plans. He wanted to call up the 'Phantom' box office. He was shaking like a child who has seen a new toy and cannot wait even a day for it. Now, now, now, please, mommy. Now! She thought of Alice with the pink shoes.

He put his spare hand onto the door knob and turned it leftward. She heard the tongue of the lock pull out of the frame. But then he took his hand off it again. The tongue clicked back into place.

"Oh well," he said.

"Oh well," she said.

"Call me Manny."

"I will, ducks. Call me Sara."

"Do I have... ur, reason to be hopeful, Sara?"

He let her hand go. He stepped back a few feet into her living space. She felt invaded.

He rubbed his thumb across the leather arm of her sofa. There was still a round bowl in the cushion where he'd been sitting.

"This is a great sofa," he said. "It's really classy."

"It's my pride and joy," she said. He had his back to her. She moved towards the stove.

"How did you know him?"

"What?"

"The kid? How did you know him?" He turned back to her. For the first time he looked right into her eyes and held her gaze. His voice did not contain an inflection of threat, but he must have known it was a reminder of why he was here in the first place.

But he already knew who that kid was! What was he fishing for?

"Would you like to stay to supper? Maybe we could talk a bit more. I'm not promising anything, mind. But I am seriously interested, if you catch my drift."

Was that pleasure on his face? Was he flattered? But he was not smiling. He looked indeed a little upset, a study of male disappointment. Perhaps he had thought they would have come to an agreement more speedily than was proving the case. After all he held all the aces.

"Not promising anything?"

"I have to think things over. It's a big step."

"Oh yeah. Sure it is. I know. I understand."

"So would you like supper?"

"No, I've got some leftovers in the refrigerator. I wouldn't want them to go to waste."

This comment, this easy escape, surprised her. She felt she had got him under her influence and was losing him again. He had the power and he was not above asserting it. She felt for the first time something other than anger. She felt trapped. This nasty little man had her over a barrel.

"Oh." She illustrated disappointment. You'd have taken it he was breaking a firm date from the purse on her lips and the sag of the eyes.

"We'll have a small wedding. Nothing fancy," he said.

"Yeh, sign a bit of paper at the Town Hall, that sort of thing. Perhaps Antony and Peter can be witnesses."

"Who?"

"Tony and Pete downstairs."

He looked disdainful. "Oh no, not them. I don't like queers." He looked deeply unattractive, the Disney animal turning sour. "I think they're immoral. It's horrible what they do to each other. It ought to be illegal."

"Oh, I agree, ducks, it's awful. But one has to be civil to the neighbours."

The Man Upstairs did not agree with this sentiment.

"I hate them. They've ruined the Village. I only live here because my Uncle left this apartment to me. I don't approve of queers. I don't mind being honest with you, Sara. I don't like them and that's a fact." His eyelids beat together. There was malevolence in the terrible unfinished vacancy of his eyes.

Sara had the far from noble but not unenviable talent of swinging her prejudices in one hundred and eighty degree arcs on an impulse. If a gay waiter was rude to her, she took an instant dislike to all homosexuals, even Tony and Pete. This could linger for as long as a week. Then Tony might lend her some sugar when she'd run out, and she'd find herself thinking, while sweetening a cup of tea perhaps, how nice gays are. They're neat and clean, and they're generous too. They're damn near perfect. If a cab driver who happened to be black sped her to her destination she not only tipped him generously, she thought for a few days more favourably of African Americans than other Americans. This was not a philosophy based on depth of thought, but perhaps the one most suited to a woman who 'lived for the moment, ducks.' Because she disliked The Man Upstairs so intensely with his Mickey Mouse voice and his Minnie Mouse eyes which were full of lostness and vulnerability and selfish need but had nothing to give, she therefore disliked all his views and any reservations she might at other times have entertained regarding gay rights were driven out. She forgot her anger over young Steve's liking for boys. She felt as affronted as if she had been gay herself.

This was not the time to say so. She was in real danger from this truly monstrous man. She enjoyed that phrase as it entered her head. A truly monstrous man, that's what you are. She could not afford to argue with him. But she was taking a soupcon of pleasure from her phrase, running it through her head. A truly monstrous man. Monstrous! Truly monstrous! YOU TRULY MONSTROUS MAN! So she did not catch the full import of his repeated question, drowned out as it was by her imagined abuse.

"How did you know him?"

She answered before she'd had time to process the weight of the question.

"I'm a friend of his Aunt Merrillee."

A splendid story shaped itself. She was supremely calm.

"He was a black sheep, dear. That's the truth of it. You saw the newspaper. No- one would put him up. I had him here for a few days. To get him back on his feet. What a tragedy. Drugs, you see. I tried to stop him. "

Unfortunately The Man Upstairs was thinking fast too.

"So you're acquainted with the Rev. Wade-Adrian?" He may as well have had dollar bills in his eyes. Money money money. Fuck! Fuck fuck fuck! You've blown it now, girl.

"No."

"But if you know the Aunt…"

"Only very slightly." How to get out of this? "She asked me to help him out while he was in En Wy. You're like another auntie to me, he said. But not really, if you see my meaning."

"Yeah." He seemed to buy this. Millions of people called old   ladies they liked their Aunts. Sara was happy for the instant to think of herself as a much-loved old lady who was everyone's aunt.

"I'm a Christian woman, Manny." She wanted to spit. "I had to help as best I could."

It was not clear from his expression that The Man Upstairs agreed that Christians should help out perverts.

"I would like an answer soon. I will go upstairs, madam, and give you time to think."

"I may need a few days.'"

He looked at his feet.

"Tonight."

"It's too fast, Manny."

"I would like an answer tonight." He was stubborn. He gritted his teeth. Then he smiled. "Tonight we can start our plans. We will be very happy together, I know we will. I'll be waiting."

He went through the door. She heard the pad of his feet on the stairs.

She wanted to scream. She wanted to cry. She clutched the air in front of her as if it was his neck. She squeezed and squeezed and squeezed. She wanted to bash his head against the wall. She wanted to throw him off the balcony. There was a painful tightening in her stomach. She wanted the creeping illness in her body to take her now, now, now.

She let an hour fly by in complete blankness. She went upstairs. She knocked on the door. She had no idea what she was going to do or say. He opened it.

She went into his apartment. It smelt of sweat and stuffiness. He probably never opened his window, except to watch naked boys on balconies.

The apartment was furnished with a fifties suite, three armchairs and a sofa. It was decorated with wallpaper of two shades of brown, in stripes. The carpet was brown too. The stove in the kitchen was sticky with spillages. A portable TV set sat in a corner. A bookcase sat in another corner.

263

The bookcase contained rows of books. Thirty-eight books.

She knew it was thirty-eight without having to count. It was a complete run of the Reverend Pat Wade-Adrian's best-selling series *The Last Days*. The most recent volume, *Sinners in Hell*, had a bookmark at the halfway point. He noticed that she noticed the set.

"A great man, the Reverend. He tells the truth. Even at the risk of offending the liberal media. It's such a strange coincidence that you should know him." He turned to her "You killed him, didn't you?" "Who?"

"The boy! You killed him! I saw it. I saw your hand."

She swallowed. "That's why I fell in love with you. When you killed him, at first I thought you were a common criminal. I was going to report you." (Then why didn't you? Because you wanted to blackmail me for money until your emotions got in the way!) "But then I saw the picture in the paper. I recognized the kid instantly. I'd seen him on the stairs. You had the courage to kill that horrible, horrible, sinful child. Right now, this very moment, he's in hell. I bet he regrets his crimes against God now!"

He clapped his hands together with enormous pleasure. Laughter emerged in three distinct globes of sound, exactly like a villain in a comic book. "Ho! Ho! Ho! The Reverend had the courage to disown him. He said, I do not have a son. I have two lovely daughters. That disgusting boy ceased to exist for the Reverend. Good for him! Good for you, lady! Good for you!" He rubbed his palms together. He looked at her with a sort of mad tenderness. "Please say yes, Sara. Please."

Sara raised herself up to her Queenliest height. She had not been a saint in her life but there were worse people than her. Everything was very clear.

"Yes."

264

He applauded. He skipped a bit. He was ecstatic. She looked around to his kitchen area. There was one cheap pan on the stove for boiling vegetables. It wouldn't harm a fly. That was all right. She didn't need it. A calendar on the wall was blank except for Thursdays. CLEANER, it said, in the square for each Thursday. Sara couldn't believe a cleaner came once a week. She wasn't a very good cleaner! Perhaps she was a fundamentalist and he employed her for that reason.

"Let's go to my apartment and we'll talk details over," she cooed. "I can't wait to be, uh, Mrs. Manny."

"I can't wait to have you." He was too stupid to know he'd made a double entendre. He followed her down. He went into her apartment. She went, swiftly but without haste to the big heavy frying pan which had been used for frying bacon. It was a well-made iron pan, and she felt its weight dragging on her wrists.

"This is for Steve," she said. He did not even have time to say, who's Steve?

What's really weird about this, she thought as she brought the pan down hard, is we've been neighbours for years and I said I'd marry you but I still don't know your last name. The skull of The Man Upstairs cracked open. The angle at which the pan hit him turned him half around and he glanced up at Sara. She struck again. A spit of white fat splashed onto his cheek like a tear. He looked not so much appalled as disappointed. Everyone seemed to be disappointed these days. He toppled forward.

She knew as he hit her carpet that she had solved a problem only by creating another. She no longer had a blackmailer. She no longer had a fiancée. However, she did have a corpse in her living room. In the first instance she enjoyed the end of the blackmailer more than she fretted about the corpse. As he lay there lifeless she felt like a moral

265

woman. She had caused Steve to die and now she had redressed the balance.

She sat down and looked at the body. Face down, one arm under the torso and the other stretched outward. The torso was very thin. The legs were thin too. They were a little short for the body. The Man Upstairs did not look as if he could ever have been dangerous. His misfortune perhaps had been that he looked too much like a Disney animal, too little like a person who could suffer. Like a Disney animal, he was not really alive. It was because he was not really alive that he could so easily hate the living and judge them. Sara did not loathe him any more, but she didn't feel any remorse. One cannot feel remorse for a cartoon creature. Or if one can it is in that limbo where more remorse can be felt for a cartoon creature than the real breathing thing, just as some people can claimed to feel love for something they called the soul while hating the human being who loves and fucks and lives in a body and is made of flesh.

What was she to do with him?

Take him upstairs? But then the wretched cleaner would find the body on Thursday! Sara, though her insides roiled, could not be sure that fate had prepared her own passing quite so soon.

She remembered something. She had an idea. She smiled. She was pleased with herself.

She felt in his pocket and found his key. She went upstairs and brought down volume thirty-eight of *The Last Days*. She laid it on his body and waited for nightfall. The gray of dusk became darkness. She heard the life of the City. She heard people going to the Mexican Restaurant. She sat there on her sofa, sat and sat and sat. She heard Peter come in from the office. She heard sirens. She heard voices. She heard the lovely chiming of bells. She heard cars hooting at each other.

266

Was it two in the morning now? Her watch said it was. How time moves on. She felt a serious pain in her stomach, the worst so far, and she rushed to the bathroom and vomited. Afterwards, she brushed her teeth and felt refreshed.

She heard chatter in Spanish. The waiters and the chefs from *Panchito's* were going home. All was as nearly silent as it could be. She tucked the book under her right arm. She put her hands under the armpits of The Man Upstairs. She dragged him to her door. She dragged him down the stairs. She dragged him outside and down the steps. She dragged him to the door of *Boyle's Travel*. She put her bottom against the door and it opened easily and she dragged him in.

The desk was there, and the chair.

She sat him in the chair. She opened the book where he had left off. She placed it on the desk. She put the bookmark next to it. She laid his palm on the book. She left him to read.

FRIENDS

It is an indisputable truth that for all the modern talk of freedom and our rights we do not choose anything that matters. We may select our donuts from a large variety of creams and icings and sprinkles, we may select a sitcom over the WWF, we may select a green rather than a blue sofa. But we cannot choose the things we would most like to choose: we are trapped in what we are. We do not choose the place or date of our birth or to whom we are born, and we do not choose the date of our death. Sara at forty-five had expected to live for another thirty years or more. This was a reasonable expectation. She had not especially looked forward to those years but nor had she on principle objected to them. But as for Steve One and Steve Two and The Man Upstairs, the end came sooner than, a few weeks ago, she might have supposed.

It wasn't a long fall nor a frying pan which brought her end. It was cruel nature herself. The pains in Sara's stomach became more intense, she vomited more and more frequently. Just as she had suspected, Sara was diagnosed with a rare, slow-acting food poisoning, well advanced by the time she consulted a doctor. She had eaten some chicken legs and wings not fit for human consumption. The doctor said, if only we'd known earlier. Only a week ago things might have been different. Sara shrugged. She didn't mind, really she didn't. Fate is fate. She would die soon and that was that. She took the news very well, better than any patient he'd had, did not bawl or cry out or curse God. She looked only a little sad and she said again, to herself more than to her doctor, "Well, it's fate, isn't it ducks? You can't stop fate."

The doctor misheard. He thought she'd said, "Well, it's fate, isn't it Doc? You can't stop fate." He was impressed by her undemonstrative acceptance of the inevitable and smiled wryly.

There may have been deep within the places of the mind which send out signals too distant to articulate, (to be discerned only by a feeling, a little jolt, a tingle of excitement,) a perception that the poison in her body had forcibly pulled her out of the cycle of *Make Someone's Day* and *Mulligan's*, a reaffirmation in a terrible final way of her physical being. She remembered Steve's love of and absorption in his own physical self. She had envied it. Now in this undoubtedly appalling way she was aware as his penis had made her aware, as no-one else and nothing else had in years and years, of her body, the physical construct called Sara Smith. For this she was grateful. The physical construct called Sara Smith was coming to its mortality as all things must. That this was so did not seem wrong, not a crime, not a shame. It felt human. It felt natural. It felt right.

Did it also feel just?

I killed him. For the first time she said this to herself in a clear   unflustered line. I killed him. He is dead because of me. Now I must die. It is only just. It is the motions of fate at work.

Lying in her final bed at St Vincent's, she did not think often of the Man Upstairs. He had brought his end on himself, she was a helpless lady defending herself from his nasty come-on. No jury would ever have convicted her. But in a cruel flash she thought how funny it would have been if

269

she had married The Man Upstairs, only to die. As he came to her as husband with his demands and expectations - or, because he was a coward, not even with those - she would have been carted off to her hospital bed. The only bed he would have seen his new wife in would have been her deathbed. He would have watched helplessly as his hopes faded away.

Well, the bugger tried to blackmail me, if I think meanly about him it's his own fault. In fact, from now on I refuse to think about him *at all*.

Steve, however, she did think of, a lot. She lived her last days with his ghost.

Unfortunately, Leanne, one of the gang at *Mulligan's*, was a nurse at St Vincent's. She came to Sara, all tears and emotion. Why hadn't she told them, Leanne wanted to know. Sara, who was feeling more and more tired now, couldn't be bothered to answer. But Leanne made what she supposed was a kindly gesture. She arranged for the core of *Mulligan's* regulars to visit Sara, as a group. Lawrence the once-punk, Ernest and Jackie and Bea, Leanne herself in her nurse's uniform, arm knitted through Lawrence's. Eddie, of course. They all stood around her bed except Eddie, who held back because he could not bear to move nearer for fear of what he might see. They'd brought between them enough flowers to fill a garden, or a cemetery. Leanne set about putting them in obese vases. Everyone was very brave; they were not going to allow tears to be shed. They were going to be bright and amusing, as they were in *Mulligan's*. Just like the old days. They could not perceive that Sara did not want the old days back.

In her cynicism Sara had thought many times, I expect the last bloody thing I'll see on my deathbed will be that bloody mouse on a screen in my hospital room or from somewhere down the corridor that pious nagging high-voiced Snow White cow shrieking her way through 'Whistle While You

Work' (while wagging a condescending corrective finger at that dwarf - why didn't he bloody slap her one like she deserved?), shattering the water glass by my bed, so I'll die dripping wet and bleeding, cut all over by tiny lethal shards.

Sara had never feared hell because she felt she'd already seen it, already heard it. Hell was a perpetual smile, perpetual vacant happiness, a merry tune which knew no melancholy. It was animals that sung and birds that flapped prettily in the trees, but which did not rend their prey and were not torn apart by the claws of bigger creatures. They didn't know of blood and flesh. They didn't even need to shit. They were horrible.

It was conceivably from the kindness of fate that this nightmare did not come to pass. Four rooms down an old lady was surfing the television. She settled on the Disney Channel. An insect sung about the stars. But her door was closed, her nurse had closed it, and the sound did not sift past the walls of her room.

Yet fate exacts a price, as Sara had already discovered, and if Snow White was not to haunt her final hours, nevertheless she experienced an unwelcome intrusion. She lay in her bed - but of course she always lay in her bed now. She was wide awake looking at the ceiling. She knew every crack in that ceiling, she knew the curve of the white plastic shade which covered the bulb, she knew the greenish yellow colour of the paint and when she closed her eyes the greenish yellow was still visible against her eyelids. Eyes closed, the colour against the lids broken by floating discs of gray and black, she was absent of thoughts. She heard the door open and the shuffling of feet. It was not a meal time, it was not time for a blanket bath or a changing of sheets. It was not time for a visit from the doctor. The nurse had no right to disturb her at any old time she chose. Sara did not open her eyes, said only,

"What is it, nurse? Can't you see I'm trying to rest?"

271

And a voice which was not her nurse's said,

"Oh my God! So sorry, wrong room," and there was another shuffling of feet, back towards the door. Two people went out. A grown-up and a child. Sara opened her eyes just wide enough to see a pair of adult shoes disappear and behind them a pair of little pink shoes. The child held a huge multi-coloured bunch of flowers, wrapped in plastic which crackled. The flowers were resting on her shoulder like a rifle. They remained on Sara's side of the door a moment after the pink shoes had gone. For a second they seemed to look back at Sara. Steve's rose tucked into his leather jacket had looked over his shoulder at her just as these flowers, two dozen or more, gazed at her now. The child must have adjusted the bunch on her shoulders because the flowers tipped down a half an inch, and the petals gathered together. It was as if... not as if they were winking back at the woman in the bed, because that would have implied affection, humour. Rather, as the petals pressed together, they were like eyes narrowed in criticism. Twenty-four eyes slitted to accuse.

Then, shifting their angle again, they unfolded and were gone.

The grown-up said in the corridor, "How embarrassing! It must be this room."

The child said,

"Will she die, momma?" Whoever it was she spoke of, to Sara it must have been of her.

"We must hope not."

"Will she go to heaven? Will she be with the angels?"

"We must hope not, Alice." They went into a room.

"Hi, Gramma!" said the girl with sickening brightness.

*

272

In her hospital bed Sara's pain became so extreme that she was unable eventually to think in words at all, only in pictures. The last thing she saw was Steve rising from the black waters of the Hudson, naked and dripping wet, beckoning to her with his young cheeky smile, his forgiveness and his promise. There was no graze on his cheek, no dark stain on his temple. A bright light took him upward and he waved to her. Did his mouth shape silently these words? "See you later, Sara. See you soon." He lit out to unknown territory.

Then pain and the morphine turned her world blacker than any earthly night with or without stars, and she saw and heard and thought nothing more at all. Did she see him later? That cannot be told.

EPILOGUE:
RANDY AND DAVID

Randy saw him looking intently at a painting in the Metropolitan Museum of Art. Most people swum indifferently from painting to painting until after an hour they felt they'd had their money's worth and went to the cafeteria. But this kid, he couldn't have been older than twenty, he was looking with great concentration at the picture.

He was a short well-shaped guy, in his denims - ripped, saw Randy - and his t-shirt. He had nice dark hair. He had a small scar on the temple, a little bit of damage which made him even more attractive. Randy thought him very fanciable. He would've just loved to fuck him. It was not lust, however, that made him approach the kid. He wasn't the kind of person who picked guys up at the museum. No, it was the boy's gentle yet intense gaze up at the picture which drew Randy to him.

"It's a great painting, that," said Randy, looking up at it himself.

"Yeah. It's beautiful."

"Memling is one of the greatest of the lesser known Dutch painters."

"Yeah. He was great."

"See, he's set the Annunciation in his own time." Randy was moved by this idea. Of course, in Memling's day, he mused, it was still possible to believe literally in the annunciation, the virgin birth, the resurrection.

If an angel or whatever came now he'd go unnoticed. He'd look like just anyone. He'd wear ripped jeans and a T-shirt.

While he could, he would give all the love he could give. He would give all the love he could give.

But.

He would give all the love he could give, sure. But it would be better for angels to keep away from this earth.

Out of the blue, Randy felt a moment of unsustainable despair. He shook. The boy clasped his arm and steadied him.

"Whoa!" said the boy.

And Randy's head cleared. The despair lifted.

"Wow, I'm sorry, I don't know what happened."

"You were telling me about the painting."

"Yes. Yes, I was."

The boy laughed gently.

"And?" Randy looked up to the Memling. So did the guy in the t-shirt.

"And see how Gabriel's clothes are like a priest's robes of the time? If he came to fifteenth century Holland, see, he'd come as a fifteenth century Dutch man. "

"I was just thinking how beautiful that is, that robe."

"Look at the red and the gold material, the folds of it. It's almost palpable. You want to brush your hand over it."

"Yeah."

"You an art student?"

The boy thought for a moment as if unsure. Then he said, definite,

"Yeah. I'm an art student."

"So was I. Been out of college three years. I'm an assistant in acquisitions."

"Cool."

"It's great." Randy ran a hand through his sandy hair. He was tall. The boy was shortish so when he looked down from the painting to Randy his face stayed upwardly inclined.

What strange eyes...

Randy stood back.

They were very dark, those eyes, but spotted with little golden discs, just as if he'd stared so long at the painting that the golden splashes on the robe had somehow melted onto his eyeballs. They were very, very beautiful eyes. And when the boy smiled it was a very beautiful, open smile. Generous.

And Randy, looking into the face, felt a momentary shadow of knowledge, lost knowledge, or foreknowledge perhaps. Then he didn't.

"Yeah," said the boy, looking back up to the picture. "It's great. Very moving."

"You Southern? Memphis?"

"Yeah."

"Been in town long?"

The guy thought for a second.

"I've been in En Wy for a couple years." Another beat, then, "I study at Columbia."

"Cool."

"I'm Dave." The boy held out his hand. He had delicate fingers, clean nails.

Randy's ex was called Dave. They'd separated unhappily. Lots of angst. It was a pity this boy should be called Dave too. Still, not an uncommon name.

"Randy."

"Hi, Randy." He smiled very sweetly.

Randy looked shyly away from him and back to him and away from him again. He looked down.

"Your lace," he said, smiling, pointing.

The right lace was loose, flopped on the floor. The boy laughed.

"Yeah! A bad habit. Everyone tells me that." He made to bend downwards but Randy said, "No, let me," and he dropped to his haunches and tied the lace up in a swift dance of fingers.

"Thanks."

"Want to go for a cup of coffee when you've finished here?" Immediately he'd said this Randy felt he was being too forward, but the boy smiled again, sweet and lovely, and said,

"Sure."

"Cool."

"Okay!"

Randy laughed and Dave laughed. They looked back up to the picture. The golden light on the cloak was exquisite. Randy felt unusual knowledge again, but this time it was different knowledge: whatever people said, sometimes you could experience perfection in life, just as this painting of the robe was perfect. Randy wanted to weep at the loveliness of the painting and the loveliness of the boy next to him and the loveliness of life.

END

Released November 2010
Matthew Waterhouse : Vanitas

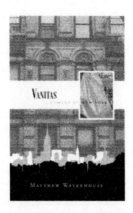

WHEN YOU WISH UPON A STAR...

Your dreams come true...? They did, at any rate, for Florinda
Quenby, though not in the way she had planned. When she flew
out to Hollywood to become a movie star, she could not imagine
the terrible struggles ahead of her, from riches back to rags, or that
fame and wealth would finally come from an entirely different
quarter, her fantastical soup factory in Harlem, modelled on the Taj
Mahal... Once she was famous, she became one of New York's
grandest hostesses and one of America's most beloved celebrities.
Her parties for the Christmas season in her huge, gold-lined
apartment overlooking Central Park were an un-missable feature on
Manhattan's social calendar. Those parties grew wilder and wilder
every year, until finally she decided to throw one last party,
designed to top all the others... This is a tale of ambition and wealth
and fame and vanity. This is Florinda's incredible story.

Pre-order a signed copy at www.hirstbooks.com

Released July 2010
Matthew Waterhouse : Blue Box Boy
A Memoir of Doctor Who in Four Episodes

As a boy Matthew Waterhouse loved *Doctor Who*: he watched all the episodes and read all the novels and comic strips. Then, at eighteen, like a lightning bolt, he found himself cast in the series, as the youngest ever travelling companion, working alongside his hero... This book tells about the whole arc of his involvement, from his childhood interest to his work on two of *Doctor Who's* most inventive seasons to the absurd, comic world of minor celebrity. This affectionate memoir is a record of what it was like to make *Doctor Who*. Written with the same verve and wit as Matthew's novels, and shedding an honest light on his time in the Tardis, *Blue Box Boy* is a must buy for everybody interested in the programme, and the BBC as it was at the time.

Pre-order your signed copy at www.hirstbooks.com

Thank you to the following people, for pre-ordering 'Fates, Flowers'

Donna Burditt
Graeme Caddies-Green
Mike Cook
Kerry Cooper
Manu Das
Robert Dick
Jeffrey Easlick
Cindy Garland
Rod Hedrick
Brad Jones
Gary Knowles
Christopher Leather
Jeffrey Miller
Dave Owen
Alister Pearson
Jackie Thompson
Kelvin Troake
Martin Wiggins
John Williams
Alex Wilson-Fletcher
Anthony Zehetner

'Look Who's Talking' by Colin Baker

A compilation of articles from 15 years of his weekly newspaper column

To many, Colin Baker will always be the sixth Doctor Who, or the villainous Paul Merroney in the classic BBC series *The Brothers*. But to the residents of South Buckinghamshire he is a weekly voice of sanity in a world that seems intent on confounding him. Marking the 15th anniversary of his regular feature in the Bucks Free Press, this compilation includes over 100 of his most entertaining columns, from 1995 to 2009, complete with new linking material. With fierce intelligence and a wicked sense of humour, Colin tackles everything from the absurdities of political correctness to the joys of being an actor, slipping in vivid childhood memories, international adventures and current affairs in a relentless rollercoaster of reflections, gripes and anecdotes. Pulling no punches, taking no prisoners and sparing no detail, the ups and downs of Colin's life are shared with panache, honesty and clarity, and they are every bit as entertaining and surreal as his trips in that famous police box... For a world that is bewildering, surprising and wondrous, one need look no further than modern Britain, and Colin Baker is here to help you make sense of it all, and to give you a good laugh along the way.

www.hirstbooks.com

'Self Portrait' & 'Naked' by Anneke Wills

One extraordinary life.
Two breathtaking books.
Countless Adventures.

A two-part autobiography from Doctor Who's original glamour girl

Did you know that Anneke Wills once lived naked in a jungle? Or that she was a follower of a **notorious** spiritual leader? Maybe the fact that she was a **child actress** who in her late teens started a relationship with the legendary Anthony **Newley**, had passed you by. Of course, you know all about her time at the heart of **swinging sixties** London, her famous friends, like **Peter Cook**, and her turbulent marriage to **Michael Gough**. Don't You? Next you'll be saying you didn't know that she's descended from an **Elizabethan** hero or that she lived in **California**, **Canada** and **India**. You are of course aware that she was a companion to the first two Doctor Whos, but did you know that she's appeared alongside four more doctors? Or that **Doctor Who** has stayed with her for over 40 years? Did you know she climbed Sydney Harbour Bridge with Colin **Baker**, partied with Paul **McGann** in Vancouver and baffled Jon **Pertwee** at a BBC party? Did you know about the mysterious death of her brother, on the trail of the **Holy Grail**? Surely you've heard how she drove a huge truck across the **Rockies**, and how she and her friends took two double-decker buses across **Europe** and **Asia** to **India**? Oh, and then there's the other two marriages, and living on the remote Canadian island. Obviously you've seen at least **100 of her works of art** and personal photos, and no doubt you've experienced her warm, **intimate** storytelling style, and found yourself moved by her honesty, touched by her **sadness** and entertained by her wit. No? **You should probably buy the books.**